dear bridget,
I WANT YOU

PENELOPE WARD
VI KEELAND

Copyright © 2017 by Penelope Ward and Vi Keeland
ISBN-10: 1682309800
ISBN-13: 978-1682309803

This book is a work of fiction. All names, characters, locations, and incidents are products of the authors' imaginations. Any resemblance to actual persons, things, living or dead, locales, or events is entirely coincidental.

DEAR BRIDGET, I WANT YOU
Cover model: Philip Van den Hoogenband –
Chadwick Models Melbourne
Photographer: Brian Jamie
Cover designer: Letitia Hasser, RBA Designs
Formatter: Elaine York, Allusion Graphics, LLC/
Publishing & Book Formatting

dear bridget, I WANT YOU

Chapter 1

Bridget

Tuesday. That's what my underwear said, even though it was Friday. Right across my ass in big, bold letters. A few months ago, when the airline had lost my luggage during my trip down to Florida to visit my mother, I'd picked up a package of cheap undies at Target. Of course, I had no idea there was anything printed on them at the time. And I wasn't about to throw away seven pairs of perfectly good underwear when I eventually realized. Plus, how long had it been since anyone had seen my underwear anyway? Two years?

The nurse came back into the treatment room to take my history. "Why don't you have a seat, Ms. Valentine?"

"Ummm. I can't."

"Oh, sorry." She smiled. "That's right."

"Do you know when the last time you had a tetanus shot was?"

"I'm a nurse over at Memorial, so I get them regularly. Last year, maybe."

"Okay. That's good. How about pregnancy? Any chance you could be pregnant?"

"Not a cold chance in hell."

Even the sixty-year-old nurse looked at me sympathetically. "Dry spell, huh?"

"You could say that."

"Well, you're in luck then. Dr. Hogue is on today."

"Dr. Hogue?"

"He's our resident. A real young hottie." She winked.

Great. Just great. I wasn't just going to be mortified in front of the first man to see my ass in years, it had to be a young, handsome doctor. "Do you have anyone else on call, by any chance? Maybe a female doctor or an older, male physician, perhaps?"

The nurse stood and closed the chart she'd started for me. "Don't worry, sweetie. You're in good hands. I'm positive Dr. Hogue has seen his share of ass."

Kill me now.

A few minutes later, I was trying to ignore the pain and distract myself by scrolling through my phone while I waited for the resident on duty, when the door opened.

I turned around and froze.

Seriously? This couldn't be the doctor. We definitely didn't have any doctors that looked like this over at Memorial.

"So, I hear you want to show me your bum, and I'm not even going to have to buy you some dinner first?"

My bum? Of course, young, hot doctor had an equally hot accent, too. Was he...*British*? I pulled the gown I was wearing closed tighter. "Please tell me this is a joke. You are *not* the doctor. How old are you even? Twenty-two?"

He didn't seem the slightest bit offended by my comment. Instead, he leaned against the desk and folded

2

his arms across his chest. "Twenty-nine. Would you like to see my driver's license?" Then...he smiled. *Oh God.* Perfect pearly whites, too. *Figures.* The man was downright gorgeous. Tall, really tall—probably at least six foot two, broad shouldered, muscular arms, bright blue eyes, a chiseled jaw, and blond hair that looked as if he'd just had sex. Jesus...the doctor had fuck-me hair. I couldn't possibly show him my ass.

"I need a new doctor."

He looked down at my chart. "No can do, Ms. V. It's three o'clock. You arrived right at the change of shifts, so it's me or the janitor with a rusty, old pair of pliers—he might be able to help you out. Come on. Don't be shy. Let's have a look, shall we?"

Ugh. It was either Dr. Dreamy or the ER across town that I worked in. And I'd never live this one down if I went to Memorial. I rolled my eyes and huffed. "Fine."

Just wanting to get the humiliation over with and get the hell out of here, I turned around and leaned over the examining table. I then proceeded to reach back and pull my gown aside to expose my left ass cheek. I'd already tucked that side of my underwear into my butt crack to keep it from getting tangled with the hook.

Dr. Hottie was quiet for a long moment, but when he spoke, I heard the laughter in his voice. "Have you been wearing them for three days?"

"What?" I turned to look back at the gorgeous doctor. His right hand was scratching at the stubble on his chin, while his left was holding onto his elbow.

"Your knickers. It's Friday. They say Tuesday. I was wondering if you'd been wearing them for three days or just got your days of the week mixed up."

I seriously would've rather kept the hook in my ass. "I bought them when the airline lost my luggage during a trip. I didn't realize what was printed on them. You know what. I'll keep the hook." I dropped the gown back down and stood.

Dr. Hogue put his hands up in surrender. At first he seemed sincere. "I'm sorry. I shouldn't have made that comment. It was inappropriate."

"You're right. It was."

"It's bad enough you're already..." He grinned. "...the *butt* of the joke. You don't need me to poke fun."

"You're an ass, you know that?"

"I'd rather *be* one than have a fish hook in one."

"Very mature. Did you say you were nine or twenty-nine?"

We had a mini staring contest and then the ridiculousness of the situation made me break out in laughter. Dr. Dreamy joined in, and when we were done, the air had shifted back. "Why don't you go on and turn around and let me take a better look this time? I'll be serious." He held up three fingers. "Scout's honor. What kind of a hook is it? A Circle? Treble? Aberdeen?"

"I have no idea." I turned back to face the treatment table, assumed the dreadful bent-over position again, and lifted my gown. "I really don't know much about fishing."

"You don't say..."

"Does the type of hook matter? I could probably find out if I need to."

I heard the slap of latex from Dr. Hogue putting on his gloves and then his large hand was on my ass. "It's pretty far in there, actually. I'm not sure the type of hook really matters. Looks like I'm going to have to make a clean slice to slip it out no matter what. How did you get the thing set so deep in there anyway?"

"I was on a little row boat out in Narragansett. I was trying to teach my son how to cast."

Dr. Hogue squeezed the area where the hook was embedded. "Oww."

"Sorry. You know teachers are supposed to have knowledge on the subject they teach."

"Just take out the hook."

"I'm going to need to numb you up first in order to slice it open."

"Can't you just thread the hook back out?"

"Nope. More than the tip is in your arse, and it looks like it's got a long shaft."

God, my body had been ice cold for two years—not a hint of heat even when I'd taken my own hands to it. And it decided to spring back to life at *this moment*. I was bent over a table talking about the tip of a long shaft going in with a man who could have been a model instead of a wise-cracking doctor. *Perfect timing, Bridget.* I was suddenly glad to be in this position I was in so he couldn't see the flush on my face. I felt the good doctor walk away and then the heat from his body returned.

"Stand by for a quick pinch."

"Ouch!" As quickly as the word escaped me, the pain was over.

"Okay, that should numb the area so we can dig in and extract the hook without too much pain."

It was quiet for a minute or so before I felt his hands on my ass again.

5

Ohhh.

His voice seemed to go lower, deeper. "Just relax, Bridget. Breathe in and out. Everything's going to be okay."

He sounded almost...seductive. The muscles between my legs contracted. God, was I really getting off from having a fishing hook removed from my ass? The answer would be yes. Yes, I was.

"You're just going to feel a little bit of pressure."

I couldn't help where my mind went. I imagined what it would be like if he came up behind me with a special surprise, bestowing upon me way more *pressure* than I bargained for.

Get your mind out of the gutter, Bridget!

"Here we go," he said.

I felt the skin of my ass stretching along with some tugging.

"It's out," he finally said. "Just going to bandage you up. Hold still."

It actually hadn't hurt nearly as much as I'd expected.

"Well, Ms. V., it looks like you are officially off the hook. Pun intended."

When I turned around, he had the hook in his hand.

"This is known as a double hook, by the way," he said.

"Good to know."

"Do you want to keep it for any reason? A souvenir?"

"No. Thank you."

"Very well, then." Dr. Hogue set the hook down on the tray and then removed his gloves, discarding them in the trashcan marked Biohazard.

He took something from his pocket and began to write something on a piece of paper.

6

"What is that?"

"Don't worry. It's not my number, just a prescription for some antibiotic cream in case you need it. I'll leave it right on the desk here. You can get dressed, and then you're free to go."

He lingered for a few seconds before he said, "Take care now. Watch your back, Bridget. Or rather, your backside."

"Wait," I blurted out.

He stopped and turned around. "Yes?"

A piece of his blond hair had fallen into his eyes. He was so handsome.

I cleared my throat. "I'm sorry if I was…"

"A pain in the arse?"

My cheeks felt hot. "Yes."

"No worries." He winked.

And just like that, Dr. Dreamy disappeared out of the room. Unfortunately for me, my sore ass had been replaced by a tingling vagina.

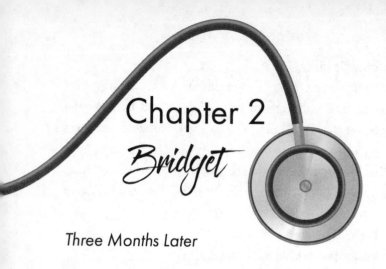

Chapter 2
Bridget

Three Months Later

The phone rang while I was getting ready to work the first of three consecutive, twelve-hour shifts.

"Hello?"

"Bridge?"

"Hey, Calliope."

"I just wanted to let you know I've given Simon the key to your flat. Is that okay?"

"Absolutely. It's empty and move-in ready. That key is for the separate entryway off the main house. The only thing the space doesn't have is a kitchen. So, he'll have to share with us. You told him that, right?"

"Yes. He's thrilled that he doesn't have to commit to a lease. So, he'll take anything flexible he can get. He says he'll start gradually moving his stuff in, if you don't mind."

"Not at all. Thanks for the heads up."

"Alright, see you at class next week, Bridge."

Calliope was my yoga instructor, who'd become a friend. Outside of classes, we'd sometimes meet for coffee at the Starbucks in town. She'd moved here to Rhode Island from the UK several years ago when her husband got a job with the American division of the bank he worked for.

When she'd told me that her BFF needed a place that didn't come with a one-year commitment, I offered the in-law apartment on my property. Apparently, he was in his last year of residency and was transferred to my hospital with less than a year to go before he would be moving out of state. So, he didn't want to sign a new lease and needed a place relatively close to work. The suburb where I lived was right off the highway and a straight, ten-minute shot to Providence.

My husband, Ben, died unexpectedly a couple of years ago, leaving our then six-year-old son, Brendan, and me behind to fend for ourselves. Despite my decent nursing salary, it had become tougher as of late to cover the mortgage for our large colonial. The life insurance that I'd collected needed to be set aside for my son's eventual college education. I'd never be able to save for that; even meeting the monthly bills was a challenge. But I refused to move, wanting Brendan to be able to continue to live in the only house he'd ever known.

I'd been thinking about renting out the vacant in-law apartment that came with the house for a while now. So, when Calliope mentioned her friend, who she said was like a brother to her, needed a place to stay, I figured it would be good extra income to rent out the space to him. And at least I knew he wasn't some psychopath.

By the end of the week, I'd slowly noticed boxes showing up whenever I peeked into the unit. Simon must have been coming in during the day and dropping things off, but we'd yet to cross paths.

One evening, Brendan was spending the night over at Ben's mother's house about a half-hour away in North Kingstown. I decided to draw myself a hot bath, since I could relax without interruption. The bathroom typically got too hot with the door closed, so I left it open, figuring I'd take advantage of the fact that my son wasn't home tonight.

I had a tendency to feel faint when immersed in hot water for too long, so I reluctantly forced myself out of the soothing suds after thirty minutes and wrapped myself in a plush towel. Sure enough, the twinge of nausea that I normally felt right before I was about to pass out hit.

I had been told that to prevent a blackout, I should put my head between my knees. But it was too late. The last thing I remembered was my towel dropping to the floor.

An indeterminate amount of time later, my eyes blinked open. I was lying by the tub naked, grateful that I was okay. It wasn't my first rodeo; fainting was just something I was prone to.

When I had passed out that one time in hot yoga class, I remembered Calliope telling me to get into Child's Pose before standing. So, this time I stayed down on my hands and knees, spreading my knees wide apart while keeping my big toes touching. My butt rested on my heels. Breathing in and out, I tried to relax.

"Bridget?"

The sound of a man's voice caused me to jump so fast that I hit my head on the tub. "Ow!" I turned around, took one look at him, and gasped.

Holy shit. What?!

I blinked.

What is Dr. Dreamy doing here? Is this a dream? Maybe I didn't really wake up?

Covering my breasts, I said, "Oh my God. What? What are you doing here?"

He reached for my towel and wrapped it around me then knelt down to immediately check my head for any injury. He'd slipped right into doctor mode. "Where does it hurt?"

Pointing to an area on the front of my skull, I said, "Here."

My nipples hardened at the closeness of his body.

He rubbed his finger along the area. "There doesn't seem to be a bump. I think you'll live."

We both sat on the floor, our backs against the tub.

I repeated, "What are you doing here?"

"I live here, apparently."

Realization hit.

"It's you? *You're* Simon? Calliope's friend?"

"Yes. And believe me when I say I had no clue I was moving into *your* house. She refers to you as *Bridge*, not Bridget and never told me your last name, so I couldn't even put two and two together. This is just as much a shock to me as it is to you."

"Then how did you recognize me so fast? I wasn't even facing you."

"You were down on the ground with your buttocks in the air. I would recognize that arse anywhere."

Utter embarrassment consumed me. "Oh, really…"

"Your derriere precedes you, luv." He laughed. "Anyway, the door to the loo was open. I had come to introduce myself and make some tea. What were you doing on the ground?"

"I'm prone to fainting, particularly when I spend too much time in heated water. I was unconscious for probably a few minutes. When I came to, I was doing a yoga pose Calliope taught me to help regulate myself before standing." A visual of what I must have looked like from the rear came to mind. He probably saw my asshole, too. "Oh my God. I'm mortified."

"It's not like I haven't seen your backside before."

"Yes, but what *else* did you see? Everything happened so fast when I turned around."

"Bridget, relax. Are you forgetting I see naked bodies all day long?"

"Yeah, well, not *mine*...ever again."

"You need to learn to lock the bathroom door, although with your syncope tendency, maybe that's not such a good idea." He shook his head in disbelief. "God, you are a walking disaster, Bridget Valentine." Simon held out his large hand. "Let's get you up."

After he helped me off the ground, I adjusted the towel around myself.

He pointed his thumb toward the door. "I'm gonna go make that tea. Fancy some?"

"Um...sure. Yeah. I'll have some tea."

Before he walked away, his eyes darted down to the pile of dirty clothes I had left on the ground before my bath.

"I see you're at it again."

"What?"

"Not changing your knickers every day. It's Saturday. The ones you took off were Wednesday's."

Those damn underpants had come back to haunt me yet again.

"I don't pay attention when I grab them from the drawer. I just put those on this morning." Crossing my arms, I said, "You know what? I shouldn't have to be explaining this in my own house!"

"Relax, Bridget. I'm just kidding you. Get some clean knickers on, whichever day you want, and join me in the kitchen for some tea."

When he finally left me alone, it all seemed to sink in.

The sexy, blond, god of a doctor whom I'd masturbated to for weeks after the fish hook incident...was now my roommate.

Simon.

Simon says...commence freak out.

Chapter 3
Simon

"I don't have to marry you now, do I?" I set two cups of tea down on the kitchen table.

"Marry me? Why would you have to marry me?"

"Fuck if I know." I pushed the hair off my face and sat down. I'd been meaning to get a haircut for the better part of a month, but never seemed to get around to it. Bridget sat across from me. "I thought maybe it was an American tradition or something. The last three women I saw naked twice seemed to think we were getting married."

"Awww...poor baby. What a terrible problem to have. The women who put out for you think you're such a Godsend that they want more of you."

I smirked. "I never thought of it that way. I thought they were just a bit loony. But you're right. It's probably because I'm so blessed...you know...in the lower anatomy, that they want to anchor their loose chain."

Bridget's skin turned pink. I liked screwing with her. It was going to be fun living here. "I'm just messing with you, luv, relax. I like watching your cheeks change color when you're embarrassed." I winked. "Both cheeks."

She shook her head. "I think we need to set some ground rules."

I sipped my tea. "Alright. I like rules. Without them, breaking them isn't nearly as much fun."

"I'm serious."

"Okay, then. Lay 'em on me. What are the flat rules, Ms. V.?"

"Well, first off, you can't talk like that."

"Like this? I'm working on losing the accent, but I don't think I'll master calling the trash *gah-bidge* or going to the *ba ba* for a trim anytime soon."

Bridget laughed. "I didn't mean you had to lose the accent, I meant you can't use bad words."

My brow furrowed. "What bad words did I say?"

"You said 'fuck if I know,' and you also talked about your lower anatomy and seeing my ass. Those are all no-nos."

"No-nos?" I arched a brow. She was really damn cute.

"Sorry. I have an eight year old and worked in the pediatric ward for years before moving to the ER. Force of habit."

I'd forgotten that Calliope had said she had a kid. She didn't look old enough for one. "How old are you?"

"That's not a proper thing to ask a woman, you know."

I folded my arms across my chest. "If I remember correctly, you asked me how old I was within thirty seconds of walking into the examining room a few months back."

"You have a very good memory, don't you?"

"Yep. It's been three months, and I could have identified your arse out of a lineup."

15

She blushed again. I could tell she was flustered. "Back to the rules. You can't say 'arse', either. No curse words, or you'll have to put money in the swear jar."

"The what?"

She pointed her eyes to the kitchen counter. Sure enough, there were two mason jars in the corner. Each had a piece of masking tape across it with what looked like a child's handwriting. The one labeled *Mom* was filled half way with coins. The one labeled *Brendan* had one lone, shiny copper penny. Bridget sighed. "It was my son, Brendan's, idea. He'd left his bike out at the curb again even though I'd told him to bring it in for the hundredth time. It was stolen, and I refused to buy him a new bike for no reason. I'd figured he'd get one for his birthday or Christmas, and by then maybe he'd learn his lesson. But he's a resourceful boy. A day or two later, I was unloading the dishwasher and didn't realize a glass had broken until after I'd sliced my finger open. I yelled, "shit," and after the bleeding stopped, Brendan came up with the swear jar idea. He'd recently taken a liking to the word damn, and I'd been on him about it. If my jar is filled to the top first, I have to buy him a new bike. If his jar is filled to the top first, he has to get a haircut."

"You don't like his hair?"

"He's going through this phase where he wants to grow it long. I think one of the girls at school told him she liked it that way, and now he won't even agree to get a trim."

I wiggled my brows and ran my fingers through my longish hair. "That's how it all starts. He'll have a selection of gel in no time."

Bridget shook her head at me and sipped her tea. "Great."

"Don't think I didn't notice that you still haven't answered my question."

"What question?"

"How old are you?"

"I thought we decided a gentleman didn't ask a woman's age."

"Well, there's your first problem. You shouldn't have assumed I was a gentleman."

She laughed. "I'm thirty-three."

"You don't look a day over thirty-two-and-a-half."

"Gee, thanks."

I caught the time on my watch. I was enjoying my chat with Bridget, but I was going to be late to work if I didn't get myself out of here in the next five minutes. Finishing off the rest of my tea, I stood and placed my mug in the sink. "I have to get to the hospital. What are the rest of the rules?"

"Oh. Let's see..." she tapped her pointer finger to her lip a few times. "Off the top of my head: Clean up your own mess in the kitchen. Don't leave dishes in the sink—either wash them or load them into the dishwasher, and even though you have your own bathroom, if you use the one off the kitchen while you're in here, put the seat down when you're done."

"Got it. Is that it?"

"Yes. For now. Although I reserve the right to add more at a later date."

I contained my smile. "Of course you do."

"Are you working a twenty-four-hour shift?"

I nodded. "Four twenty-fours this week."

"I don't know how you guys do it."

"You get used to lack of sleep."

"I suppose. I guess we'll be seeing a lot of each other from now on. I'm working a twelve-hour shift tomorrow, too."

"You're a lucky woman. And I'm not referring to the twelve-hour shift."

Bridget rolled her eyes. "Goodbye, Simon."

"You have a good night. And try not to pass out anymore." I was halfway out the door when a thought dawned on me. Turning back, I asked, "Is it body temperature or external temperature that makes you pass out?"

"Both, I guess. It's usually the external temperature that makes my body temperature rise and then it hits me all at once."

"So do you ever pass out while shagging?"

"Excuse me?"

I honestly thought she didn't understand the term. "Shagging...you know...fucking."

"I know what the term means. And even though it's none of your business, no, I've never passed out while having sex."

I dug into my pocket and pulled out a single. Holding it up, I walked over to the counter where the swear jars were and deposited the dollar into one.

"What's that for?"

"Consider it a credit. You're so fucking adorable the way your skin pinks up when I say *fucking*, I'm definitely going to say it again."

Why didn't I visit my BFF more often? During my lunch break the next day, I took a walk over to Calliope's yoga studio, which was only a few blocks from the new hospital I worked in for my final rotation. I'd picked up a smoothie before heading over and sat in the back of the class watching a room full of women in tight yoga pants bend over. She smiled and motioned that she'd be a few more minutes, but I was pretty damn content where I was. I got to sit and give my dogs a rest and take in the view.

I mentally graded the rows of arses while I sucked on my strawberry banana smoothie with a double shot of energy boost enhancer. It was like the Olympics, only a fuck of a lot better than synchronized swimming. I liked a full derriere. From the right, I started my grading in the back row. There was a skinny seven with a nice shape, followed by a buxom eight in a pair of pink trainers, and a five who definitely needed to eat a little more pizza. When I got to the fourth rear end, I gave myself a brain freeze sucking on the straw while staring—*now that's a nice plump ten*. Damn. I was in the wrong line of work.

Calliope finished up her class, hit some stupid gong, and walked to me wiping her forehead. "You're such a pig, you know that?"

"What? I came to visit my BFF."

"You looked like you were judging an ass contest the way you were staring."

I smirked. "Number four, purple Nike leggings. She won. I'm going to give her the gold medal when she comes out from the locker room."

Calliope elbowed me in the ribs. "Help me clean up while we talk. I have another class in fifteen minutes and need to collect all the balance blocks."

I picked up a total of three of the silly styrofoam blocks and used those to juggle while she cleaned up the rest.

"So, to what do I owe this pleasure?"

"Tell me about this woman, Bridget, I'm living with."

She held up her hands. "Oh no. You can't do that to Bridget."

"Do what?"

"Remember what happened with Suzie McInerney, when we were fifteen? I don't have a lot of friends here in the states yet. Bridget's a good friend. You can't screw her over."

Suzie McInerney. Now that was a name I hadn't heard in a long, long time. She'd been our mutual friend before *the incident.* Suzie was a year older and had the most fantastic set of tits I'd ever seen. One night when we were all hanging out in my parents' basement, Calliope fell asleep early. Suzie let me feel her up. It was my first time copping a boob.

The following week, the same thing happened. Only it was Hazel Larson who let me feel hers while Calliope was snoring. Hers weren't half as nice as Suzie's, but Hazel let me feel them *under* the shirt, unlike Suzie. So, when Hazel told me that if I was her boyfriend, she might consider letting me touch her in *other* places, I didn't think twice about asking her out. But apparently I should have. Because Suzie assumed I was already *her* boyfriend just because she let me play with her boobs over her shirt for twenty seconds. Needless to say, when Suzie found out I was going out with Hazel, she never spoke to me or Calliope again. They'd blamed Calliope since I was the BFF she'd always have hanging around whenever she hung out with her girlfriends. *Women.* I still didn't understand them.

"I'm not planning on copping a feel. Bridget's cute and all, but she's got a kid—you know me and kids." I wasn't planning on having my own, so dating someone with a rugrat was definitely not on my agenda, either.

She looked at me suspect. "That's true...I guess. What did you want to know about Bridget, anyway?"

"I don't know. For starters, what happened to her husband?"

Sadness crossed over Calliope's face. "She hadn't started coming to yoga yet, so we weren't friends when it happened. But she told me about it. Sounded horrible. She was down in Florida with her son visiting her mother when she got a call that he'd been in a terrible car accident. He died before she even landed back in Providence." Calliope shook her head. "He was only thirty. They were college sweethearts."

"Wow."

"Yeah. Awful."

I scratched my chin. "I wonder if that was the trip she got the knickers on."

"What?"

"Nothing."

"Other than that. There's not much to tell. She's devoted to her son, Brendan. He's a sweet, little kid who's really good at baseball. Works at the hospital, and picks up as much overtime as she can, but money's tight living on only one salary. Her husband didn't have much life insurance."

When her next class started to trickle in, it was time for me to get back to the hospital anyway. I leaned down and kissed my friend's cheek. "I'll be back next week—same time, same ass. I mean class."

Chapter 4
Bridget

The ER was busier than usual for a Wednesday afternoon. I hadn't seen much of Simon in the hours before he snuck up behind me.

"Hey, Roomie. I hear you have a chart for me to look at."

Handing him the clipboard, I said, "Yes, this is Eileen McDonough in Room 3. Suspected appendicitis. And can you not say that too loudly?"

He smirked. "What…'Roomie?'"

"Yes. 'Roomie.'"

"Why is that?"

"Because it's not really professional for people to know that we live together. You need to pretend we don't."

"It's not like we're shagging."

"Don't say that," I whispered.

He raised his voice a little. "Excuse me…*fucking*."

"Shh."

"Relax. No one is in the vicinity." Simon chuckled. "Alright, in all seriousness, you don't want me to say anything. Fine. I'll consider it another one of your rules."

"Thank you."

When Simon walked away, I couldn't help but stare at the curvature of his rock solid ass. His thin, blue scrubs left little to the imagination. As much as he'd joked about my rear end, he truly had a beautiful one himself.

One of the other nurses, Julia, caught me in the act. "Hard to focus lately, huh?"

"Hmm?"

"I don't know about you," she said. "But I find myself very distracted whenever Dr. Hogue is on shift."

I couldn't have agreed more. It was definitely distracting. Work hadn't been the same since his transfer to Memorial.

"Well, he's definitely different than the doctors we're used to," I said.

"He never seems to let his fatigue show, either. All of the patients love him. Seriously, I've seen him put smiles on the faces of people who were near death."

I reluctantly agreed. "He does have a way about him."

Julia leaned in. "He's apparently not gay, either."

"Why would you think he was gay in the first place?"

"Someone like that—a hot, single, doctor? I just assumed he would have to be gay, otherwise it's almost too good to be true, right?"

Even though I damn well knew he wasn't gay, I asked, "How can you be so sure he's *not*?"

"Well, I heard Brianna say she hooked up with him once and apparently she's going out with him again one night later this week."

"Really..."

Brianna was one of the newer nurses. She was younger than most of us and fresh out of nursing school. She was pretty, and it didn't surprise me that he was attracted to her. I truly hated that my stomach was now in knots, though, upon hearing that bit of news.

Julia crossed her arms over her butterfly-covered uniform. "Lucky girl, huh?"

"I suppose." I needed to get out of this conversation. "Excuse me. It's time to check Mr. Maloney's vitals."

As I pumped the sphygmomanometer that was wrapped around the old man's arm, I listened to the conversation next door. A thin curtain separated me from the space where Simon was with a different elderly patient.

Simon spoke, "Alright, lovely. Here's the deal. The X-ray came back showing some fluid in the lungs so we're going to have to admit you."

"I can't stay here," the woman protested.

I could hear her daughter say, "Mom, you don't have a choice." She addressed Simon, "She's terrified of hospitals, convinced she'll never return home if they admit her. You have no idea how hard it was to get her to agree to let me bring her here."

It sounded like Simon took a seat on a stool before he said, "We have to get you better, Mamie. We can't send you home like this. What can I do to make you feel more comfortable here?"

The old woman started naming a laundry list of items that she wanted for her room.

"I can go get them for you, Ma."

"No, you can't leave me," Mamie insisted.

Simon interrupted their arguing, "How about this? I'm breaking for lunch soon. How about I pick up some of the items you need from CVS?"

I laughed at the idea of Simon purchasing the "Revlon Stormy Pink" lipstick and the "Jean Naté After Bath Splash Mist" she asked for.

"You would do that for me?" the old woman asked.

"Anything for you, gorgeous."

Smiling, I rolled my eyes and shook my head as I loosened the Velcro from Mr. Maloney's arm.

Simon, you fucking charmer, you.

───────

The last thing I expected when I opened the dishwasher was to see something jump out at me. Quickly realizing it was a mouse, I screamed at the top of my lungs.

I climbed on top of the kitchen table as I watched the little, furry terrorist scurrying across the wooden floor.

I yelled, "Shit. Shit. Shit. Shit. Shit!"

Simon and Brendan both seemed to appear at almost the same exact time.

"What's going on, Bridget?"

"Mommy, what's wrong?"

Waving my arm, I said, "Stay back, Brendan. There's a mouse in the kitchen."

My son beamed. "Cool!"

"No, *not* cool. Mommy won't be able to sleep with a mouse in the house." After spotting it running past me again, I pointed and squealed. "Oh my God, there it is."

I looked at Simon, who seemed really amused by my reaction.

"I need you to catch it and kill it, Simon."

He scratched the stubble on his chin. "Per your request, I was supposed to be *pretending* I don't live here...so perhaps, now would be a good time to disappear?"

"Don't you even think about it."

"I'm kidding. I'll get it. But I'm not killing it. I'll rescue it from this crazy kitchen and send it back into the wild." He bent down. "If only I can find it."

Pointing, I said, "It was just in that corner a minute ago." I looked around. "Oh, no. Where did it go? We have to find it."

Brendan pointed to under the table where I was standing. "Over there!"

I closed my eyes and cringed at the thought. When I opened them, Simon was on the floor. He looked so funny crawling around with his long arms and legs.

"I wasn't expecting to play *Tom and Jerry* today." When he stood up, his hair was disheveled. He was holding the mouse by the tail as its little arms and legs wiggled around aimlessly. "Got it! Come see, Brendan." Simon then cupped the rodent as my son pet it. It was totally skeeving me out and warming my heart a bit at the same time.

Brendan looked at me. "Can I keep it?"

"No!"

"Brendan, I think it's best for your Mum's sake if we set it free. Go grab your coat."

I watched from the window as Simon led Brendan to the wooded area behind our house. Simon knelt down, and I could see Brendan talking to the mouse and waving goodbye to it. Simon then rustled my son's hair before they high-fived each other.

I fought the tears forming in my eyes as the thought occurred to me that Brendan had really been missing a male influence in his life. He was only six when Ben was killed. He could barely remember his dad already.

When they returned to the kitchen, Simon counted five singles then stuffed them into the swear jar labeled *Mom.*

"What's that for?"

"Five dollars donated to Brendan's cause for your S-word recited five times." He turned to Brendan. "You might just get to keep that hair, after all."

Brendan looked over at me and smiled. "I want my hair to grow like Simon's in the front."

I crossed my arms. "Great."

Simon bent his head back in laughter.

After Brendan ran back to his room, I turned to Simon. "Thank you for helping with that. I definitely don't do well with rodents."

"You don't say?" He placed his hands on my shoulders in a firm grip. "You alright now?"

My heart raced upon the brief contact. "Yeah, I'm fine. I'm really glad you were home."

"If you ever need anything, don't hesitate to yell."

I let out a breath. "It's been two years, but I still haven't fully adjusted to not having a man around to handle certain things. I've really tried my best, but clearly I would've totally failed at that one. Literally, I think it would have kept me up all night."

"I think you're handling things just fine—way better than I would be, working the hours you do, then coming home to parent. Your son is a good kid. You're doing a damn good job. But do you ever get to go out, make some time for yourself?"

"Ha!" I laughed. "That would be a no."

"That's not very healthy, Bridget."

"I know. But it's tough. I pay a sitter to watch him while I'm working, so I hate to leave him when I don't have to. It might be different when he's a little older, but for now, I just have to make him my priority."

He leaned against the counter. "That's commendable, but you also have to think about yourself and your sanity. You deserve a break once in a while."

"Have you been questioning my sanity?"

"Maybe a tad." He winked. "Seriously, though, when was the last time you've been out on a date?"

It wasn't difficult to figure out the answer. "I haven't. I mean, Ben's only been gone two years. I just haven't felt ready."

Simon's expression grew sullen. "I'm sorry that you had to go through that. Calliope...she told me, you know, what happened."

"Yeah, I really don't like to talk about it."

"I don't blame you."

Simon seemed to be quietly observing me for a few seconds, and I was starting to feel hot.

I didn't know what came over me when I asked, "Would you want to have some tea with me?"

He looked at his watch. "Shit. I'd really like to, but I'm supposed to meet someone in Providence in twenty minutes."

Trying to mask my disappointment, I said, "You said 'shit.' Money in the Brendan jar, please. Since you and he seem to be ganging up on me as far as the swear words go, it's only fair that I get commission for your swears."

"You got me," he said as he fetched a single from his wallet and placed it in the jar.

"Are you going out with Brianna?"

"How did you know that?"

"The nurses' station is basically a gossip den, Simon. You'd better be careful. You're definitely on everyone's radar. They talk about you a lot."

"Is that so?

I was oddly feeling a bit protective of him.

"Seriously, just be careful what you do. It *will* get around."

"Thanks for the fair warning, Nurse Valentine."

"Where are you going tonight?"

"WaterFire. Apparently, it just opened for the season."

"Ah. I've never been there. Always meant to go but never got around to it. What is it like?"

"It's awesome. Picture like a hundred bonfires on the surface of the river in the middle of downtown. There's music and performances. You really should see it sometime."

"Do you take all your dates there?"

"It's not always in season."

I'd always hoped to go with Ben.

"Well, you'd better go, or you'll be late."

He lingered at the doorway for a bit before he said, "Have a good night, Bridget."

"You, too."

30

As I stared out from the kitchen at the sun setting in my backyard, I once again felt myself getting teary-eyed. I couldn't pinpoint exactly why I was so emotional tonight. Was it because I missed Ben? Or was it because my jealousy over Simon's date meant that I was finally starting to move on? I wasn't sure, but I somehow felt happy, hopeful, and terribly sad all at the same time.

Chapter 5
Simon

Brianna and I strolled along the river walk surrounded by the flames of WaterFire. It was a breezy May evening in Providence, and her long, black hair was blowing around into her face. At one point, I stopped to take some video footage of the flickering lights before we continued walking.

As she was talking my ear off, I was zoning out. I couldn't stop thinking about Bridget, about the sadness in her eyes earlier when we were talking about her husband. I couldn't imagine having to endure that kind of tragedy at such a young age. I also couldn't stop thinking about the fact that I had refused her offer to have tea. Just when she finally seemed to be warming up to me, I had to leave.

Brianna was only twenty-three and definitely not looking for anything serious. It was exactly why I'd pursued her. We'd had sex one time, and while it was good, I couldn't help wanting to find a way to get out of going back to her apartment tonight. I just wasn't into being with her right now, and I couldn't figure out why.

I didn't want to admit that maybe it had something to do with a certain widow, because that would have been dangerous. As curious as I was about Bridget Valentine, I couldn't do anything more than just fancy her. She was someone's mum, for Christ's sake. You don't mess with that. I'd be leaving town in a matter of months when my residency ended. So, the only women safe enough to date were those I was certain weren't looking for anything more than a casual fling.

Brianna turned to me. "Dr. Hogue, did you even hear what I said?"

"Huh?"

She liked calling me Dr. Hogue instead of Simon. It might have been cute while we were screwing, but it was starting to annoy me.

She continued, "I was saying we should try this new bar that opened on Wickenden. It's right around the corner from my apartment."

I knew she assumed I'd be going back to her place. But I really didn't want to.

"Actually, I have an early morning appointment. So, unfortunately, I have to head back to my apartment."

"Aw, you suck, Dr. Hogue." She giggled. "Just kidding...I still love you," she teased as she wrapped her arms around my neck and reached up to kiss me.

After dropping Brianna off at the bar where she planned to meet up with some friends, I drove over the bridge back to our sleepy suburb.

As I passed the white church with its high steeple near the center of town, I was reminded of how nice it was to be able to escape the city yet still live close enough to enjoy it when I wanted. We lived on a peninsula and were surrounded by water.

When I pulled into the driveway, I noticed that Bridget's living room light was still on. Although I knew she liked her privacy, I wondered if she might be up for a late tea. I could show her the videos of WaterFire I'd taken. After all, if I was being honest, I took that footage for her, because she said she'd never had the chance to go.

I'd had a bag of leftover chicken dinner sitting on the passenger seat. It was lined in aluminum to keep the food warm and had roosters all over the exterior of the bag. The restaurant we'd gone to was known for serving fifty different varieties of chicken. The meal was delicious, but they'd given me way too much food. Maybe she would want some.

Ringing the doorbell might have woken Brendan, so I opted not to.

While I had a key to the entrance of my studio apartment, I didn't have a key to the main house. Even though I could access Bridget's kitchen from a set of stairs in my space, I opted to knock on her window.

She'd been reading on the couch and jumped up to let me in.

When she opened, I lifted the bag of chicken. "Care for some cock?"

━━━━

"Wow. Does it taste as good as it looks?" Bridget bent over the oven to remove the tray of food she'd popped in to reheat. She was wearing thin, little shorts, and I swallowed finding myself mulling over the question inappropriately. I cleared my throat and forced my eyes from her ass.

"Even better, actually."

She removed the oven mitts and grabbed two plates from the cabinet. "Will you join me? I hate to eat alone."

Of course, I'd already had my meal earlier. But I could almost always eat. "Sure." I walked to the refrigerator. "What would you like to drink?"

"Actually, I'd love some wine. There's an unopened bottle in the door. I don't get to drink too often because I make it a rule to never drink alone. After...the accident, there were a few tough months that I started to do that, and I realized it would be very easy to make it a daily habit with no one to answer to. So I made it a rule to only drink with others."

"I suppose that's a good rule." I didn't drink often either, but that was more for a lack of time and a lack of tolerance for feeling like shit while working a twenty-hour shift. I removed the Sauvignon blanc from the refrigerator and rummaged through a drawer until I found a corkscrew. It opened with a loud pop that made Bridget smile.

"I love that sound," she said. "I don't know why."

I poured two glasses, and Bridget asked if I would mind eating in the living room on the coffee table because Brendan was a light sleeper and would hear us less in there. She set the plates on the table, and I brought our wine glasses, as well as the bottle.

When I'd knocked and nearly scared the crap out of her a few minutes earlier, she'd been reading, so I picked up her book. "And what are we reading here?"

Bridget practically lunged at me to grab the book out of my hand, which only served to make me even more curious. I held it above my head, out of her reach. "It seems like you don't want me to see what you're reading."

"Give me my book."

I smirked. "Reach it."

Bridget was tiny. I'd guess a good foot shorter than me. There was no way she was reaching the book, even if she jumped.

Her hands went to her hips. "Simon Hogue. Give me my book or else."

"Or else, what?"

"Or else...so help me, I'll climb you like a tree and get that book myself."

Maybe I should have gone home with Brianna and gotten my fill...because I sort of fancied the thought of Bridget climbing me like a tree. "You're welcome to climb me, luv, but be careful, some trees have thick wooden branches and you could get poked."

Her face pinked, and I wasn't sure if it was from my lewd comment or if she was pissed. Either way, it worked for me apparently, because I felt a twitch in my pants. Afraid I might be having a twelve-year-old boy uncontrollable reaction, I thought it best to give in sooner, rather than later. "Here you go. I was only screwing around."

Bridget snatched the book out of my hands and shoved it into the drawer of an end table.

"What's so private that I can't read it, anyway? Are you reading porn?"

Her already pink face turned a deep crimson. I'd hit the nail on the head.

"It's not porn. It's a romance novel."

"That you get off to."

Her eyes widened.

I shrugged. "What's the big deal? I like porn. Have myself a decent collection if you ever want to share. Maybe I can borrow your book, and you can borrow my DVDs. I'll even wipe 'em off before I give 'em to you."

She added a scrunched up nose to those eyes that were already saucers. "Please, tell me you're joking?"

"About the DVDs? Yes."

She looked relieved, so I clarified what I'd meant. "It's the new millennium. No one buys porn on DVD anymore. It's all on my MacBook from downloads."

Bridget shook her head and sat down on the floor. "I think I need that wine now."

I had to move the table out a bit to be able to fit between the couch and the coffee table, but once I sat down, it felt good to stretch out my legs. Bridget plated us food, and the chicken tasted even better the second time.

"Mmmm. This is so good," she said.

"I'll bring you home my leftover cock from now on."

She rolled her eyes. "Must you do that? Always make everything a sexual innuendo."

"It's just *so hard* not to when you like my sexy talk so much."

I caught her smirk before she shoveled her mouth full of my cock. *God, I need to stop even thinking about that.* I pretended to make myself more comfortable but I was really discreetly adjusting my jeans that were growing snug in the crotch.

Bridget sipped her wine to wash down the chicken. "So, why are you home so early. I figured you'd...you know...be with Brianna for a while."

"Are you saying you thought I'd be getting laid right now? You just assume I'm easy and put out on the second date?"

She squinted. "You're so full of shit."

I leaned in with a big goofy grin. "You owe the jar a quarter."

"You're impossible."

"Maybe." I shrugged. "But you like me anyway."

"You didn't answer my question."

"Why am I home so early?"

She nodded.

I debated my answer, just like I'd done for the entire drive home. Scratching my chin, I said, "Let me ask you something first. If you could pick any animal to be, what would you select?"

Rightly, Bridget looked at me funny. "I don't know. Off the top of my head, I guess a stallion."

"Why a stallion?"

"Because they're strong, wild, and free."

I nodded. "Good answer."

"What would you pick?"

"A lion. Because they're king of the jungle, of course." I brushed back my hair that still needed a haircut and winked. "Plus. They have a good mane."

Bridget laughed. "Figures."

"Wanna know what Brianna said when I asked her?"

"Absolutely."

"She said a Pomeranian."

"The little dog?"

Bridget's wine glass was empty, so I refilled it. "Yep. And before you ask, her logic was *because it's so cute*."

"So it's not the most well thought out answer, but you cut your date short because of that?"

"Just wasn't feeling it, I guess. So it didn't feel right to *feel it*. If you know what I mean."

"You're bizarre, Simon Hogue, you know that?"

"I'm glad you said stallion, or I might have had to move out."

Bridget and I sat in the living room and polished off the chicken and almost a full bottle of wine—most of it consumed by her. I realized she was starting to get tipsy when she loosened up a bit.

"Let me ask you something." She pointed her wine glass at me and nearly spilled it. "Have you ever done online dating?"

"You mean like Match.com?"

"Yes."

"No, I haven't."

She sighed. "You probably don't have to. You're..." She waved her hand up and down at me. "Tall and all hot and stuff. And you're a doctor."

"You think I'm hot?" I smirked.

She rolled her eyes. "Of course you don't have to use Match to get a date. What was I thinking? You probably just snap your fingers like Fonzie and the girls come flocking."

"Who?"

"Am I that much older than you? Never mind. Don't answer that."

"Alright. But are you really thinking of joining an online dating site?"

"I was thinking about it."

"I'm not sure if that's a good idea."

"You think it's too soon?"

"No. I'm not sure if online dating is safe."

Bridget waved me off and then gulped back the balance of the wine in her glass. "It was a stupid idea anyway. I don't even *know how* to date. It's been so long."

"Well don't worry about that. It's like riding a bicycle, you'll get right back on."

She mumbled. "I haven't taken a ride in a very long time, either."

Yep. Bridget was definitely drunk. "What about a fix-up?"

"You mean like a blind date?"

"Yeah. It's safer than meeting a stranger."

"I guess..."

"I'll tell you what, Bridget, you let me fix you up, and I'll let you fix me up. We can go out on a double date."

"A double date?"

"What's the worst that can happen? If you don't like the bloke, at the end of the night you're stuck coming home with me."

She grinned. "Okay."

Chapter 6
Bridget

God, I feel like crap.

Lifting my head from the pillow, my initial thought was that I must have the flu. Then I remembered the bottle of wine I'd polished off last night with Simon. I groaned as I reached for my phone from the nightstand and squinted at the time. 8:45!

"Shit!" I jumped out of bed. Brendan was going to be late for school. Darting across the hall to my son's room, I whipped the door to his bedroom open and found it still dark. "Brendan! Get up, buddy! We're late." Flicking on the light, I was surprised to see an empty bed, so I checked the bathroom before heading to the kitchen.

A shirtless Simon was standing at the stove. With just the flick of his wrist, he flipped a pancake over in the pan, before turning to see me.

"Morning, sleepyhead."

Good Lord, the man had some body. Smooth, tanned skin, chiseled abs that looked like they belonged on a magazine cover, and a deep-set V that made it rain inside the desert of my hungover mouth. *Jesus—I don't remember men looking like that.* Not in real life, anyway. I had to look away. But taking in the rest of the room just added to the strange scene. Music was playing from the countertop kitchen speaker. Brendan was beating a drum on the table with one hand and finishing up his breakfast with the other. Simon pressed a button on some contraption on the counter, and a loud whirring sound blared for a minute. Then he poured whatever he'd made into a glass and turned to me. "Juice?"

"What is that thing?"

"It's a juicer."

"Where did it come from?"

"I brought it in. I like fresh juice in the morning." He winked. "Plus, I thought you might be needing some extra Vitamin C and potassium this morning."

I took the glass from Simon's hand, while he spoke to Brendan. "Go get your backpack, kiddo, or we're going to be late."

Brendan took off running. "Late?" I was so confused.

"For school." Simon plated the pancake and set it down on the table. He then pulled a bottle of Motrin from his scrubs pant pocket and pointed to the chair. "Sit. Eat. I'll drop Brendan off and be back to clean up before I go to the hospital."

I was still sitting at the kitchen table when Simon returned from dropping Brendan at school. He leaned one hip against the counter and folded his arms across his chest—which was, unfortunately for me, now covered with a shirt.

"Thank you so much for covering for me this morning. I can't believe I overslept. I didn't even hear my phone alarm go off."

"That's because it didn't."

"It didn't? How do you know?"

"Because I turned it off last night before you turned in."

"Why did you do that?"

Simon shrugged. "So you can sleep in."

"Well, thank you. It's been a really long time since I did that. And, God, it's also been a really long time since I had a hangover. That wine really went to my head last night. I hope I wasn't talking your ear off or anything. To be honest, it's all a bit fuzzy."

Simon took my empty plate to the sink. "Not at all. We had a nice chat and then you went off to bed."

I sighed. "Oh, good."

"After you read me your book."

I froze. "What?"

Simon chuckled and put his hands on my shoulders. "Relax, luv. I'm teasing."

"Thank God."

He went back to finish loading the dishes. I didn't have the energy to even offer to help. Plus, when he bent over in his scrubs, I could see the muscles in his ass flex. I might have been hungover, but I wasn't blind.

When he was all done, he swung a chair around backward and straddled it at the table. "So, tell me your criteria for a bloke?"

"What?"

"Our double date."

Crap. I'd forgotten all about that conversation last night. It was the wine talking. And maybe a bit of jealousy watching Simon go out on his date, too. "I'm not ready for that yet, Simon."

He squinted. "I don't believe you. I think you're just afraid to get back in the saddle."

For a guy I'd only known for a week, he'd figured me out pretty quick. Although I wasn't about to admit that. "I'm not afraid."

"Good, so it's settled then." He pulled a folded-up piece of paper from the chest pocket of his scrubs. "And here's my wish list."

"Your wish list?"

"For my fix-up. I thought you'd like some guidelines."

I unfolded the paper. He'd written out a checklist of about five sentences. "They're not in any particular order."

His chicken scratch was barely legible. "Do they teach you to write like a seven year old in medical school?"

"Give me that. I'll read it to you." He reached over to take the paper from my hands, but I pulled it out of his reach.

"I'm a nurse. Just give me a second, and I'll decipher it. It's part of my job, apparently. Let's see. Number one— no Pomeranians."

Simon elaborated, "Better make that no little dogs, in general. Do you want a pencil to take down notes?"

I laughed. "No, that's okay. I think I can handle remembering. No cute dogs as animal soulmates. Got it. What's next? Let's see. Number two—Apple bonnet?" My brows drew together.

Simon corrected me. "That's apple *bottom*. I like a full rear. I was going to write badunkadonk, but I wasn't sure how to spell that."

"You want me to check out a woman's ass before I fix you up?"

"Oh, come on. You women are always sizing each other up."

"We are not."

"Sure you aren't. Go on, read number three. I don't have all day. I have to get to the hospital and save lives like a superhero."

"Number three—must like the outdoors. Well that one is a reasonable request."

"All of my requests are reasonable."

I ignored him in favor of continuing with his list. "Number four—must dislike Celine Dion." I looked up at him. "What's wrong with Celine?"

"She annoys me."

"Her singing?"

"Nope. Just her, in general."

"You're bizarre, Simon Hogue."

"So you've said."

"Alright, what's the last requirement? Let's see, number five. No starfish." I scrunched up my nose. "What do you have against starfish? They're so pretty and harmless."

Simon chuckled. "Not the marine echinoderm. A starfish. You know..." He leaned back from the chair, balanced on his ass, and spread all four of his arms and legs wide. "A woman who spreads her arms and legs during shagging and doesn't get into it. She just lies there like a starfish. They're usually silent, too."

"Are you joking?"

"I wish I was." He pointed to the paper. "Make that number one on the list if you're prioritizing. It sorta freaks me out."

Simon stood and looked at his watch. "Gotta run. You going to make me a list, or do I have carte blanche."

"As amusing as I find your list, I'm really not ready for a fix-up yet."

Simon smiled from ear to ear. "Carte blanche, it is."

I was really doing this.

Exhaling, I waved to Brendan after dropping him off at my mother-in-law's. It had taken a few weeks to find a night that both Simon and I had off for this double date.

Was I crazy for letting him set me up blind?

I'd chosen an acquaintance from the yoga studio for Simon. Her name was Leah, she was around my age, and was the only single person I knew in town. Her job in finance kept her pretty busy, and she'd always put her career first. But I remembered her telling me that she was looking to get into the dating game, although not looking for anything serious or to really settle down. And I knew that was what Simon wanted. In all honesty, I hadn't bothered to check off any of the other criteria on Simon's list. I'd felt funny asking her the animal question. And how on Earth was I supposed to ask her if she was a "starfish" in bed?

For all I knew, she had probably met Simon before, since he'd gone to visit Calliope at the studio in the past. All I'd told her was that my roommate was a hot, British doctor nearing thirty and that I was looking to set him up on a blind date. She jumped all over that without questioning anything else. I probably would've done the same.

Each of us would be arriving separately to the restaurant on Federal Hill, an area of Providence known for its fine Italian dining. Simon and Leah would be coming straight from work, and I would be heading straight there after dropping Brendan off.

I spent the ride from North Kingstown to Providence obsessing over whether or not this date was a good decision. I suppose it was too late for that to matter, in any case.

My roommate had given me no details about my date, so I was definitely on edge by the time I pulled up to Il Forno Ristorante.

I remembered Simon saying he had made a reservation.

"Hi, do you know if someone named Simon Hogue checked in? Tall, blond, British accent..."

The hostess grinned and grabbed a menu. "Yes. He did. Right this way."

He'd picked a really nice place. The lights were dim, and there was someone playing piano. Simon and another man were sitting at a table in the corner. When I got a look at my date, my spirits dampened immediately. I never considered myself a superficial person, but there just wasn't an iota of attraction for the man sitting across from Simon.

There's still time to turn around.

They both stood up as I approached.

Too late.

Give him a chance.

"Bridget, glad you made it in good time," Simon said.

I nodded. "Simon."

To make matters worse, Simon looked absolutely gorgeous in a fitted, ribbed sweater and dark jeans as his manly scent wafted in the air and floated right between my legs. It was hard not to compare the two guys.

"I'd like you to meet my good friend, Dr. Alex Lard."

I held out my hand. "Hi, Dr....Lard."

Lard? Like the grease.

What a name.

"Please, call me Alex."

"Alex." I smiled. "Good meeting you."

He let out a single cough. "The pleasure is all mine." He coughed again.

Simon gestured to the seat. "Let's sit, shall we?"

Alex Lard coughed another time before sitting down. Was this a nervous habit, or was he ill?

Either way, this was going to be a long night.

Chapter 7
Bridget

Full disclosure...Dr. Lard, the unattractive incessant cougher, was probably the wrong choice for Bridget. *I knew that.* Now before you judge me for setting her up with him, keep in mind that it wasn't easy finding someone whom I could honestly deem a decent human being. I was operating on limited time.

I'd promised to find her a date, and it was either Lard or someone I didn't fully trust, which if I was being honest, was pretty much everyone else. At least I knew Alex wasn't a scumbag. In fact, he was a well-respected Providence physician and Brown University professor. He was a lot of things—sexually appealing just wasn't one of them.

The initial conversation at our table was very awkward.

I sipped my wine. "Did you hit any traffic?"

Bridget looked behind her shoulder then checked her watch, seeming incredibly tense. "No, but Leah must have. She's fifteen minutes late."

I lifted my brow. "Leah, huh?"

Dr. Lard turned to Bridget. "So, Simon was telling me you have an eight-year-old boy. *Cough.* He must keep you busy. *Cough.*"

"Yes. He's a great kid. Not sure if Simon also mentioned that my husband died a couple of years back, so it's been tough on Brendan, but he's doing remarkably well considering."

Before he could respond, we were interrupted by my date, Leah's, arrival. I squinted. She looked familiar.

She flashed a smile as she looked over at me. "Oh my God. It's you."

"You know me?"

"Calliope's friend."

"I am."

"I've seen you when you've come to visit our hot yoga class."

That's right. That was where I knew her from. I immediately realized she was the bony-assed one in class, too. Great.

Leah sat down, and the four of us made small talk until our food arrived. To be frank, from the get go, it was pretty clear this double blind date was a dud. I knew it. Bridget knew it. And If I were being *really* honest, it was hard to concentrate on anything besides how fucking stellar Bridget looked tonight. Her full lips were painted a hot shade of pink. She'd put waves in her hair, which I'd never seen her do before. It was down, but she'd pulled some of the honey brown strands back with a barrette at the front. That accentuated her green eyes. I'd normally marveled at how naturally beautiful she was with no makeup and bone straight hair, but I had to say, this look was working for me, too.

Really working for me.

Not to mention her strawberry creams looked damn good squeezed together with just a hint of cleavage showing.

She deserved better than this boring date with Alex Lard. He was a good man, but he wasn't going to be the one to give her the earth-shattering orgasm she really needed.

Fuck. Don't think about how sex-starved she is and how amazing it would be to make her moan for the first time in years.

Wouldn't that have been the bollocks...one night of non-stop shagging with Bridget sans consequences, making her scream out over and over. Of course, that scenario was never going to be possible.

To deter from my clearly inappropriate thoughts, I decided to ask Leah *the question*.

"So, Leah. Question for you. If you could pick any animal to be, what would you select?"

"What a strange question." She laughed. "But okay, let me think." She scratched her chin with her long, fake nails. "I would have to say kitten. Because they're so cute. And I love cats, in general."

Bridget looked at me and was smirking. She knew that "kitten" was probably the only answer worse than Pomeranian. At least Pomeranian was somewhat original.

"What a coincidence because Simon loves pussy," Bridget joked.

I smiled at her mischievously. "That I do, Nurse Valentine."

The remainder of the date was basically torture aside from Bridget and my flirtatious glances at each other.

51

She'd done nothing to really get to know Alex—he never stopped coughing—and Leah had lost me at "kitten."

The dinner wrapped up on the early side, and we all left in separate cars with empty promises to "keep in touch" with our dates.

The second I got back to the house, I headed straight for Bridget's living room.

She was already standing there waiting with her arms crossed. "Meow." She laughed.

I shook my head. "Kitten. Just awful. Not to mention, you set me up with the one woman in the entire yoga studio with the flattest arse. Who doesn't fill out spandex? That woman! Even Spandex are baggy on her. Probably a major starfish as well—although I don't intend to find out."

"I didn't choose those things intentionally, Simon. I don't have a lot of single friends. And you have some nerve talking to me about physical attraction right now. You knew I wouldn't feel it for Alex Lard. So, why bother setting me up with him?"

"Look, he's a nice guy. I couldn't bear to fix you up with someone who might have even a remote chance of taking advantage of you."

"Well, you got that part right...because Dr. Lard had zero chance of getting lucky with me tonight or *ever*. And what was with that cough?"

"I don't know. It's his thing. It's bizarre."

"I would prefer to go on dates where I don't have to wear a mask to protect myself from germs."

I belted out in laughter. "I know, Bridget. I fucked it up. You said you were going to do online dating, and that freaked me out a little. There are a lot of bad people out there."

"Online dating is the only way to do it when you don't have the time to go out every night. It's very common now. Someone like you doesn't have to resort to that because you have women falling at your feet."

"Trust me, if you put yourself out there in any manner, you would have no problem finding a man. You're extremely attractive."

"Well, thank you, but you don't have to say that."

"No, I don't, but it's the truth. You're naturally beautiful, even when you're not done up like tonight. You have gorgeous lips, ample tits, a fit body, and a mighty fine apple bottom."

The bluntness of my words surprised me. She looked a little taken aback as well.

She waved her hand. "Oh, go on."

"You think I'm kidding."

"No, I meant, go on and on. Keep going." She laughed.

We just stared at each other for a bit. She looked embarrassed, and I wished I could have kissed her and made it worse.

Simon, what the fuck are you doing, you wanker?

"I probably should stop talking, actually." I said. "You might evict me. I'm being inappropriate, given our arrangement and your life situation. I shouldn't be staring at Brendan's mum's apple bottom."

"See, you hit the nail on the head. It's not easy as a single mother to find someone willing to see past my 'situation.' It's part of why I haven't really considered dating until recently. Not only has it seemed too soon after Ben's death, but realistically the chances of finding someone physically attractive, smart, honest, who would also want to take on this massive responsibility is basically nil. Honestly, I don't know if I would really want to deal with my situation if I were a guy. So, it's hard. And it gets lonely sometimes."

This woman wore her vulnerability on her sleeve. But I loved that she was so honest.

She let out a deep breath. "God, I'm telling you too much. I didn't mean to bear my soul like that."

"It's apples and oranges."

"What is...something you're juicing in the morning?"

"No. You and most of the women—girls, really—who I date. It's like apples and oranges. You're a real *woman*, Bridget, in every sense of the word. Someone like you knows exactly what she needs. You have your head on straight and your priorities in the right order. You appreciate what really matters in life because you've experienced the worst of it. You've had a lifetime of experiences at a young age. You're amazing, really."

And that's why I can't fuck with you.

She looked like she didn't know how to take the compliment. "Will you stay and have a drink with me? I really feel like one, and you know my rule about never drinking alone."

As much as I knew I probably should've gone back to my unit, my *other* unit was really enjoying being with her. I couldn't say no.

"Sure, I can."

Bridget disappeared into the kitchen to fetch some wine. She was taking an unusually long time to return, so I decided to check on things.

"Everything okay in here?"

I noticed that she was holding a piece of paper in her hands. She stood there frozen, looking gutted.

"I found this in the trash. Brendan must have discarded it when he came home from school."

My heart sank when I took the bright orange flyer from her hands, which read: *Father Son Field Day.*

Oh, shit.

She continued, "I could only imagine how he must have felt. How could they have even let him go home with this in his backpack? They all know his situation."

"I'm sure they didn't mean to hurt him intentionally, but it was stupid."

She closed her eyes then let out a breath. "You know, you go about your life as best you can, trying to forget the pain and then something like this comes along and just throws it all in your face again."

Not knowing what else to say, I simply placed my hand on her forearm. "I'm sorry."

She sighed. "God, you must find this house so depressing sometimes, constant reminders of death."

"Yeah, well, there's a lot of life in this house, too. Living here has been a learning experience for me. Before I moved in, I was just some bloke living alone who did nothing but work, sleep, and screw around once in a while. It's eye-opening to see what you go through."

She took the flyer back from me. "I don't even know what to do about this."

"You can't fix everything, unfortunately."

"I would want to just keep him home from school that day, but that's sending the wrong message, too. I don't want him treated any differently because he doesn't have a dad."

"Will you talk to him about it?" I asked.

"I'm not sure whether I should. He clearly didn't want me to see this."

"Do you think, in some way, he was trying to protect your feelings, too?"

"You know, it's funny you say that. As young as he is, he does have a protective way about him. There are times when I've broken down, and he's been the one to comfort *me*."

"You have a great kid there, very wise for his age and respectful. That's all you."

"Thank you. He was very difficult to conceive, but he's been an easy child since he was born. I'm pretty lucky." She put the flyer back into the trash and began to massage the tension in her own neck with one hand.

"Turn around for a minute."

She was skeptical. "What are you gonna do?"

"Check what day of the week's knickers you're wearing. What do you think?"

"What are you really going to do?" She laughed.

I cracked my knuckles. "Let's get some of those knots out of your neck and back."

I felt her tension lift as soon as my hands went to work. Massaging her upper back, I pressed my thumbs especially hard into her. She hung her head low as she relaxed her body, giving me full control. The sounds she was making were driving me a bit mad. This woman was wound up and needed a hell of a lot more than my hands. It took everything in me not to bend down and devour her neck. My fingers were definitely working on behalf of my cock that unfortunately couldn't be here to accept this award tonight.

Her breathing became a bit more labored at one point and she turned around, stopping the massage. "Thank you for that. I should get that wine now."

"Let me help."

"No, I got it."

I returned to the living room and sat down on the couch, noticing something under me. It was Bridget's e-reader. I opened it to the home page, which showed a romance novel featuring a salacious cover. Clicking on it, I could never have imagined the words that would meet my eyes.

Holy shit.

What's this now?

Chapter 8

Bridget

Oh no.

When I returned to the living room with two glasses of Zinfandel, Simon was nose deep in my Kindle reading my book.

"Simon, stop."

"You've been holding out on me, Bridget. *This* is the stuff in your books?"

Feeling the heat rise in my face, I said, "What did you *think* was in my books?"

"I figured it was some Fabio shit, you know, woman blushes, follows the guy to the bedroom, he makes love to her. This chap has his cock between her tits, and he just shot his load on her face."

"He did?"

"Oh, that's right. I read past your bookmark. I guess you hadn't gotten there yet."

"Apparently not."

"Let me back up and read it to you, then."

The expression on my face must have looked like a mixture of terror and amusement. At least, that was how I felt. "Simon…"

"Come on. I promise. I'll be serious. We can have Storytime with Simon. Sit back with your wine and I'll read to you."

Oh my God. He was serious.

I had to admit, though. The thought of listening to him reciting the sex scenes for me in that accent was too enticing to pass up. So, against my better judgment, I did as he said, took my glass of wine, sat down, leaned my head back and just listened.

"Let's see now. Looks like your bookmark begins right here." Simon cleared his throat dramatically. *"Ahem"* And then began...

"His fingers dug deep into my tense shoulder muscles."

Oh my God. I'd completely forgotten that I'd left off in my book at a point where the hero was about to give the heroine a massage. Just like Simon had done to me not two minutes ago. "This isn't a good idea." I began to jump up from the couch, but Simon caught me. He hooked one arm around my waist and pulled me back down. Only now we were sitting much closer on the couch. Our thighs were touching, and the warmth from his body transmitted to my leg and shot down to an interesting place.

"Rubbish. You set me up with a boney-ass, wanna-be kitten. Now I'm going to get some action tonight, even if it has to come from your e-reader."

I smirked. "Her ass was kind of boney, wasn't it?"

"Did you even inquire if she was a starfish?"

I giggled. "No."

"Alright, then. You owe me. And as payback, I'm going to read this little hot scene and then when we're done, I'll go back to my place and enjoy a good wank, and you'll do whatever it is that you do."

"A good wank?" I questioned.

"Masturbate. You know..." Simon formed a C with one hand and pumped it back and forth, simulating a hand job. "Jerk the gerk. Choke the chicken. Pump the stump. Do the five knuckle shuffle. Flog the lizard. Burp the worm. Charm the snake...whatever you Americans call it these days."

If I had any common sense, I probably should have been offended that my tenant was suggesting that he read me the dirty parts of my book and then we go our separate ways and masturbate. But...it did sound sort of appealing. God knows I was tense. Simon smirked. "You're in. I can read it all over your face. You won't deprive me this simple pleasure after the catastrophe of my date."

"Fine," I huffed trying to sound like it was a sacrifice.

Simon started to read again. I didn't bother to move from my new position snuggled against him.

His fingers dug deep into my knotted shoulder muscles. "You're so tense. Why don't you remove your blouse so I can really work my fingers into you?"

"Okay." I unfastened the small pearl buttons and slipped my blouse from my shoulders.

"Christ, you have no bra on underneath your shirt, Cheri."

"I'm perky enough that I don't need to wear one."

"Perky, huh? Perhaps I should be the judge of that." Andrew reached around to cup both my breasts. He pinched one nipple hard. "These are pretty damn perky.

How about if I massage these for a while instead of your neck?"

Simon stopped reading. "Wait. So that was an option? I only got to rub your neck?"

I elbowed him in the ribs, and he chuckled while speaking. "Let me ask you, does this thing have a word search feature?"

"The e-reader? Yes, why?"

"Do you ever just search for cock or tits and skip right to the good parts?"

"No! You think I read it for the sex...but I need the full story. I can't just jump into that stuff without any build up. That would be like having sex without any touching first—no foreplay."

"I rather like the thought of having sex without actual touching first."

"You would. You're a man."

"What's that supposed to mean?"

"It takes less to...you know...get you off. You can pretty much put it in any hole and get the job done."

"If that were true, I'd be home with Miss Kitty right about now, wouldn't I?"

"I guess..."

"Men need foreplay as much as women. It just doesn't have to be an actual act of touching for me."

"What do you mean?"

"Foreplay can be the way a woman looks." Simon's eyes dropped to my body. "The way her mouth moves." His gaze flickered to my lips. "With the right woman, I could be dreaming about what it might feel like to have her painted lips on me the entire time we're sharing a meal. It could even be in a crowded restaurant. By the time I'm done with dinner—I've had all the foreplay I can take, and I'm ready to get down to business."

I swallowed. "But what about the woman? What's her foreplay?"

"With the right person, it's the same." His gaze returned to meet mine. "If the chemistry is there, if there's a mutual attraction and she's watching me watch her, just knowing what I'm thinking can be foreplay. I drive her home. Neither of us speaks. Tension builds. Then we shag right up against the door the minute we walk in because we can't control ourselves anymore."

God, it was warm in the house. I felt like fanning myself. "I think maybe you could *write* one of my books, Simon."

"Ah. That sounds like a challenge. Don't be surprised if I jot some sexy scenes down on my prescription pad and slip them under your bedroom door. You can tell me if what I prescribe works better than your books."

"You're crazy enough that I wouldn't put it past you."

Simon lifted the e-reader. "Where were we? I need to brush up on my sex scene writing."

"I think he was giving her a massage."

"Ah, yes. Nipple pinching." His finger scanned the page of the tablet, stopping half way down the page. "Here we go."

I bent my head back offering Andrew my mouth as he kneaded my aching breasts. His tongue tasted like the whiskey he'd been drinking over dinner. Whiskey and Andrew—it was a combination that really worked for me. He broke the kiss, walked around from behind, and began unbuckling his belt directly in front of me. Sitting,

I was eye level to his thick bulge. "You know what I've been thinking about all night?"

"What?"

"How good it would feel to slide my cock in between your perky tits. I bet you're wet right now. I'm going to put my fingers inside of you, coat my hand with your juices and rub it between those tits before I pump my cock in and out. How does that sound, Bridget?"

Bridget? Did he just say Bridget, or was I hearing things?

Simon cleared his throat again. After a long pause he started to speak, only his voice was heavier and gravelly. *"Yes, please, Andrew. Please."*

Licking my lips, I unzipped his pants. I was so needy that I couldn't even waste the time to lower them. Instead, I tugged on the waistband of his dark boxer briefs and slipped my hand inside. Simon was hard as a rock when I wrapped my fingers around his thick arousal.

I'd thought he was teasing me the second time. "Simon and Bridget. Very cute, Dr. Hogue. You had me there for a second. I thought I'd imagined it the first time."

Simon turned to face me. His face wasn't playful like it normally was. "Huh?"

I squinted. "When you called the heroine Bridget instead of Cheri and the hero Simon instead of Andrew?"

He blinked a few times. "Yes. Uh. You caught me." Simon stood abruptly. "I think that's enough reading for tonight."

I was confused at the sudden turn of events...until...I looked forward while Simon was standing and noticed a considerable bulge.

Oh my God. Simon was hard from reading my book.

63

Chapter 9
Simon

I needed to get laid. *Badly.*

Last night I wanked off twice and still couldn't catch shut-eye for hours. Normally, after a good release, I could pass out for days. Finishing my morning run, I leaned over panting with my hands on my knees. Eight miles and it still did nothing to release the feeling of frustration inside of me. My neck was tense, jaw was clenched, and I had the urge to go box a few rounds with the heavy bag.

After I caught my breath, I tugged off my shirt, used it to wipe the sweat off my face, and walked the last block back to the house. I'd intentionally left while Bridget was in the shower so I didn't have to face her, figuring she'd be gone by the time I got back. I had a certain amount of guilt about visualizing her while I wanked—obviously not enough to stop me from doing it. *Twice.*

I was surprised to find her car in the driveway this late. Even though I'd planned to avoid her, I knew it was later than she normally left, so I stopped in to make sure everything was okay. Bridget was hopping on one foot attempting to put a shoe on while brushing her teeth at the same time.

"Everything okay?" I looked at my watch. "Don't you have to be at the hospital in five minutes?"

She mumbled through a foaming mouth of toothpaste. "Yes. I overslept."

I couldn't help myself. I grinned. "Oxytocin surge."

"What?"

"Orgasm causes an increased production of oxytocin which triggers endorphins that make you sleepy."

Bridget almost fell over getting on her shoe and immediately headed for the bathroom to spit out her mouth full of paste. I followed, watching from the doorway as she rinsed. Wiping her mouth on the hand towel, she said, "Is anything not about sex with you, Simon? I overslept because I'm a working, single mother."

"Sure you did."

She growled at me. It was cute.

"Is Brendan still home, too?"

"He's in his room getting dressed."

"Why don't you take off? I'll drop Little B at school to save you some time?"

"You'd do that?"

"Of course. I owe you one."

Still in rush mode, she brushed past me and went to the kitchen to grab her work ID and keys. "That would be great. But why do you owe me one?"

"Let's just say you helped me out last night. Actually... maybe I owe you two."

I saw her blush as she ran out the door. "Kiss Brendan for me!"

"Simon, can I ask you something?"

"Sure, buddy. What's up?" Brendan was in the backseat of my car as I headed toward his school.

"You're kind of like an uncle since you live with us, right?"

I wasn't sure where this was going. "An uncle is the brother of one of your parents usually."

"But Mark Connolly's parents are divorced, and his mom just had a guy move in and he calls him Uncle Sam."

"Ummm. I think that's a little different than a real uncle. Sometimes kids call close friends of their parents Uncle or Aunt."

"So, couldn't *you* be my uncle, then? You and my mom are friends, right?"

"I guess so. In that sense of the word uncle, sure."

I heard the smile in his voice. "Great. Can you come to field day this afternoon, then? Miss Santoro says if your dad can't make it, an uncle or a grandfather can come."

"Sorry, buddy. I have to work this afternoon." I pulled up to the light and looked in the rearview mirror. The kid's face almost broke my heart. "You know what, let me make some calls. Maybe I can get someone to cover my shift for a few hours."

His face lit up. "Really?"

"You bet." Two minutes later, I pulled to the curb at the front of the school and turned around. "What time does field day start?"

"Eleven."

I nodded. "I'll do my best to be there."

The kid was grinning from ear to ear. He strapped his backpack on and scooted over in the seat to open the door. "You're going to beat all the dads in tug of war. None of them look like you!"

Dan Fogel was a bastard. In exchange for covering my shift, I had to cover *two* Saturday nights and pick him up a pile of Chinese food on an evening of his choosing. He'd initially said no, and my begging told him to up the cost. But it was all worth it when I walked into Miss Santoro's classroom. I scanned the room for Brendan. There were a few dads milling around the room already. Little B was in the back of the class with a group of boys when he spotted me. Pointing, he said, "See, I told you my uncle was *huge*. Look at his muscles. We're gonna cream you in tug of war."

I would've covered twenty shifts for the way he beamed and ran over. Brendan gave me a fist bump and introduced me to all his buddies. They formed a circle around me, which made me feel a bit like Gulliver next to all the little peanut-sized boys.

"Are you really a doctor?" A suspect little redheaded freckle face squinted at me under his glasses.

I kneeled down. "I am. Do you have an ailment?"

"A what?"

"An ailment. You know...does your tummy or something hurt?"

"No. But sometimes Brendan lies."

My eyes flickered to Brendan and back to the little boy. "I highly doubt that. Brendan is a stand-up mate."

Little redhead put his hands on his hips. "Do you also fly planes?"

From my peripheral view, I caught Brendan's eyes widen at the prospect of my exposing him. "Just small ones. You should come along for a ride some time. As long as you don't mind Brendan taking the helm once in a while."

The kid's glasses nearly knocked square from his face when his eyes bulged. "You let Brendan fly the plane!"

I looked around and winked. "Shh...let's keep that between us boys. I wouldn't want Brendan to get in trouble—underage piloting and all."

The crew of kids ran off to play after that, and I was greeted by a very pretty lady. She extended her hand. "You must be Dr. Hogue, Brendan's uncle."

"That's me."

"I'm *Miss* Santoro, Brendan's teacher. He talked about you all morning. He's super excited to have you here. I'm glad you could make it."

"Thank you. I'm happy it worked out."

"Do you live here in town? I work the drop off circle in the mornings, and I've noticed you dropping him off a few times."

"Yes. I live with Bridget and Brendan. I'm finishing up my residency at Memorial and staying with them until I'm done."

"Oh. You must be Mrs. Valentine's brother, then?"

"Ummm. Yes. Bridget's my big sis."

"Were you both raised in England? I've never noticed an accent before from her...but yours is very strong. It is British, isn't it?"

Shit. And one lie snowballs into two. What the heck? In for a penny, in for a pound. I might as well have fun with it. "I went to college and med school across the pond. I guess I picked it up over the years. Harry, my flat mate, had a pretty royal sounding accent. His brother William was even worse."

She smiled. "Well, I like it."

My flirting came out on autopilot. "Then I think I'll keep it."

Little B and I won the two-on-two basketball tournament. We romped in the egg on a spoon game, and the three-legged race wasn't even a challenge—we pretty much walked to victory. Brendan was having the time of his life when we broke for lunch. The teachers had set up a table full of blankets and sack lunches. I grabbed our loot, and we went to sit under a tall oak.

Brendan sat Indian-style while I stretched out on the blanket, leaning up on my elbows. "Ah. It's good to be the king, isn't it, buddy?"

He smiled. "It's awesome. Mark Connolly usually wins everything. He thinks his dad is the coolest because he works on airplanes. But he's a mechanic, not even a pilot."

I took a bite of my sandwich and eyed my little buddy. "He's not a pilot like me, huh?"

Brendan's face dropped. I hadn't meant to make him feel bad. I was just teasing—all boys tell tall tales when they're his age. "You're not going to tell my mom, are you?"

"Of course not. Bro code. We stick together." I offered my fist for a bump.

He looked relieved. "I didn't mean to lie...I just couldn't take it anymore. They're always talking about how great their dads are. This morning, Mark made fun of me because I don't know how to throw a spiral, and it just sort of came out."

I mussed his hair trying to make light of it, even though I felt a crushing sensation inside my chest. "They're all just jealous because you have this cool, long hair going on."

After lunch, we did a few more activities and then the kids all went to do some water balloon squashing thing, and the parents stood around talking. Miss Santoro found me fiddling with my phone.

"If you win anymore events, I might have to tie one arm behind your back to make it fair for the other kids."

It was a hot one today, and Miss Santoro had changed out of her dress and heels into cute little shorts and a t-shirt to spend the afternoon outside. None of my teachers looked like her growing up. I wondered if Little B had a crush on his teacher. "Oh yeah? You're going to tie me up?"

She blushed. "When it comes out of your mouth, it sounds dirty."

That was because my mouth *was* dirty. And sometimes, I acted like an ass. "Sorry about that. I didn't mean to offend you."

"You didn't." She looked up from under her thick lashes. "It sounded kind of sexy, actually."

Oh shit. I was just screwing around. The last thing I needed was for Brendan to think I was hitting on his teacher. *Or Bridget.* Luckily, Little B was heading my way with two balloons.

"Can you throw these at the dunk tank, Uncle Simon?"

"Sure, buddy." I nodded at Miss Santoro. "Don't worry, I'm only going to use one hand."

Field day ended at three o'clock, and all of the dads were taking their kids home with them. Brendan usually went to an afterschool program because Bridget worked, but I didn't want him to be the only kid there today. So, instead, I took him for ice cream and then headed to the hospital. There was less than an hour left to Bridget's shift, so I figured he could hang around in the staff lounge and raid the snack machines while he did his homework. We were both excited to surprise his mom.

Bridget was behind the nurse's station when we walked in, typing away on the computer, so she didn't see us come into the ER.

I leaned down and whispered to Brendan. "You wanna sneak up and scare her or should I?"

He grinned. "Me."

Bridget nearly jumped out of her skivvies when he snuck up on her and growled. "Oh my God. What are you doing here, Brendan?"

"I came with Simon."

"Simon? Why were you with Simon?" She turned to me. "I was wondering why you weren't here yet."

"Simon was my uncle today. He came to field day and beat all the other dads."

"He did?"

"Yep. And that's not all. You wanna know what else happened?"

I'd assumed he was going to spill about our getting ice cream.

Bridget said, "Of course. What else happened that I don't know about? It sounds like I'm in the dark on a lot of amazing stuff that happened today."

Brendan scrunched up his nose. "Miss Santoro was making googly eyes at Simon. I think she wants to marry him."

Great. What happened to bro code, Little B?

Chapter 10
Bridget

The entire ride home from the hospital, I couldn't stop thinking about Simon attending the field day event and what that meant to Brendan.

On one hand, I thought it was the sweetest, most heartfelt thing anyone had ever done for us. On the other hand, it was a bit irresponsible. I didn't want Brendan becoming attached to Simon only to be devastated when he ultimately moved away. Simon being there for Brendan was like a temporary Band-Aid for a wound that wasn't going to go away, and there was a very good chance that my son could end up hurt even more. *Simon leaves and then what?*

But through my rearview mirror, the smile on Brendan's face couldn't be ignored. He seemed to be mentally reviewing the day's events. He deserved these moments of joy, which were few and far between. Thus, my conflicted state.

Simon had apparently switched shifts with another doctor in order to attend the field day, so he wasn't working tonight. He was already home when Brendan and I arrived back to the house.

Simon didn't join us for dinner that night, though, like he sometimes would. I assumed he must have been exhausted from his role as a human punching bag for a bunch of grade schoolers. So, I didn't bother him, even though I was itching to talk to him.

Around nine-thirty, after Brendan had gone to sleep, I heard Simon in the kitchen.

After lowering the volume on the TV, I got up from the couch and tied my cardigan around my waist before venturing into the kitchen. "Hey."

"Hi," he said. "I was just going to make some tea. You want some?"

"Sure."

The tone between us tonight seemed different, less playful. There was definitely an awkward tension in the air.

"Thank you for being there for him today."

Placing the teabags into the cups, he shrugged. "It was nothing. It was his idea. I couldn't disappoint him."

"I know. He told me he asked you to go."

Simon looked at me. "I didn't want you to think I overstepped any boundaries because I happened to see that flyer. If he hadn't come up with the uncle idea...I would never have—"

"No, I understand what happened. He's very hard to say no to when he gets excited about something. I get it."

He could apparently sense that there was something more on my mind.

"What's wrong, Bridget?"

"I'm just a little concerned he's going to get attached to you."

"You think it's bad that he's getting close to me…"

"I don't know." I just kept shaking my head. "I don't know what the right answer is."

"If he looks to me like a favorite uncle, I suppose there's no harm in that. As long as it's not like…" he paused.

I finished his sentence. "As long as he doesn't look at you like a father."

"Yeah. I suppose that's what I was getting at."

"The only problem is, I know my son, and there's really no limit to how he loves or gets attached. I don't know that he's truly able to compartmentalize. I think the longer you're around, the more attached he's just going to get regardless of what label he places on you."

"What are you suggesting, then?" he asked.

"I don't know. I'm struggling with this myself."

"If you think it's best that I keep my distance from him, I—"

"I didn't say that, Simon. I'm just confused."

He held out his hand. "I get it."

Simon seemed a little upset, so I attempted to change the subject.

"So, Miss Santoro was smitten with Uncle Simon, I take it? She's attractive, too."

"Yes, she is. And she wants to tie me up."

"What?"

"Just kidding. Sort of."

I felt like my jealousy was smoking out of my ears. "So, are you gonna go for it?"

"No."

Swallowing, I asked, "Why?"

"Not gonna cross the line with Brendan's teacher. But moreover, I don't want to piss my sister off."

"Your sister?"

"You. I told her you were my sister."

"Oh God. Are you kidding? How did you explain the accent?"

"I spent some time in England while you stayed back here?" He flashed a crooked smile.

"Goodness. You're teaching my son lying?"

"He's a pretty good fibber all on his own. Trust me on that one."

Rolling my eyes, I said, "I don't even want to know." I watched him steep the tea then continued harping on the Miss Santoro issue because I just didn't know when to stop. "So, you really wouldn't ask his teacher out?"

"Even if she weren't his teacher, she strikes me as the type who wants to nail down a man, settle down."

I used the opportunity to ask, "Have you *ever* had a serious girlfriend?"

"Once."

"What happened?"

"We realized we were much better off as friends. Then we went off on our separate ways to different colleges."

"Do you ever think about her?"

"Only when I'm interrupting her yoga class to stare at the variety of apple bottoms."

It took a few seconds before it hit me like a ton of bricks.

Wait.

Simon dated Calliope?

"Oh my God. Calliope? You...and Calliope?"

He laughed at my reaction. "She's my best friend, but she was my girlfriend for a brief time. I like to think of it as a small lapse in sanity."

"Wow. She never told me."

"It was a long time ago, long before she ever met Nigel."

"Does Nigel know?"

"Yeah. We make jokes about it. He's cool with it."

My mouth was agape. "Wow. I don't even know what to say."

"There is nothing to say. It was eons ago."

My face was hot with jealousy. "No other steady girlfriends?"

"No."

We moved to the table to sip our tea and carried on a casual conversation about happenings at the hospital until I decided I wanted to delve a little deeper.

"What made you decide to become a doctor?"

He kept steeping his tea and staring into his cup until he looked up at me and said, "I have an unhealthy and incessant need to save people, I guess."

That was sort of an odd answer.

"You wanted to be like a real-life superhero?"

"It's a bit more complicated than that," he said, almost under his breath.

"Did something happen?"

Simon didn't answer and simply looked down at his watch. "Actually, I forgot I have an early meeting tomorrow with hospital management before my shift. I've got to be up at five. So, I'm gonna turn in, alright?"

"Okay," I whispered, hoping I hadn't upset him.

He left me alone in the kitchen. I looked at the clock. It was late, but I decided to text Calliope, knowing she'd told me once that she stays up pretty late.

Bridget: Are you awake?

Calliope: Yup. Just watching the telly. What's up?

Bridget: Can I call you?

Calliope: Sure.

She answered, "What's up, Bridge?"

I came right out with it. "You never told me that you and Simon dated."

Calliope sighed. "It was so long ago. I didn't think it was significant. Are you mad?"

"No...no. I just...I'm surprised. That's all."

"Honestly, we started out as friends and have remained friends. The romantic relationship was sort of like a strange detour in the middle that didn't work out. We were always meant to be just what we are—friends. He's very special to me, not someone I could ever see disappearing from my life."

I could kind of relate to feeling that way about him.

"I can understand that."

"Nigel is the love of my life. Everything turned out the way it should have in that respect." She paused then said, "Bridget..."

"Hmm?"

"Are you falling for Simon?"

I hesitated. "No."

"Be honest."

I sighed. "I don't know what I'm feeling. I'm very attracted to him, though."

It was the first time I'd ever admitted that out loud to anyone.

"Enough time has passed since Ben died. It's okay to have feelings for someone, you know. Especially someone who's truly a great guy."

"I thought you agreed he was a manwhore."

"Well, he is." She laughed. "Or at least, he *was*. But that's not necessarily because he's a bad person. Simon thinks he doesn't want kids, doesn't want to settle down. He's always said that. But I don't truly believe him, because a lot of his actions contradict that. I think he's just scared of hurting people or getting hurt—one or the other, maybe both."

"Why?"

"He has his reasons. Not my place to talk about it, though."

What does that mean?

I chose not to pry. "Okay."

"But I can assure you of one thing," she said. "Deep down, underneath all that brawn and wild personality...is a really decent human being. I don't know exactly whether that makes him good boyfriend material or not, but Simon is certainly someone I would trust with my life."

Chapter 11
Simon

I just kept fucking up.

First...it was the Adventures of Uncle Simon. Bridget was right. There was no way I wanted Brendan to become attached to me, only to be devastated when I moved.

Second was the issue of my attraction to Bridget. I hadn't wanked off to anyone but her in weeks, and it was pissing me off. Every time I would try, the woman in my head would morph into her. What the fuck was wrong with me?

Third, I almost messed up and told her about Blake. We were having tea, and she'd asked me about my reasons for entering the medical field. I found myself really wanting to tell her, which was strange, because I normally avoided talking about it at all costs. But Bridget had a way about her that made you want to bare your soul. She emitted an air of motherly comfort or something that made me want to just place my head on her lap and tell her all of my secrets and woes. (And yes, my dirty mind did wander to some of the other things I could do with my head in her lap.) Anyway, I suspected she wouldn't judge me.

Especially since she knew a thing or two about devastating life circumstances. But I stopped myself, mainly because I really couldn't risk opening up to her, getting closer to her. I needed to consider what would happen when my residency was over and I moved back to the UK, which was the plan all along.

So, lately, I'd been distancing myself a bit, just spending more time out of the house or at least when I was home, keeping to my own space. The problem was: I was physically distancing myself, but mentally still focusing on her. I missed her and if I was being honest...Brendan, too.

Feeling frustrated, I spent my morning off at the yoga studio, arse-gazing until Calliope finished her class.

Helping myself to the smoothie station, I sliced up some fruit and vegetables and blended a concoction as she pulled up a stool to join me.

I spoke through the blender. "Care for some pineapple banana spinach flaxseed Nutella shake?"

"No, thank you." She cut right to the chase. "So, you told Bridget that we used to date..."

I suddenly stopped mixing the smoothie. "She mentioned it to you?"

"Yes. She called me the other night, wanted to know why I'd never relayed that information."

"What did you tell her?"

"I just reiterated how long ago it was, but I think she might have been a little...jealous. I could sense it."

"What else did she say?"

"Nothing, really."

"Come on. Don't hold back on me, Calliope. Don't forget I can tell when you're lying."

"I'm going to go to hell for this, but she said she's very attracted to you."

Fuck. Me.

It wasn't like I couldn't sense that already, but getting that confirmation was something entirely different.

I swallowed. "She did?"

"Yes."

"Did she say anything else?"

"Not really. I think she's confused about you. And to be honest, aside from assuring her that you're a good person, I didn't really know what to say because I don't know what you're doing, Simon. I will say this: that woman is not someone you have a quick fling with. I don't think she's capable of that."

"You've said that before, and you're not telling me something I don't already know."

"Do you have feelings for her?"

"This was just supposed to be a simple living arrangement. I wasn't supposed to have *feelings*."

She crossed her arms. "That's not really an answer, but now I've drawn my own conclusion, thanks."

Sexual frustration can turn ugly at times.

Bridget and I hadn't seen much of each other aside from the shifts we were on together, which were unavoidable.

During one of those days, we'd gotten into a fierce argument over my deciding to prescribe a particular type of antibiotic for a patient.

Bridget followed me out of the examination room. "You're overprescribing. She'll become resistant. It's clear to me that she doesn't need another round. I wouldn't do that if I were you."

I turned around fast, startling her. "Well, it works out that you're *not* me, then, doesn't it? Last I checked I'm the doctor in this situation."

She looked around us to see if anyone was watching and whispered, "That doesn't necessarily mean you know what you're doing."

I resumed walking as I looked down at my chart. "I think nearly eight years of medical school and residency *does* say I know what I'm doing. So, I don't really need Nurse Know-It-All second-guessing my every move."

"Don't call me that."

"Then don't be a pain in the arse."

"A pain? I think there must be a pill somewhere you can prescribe for my attitude, seeing as though you're drug happy, Dr. Hogue?"

"You *are* a pill, Nurse Valentine. And yes, I'm going to write you out something right now."

Wearing the burgundy scrubs that hugged her ass just right, she placed her hands on her hips. "Oh, yeah?"

Gritting my teeth, I dug my pen into my pad and wrote in swift, angry strokes.

> *Take three hard poundings against wall twice daily. Repeat for seven days until stick from arse falls out.*

I handed it to her, watching her read it as her face turned as red as her uniform.

Smirking, I then proceeded to walk away.

———

A few days later, Bridget was outside doing yard work, so I used the opportunity to pop into the kitchen without having to run into her.

Deciding to use the bathroom in the main house first, I stopped short at the sight of Brendan standing on a stool in front of the mirror. He had shaving cream all over his face. You could see nothing but his eyes. And he was just about to take a razor to his cheek.

I held out my hands. "Whoa, whoa, whoa...what are you doing, buddy? You'll cut yourself."

"Shaving."

I carefully took the razor from his grasp. "Does your mother know you're playing with this?"

"No. She thinks I'm in my room reading while she's working outside."

"Why are you trying to shave? You don't have any hair on your face."

"Mark Connolly told me if I start shaving, I might grow hair. He said it happened to his grandmother. She started shaving her face and got a full beard."

Stifling a laugh, I asked, "Why do you want a beard?"

"I want to be older."

"You're going on nine. There's only so much you can do, but I assure you growing a beard wouldn't make you any more mature."

"How old were you when you first got hair on your face?"

"I don't remember...probably a teenager. Listen, this has a sharp blade. It's very dangerous and not something you should ever be playing around with."

He stepped down off the stool. "My daddy used to shave a lot."

I knelt down and softened my tone. "Yeah?"

"I don't remember too much, but I remember him shaving right here. Are you gonna tell my mom?"

"Nah. Bro code, remember? But just promise me you won't play with razors anymore."

"I won't."

"Here, let's wash your face."

He stood back up on the stool as I ran the faucet.

I cupped the water in my hand and began removing the cream from his face as I said, "Trust me, you should be enjoying just being a kid. You're gonna grow up faster than you know. It's life experiences that make you a grown-up, not some hair on your face. We never really stop growing, actually. I think I still have a lot of growing up to do myself sometimes."

"You look grown up to me."

"Is that so?" I pointed to my head. "Well, I was referring to what's in here. Sometimes, I still feel like a kid myself. Anyway, someday, you're gonna look back at this and laugh because you'll dread having to shave all of the time just so you don't end up looking like Santa Claus."

"If you didn't shave, would you look like him?"

I grinned. "I guess I would, like a tall, blond, trimmer Santa, yeah."

"That would be really funny."

I grabbed a towel. "Let's dry your face."

"Are you mad at me?" he suddenly said.

"For the shaving? No, I get it."

"No, I mean, you stopped having breakfast with us and taking me to school sometimes. Did I do something bad?"

Bloody hell. My heart felt like it was going to break in two. I guess I had secretly hoped that Brendan wasn't wondering what was up with me. I knelt down and placed my hands around his cheeks.

"No, little guy. Of course, not."

"Why did you stop playing with me, then?"

I didn't want to lie to him and tell him I'd been busy. I honestly didn't know how to answer him. I certainly couldn't admit that I'd been avoiding him so that he wouldn't get attached to me. I just froze.

"It has nothing to do with being mad at you." When he still looked a bit sad, I gave him a hug. "Come here." Pulling back to face him, I said, "I'll tell you what...I have tomorrow night off. Why don't you and I go throw around a football at the park after school or something, maybe get some ice cream. Would you like that?"

He jumped up and down. "Yeah!"

Feeling conflicted, I smiled. "Okay."

Bridget's voice came from behind me. "What's going on in here?"

I looked her up and down, taking notice of her wind-blown, light brown locks. "Uh...we were just having a man-to-man chat."

"Oh, really." She looked skeptical. "What's the razor doing out? And there's water all over the sink."

"It's fine, Bridget. Everything's under control."

She looked down at her son. "Brendan, I thought you were supposed to be doing your reading homework."

"Sorry, Mom."

"Go to your room, please."

After Brendan ran to his room, I followed Bridget out to the kitchen.

"What was he really doing in there?" she asked.

"I told him I wouldn't tell you."

She glared at me. "Tell me, Simon."

"Alright, don't tell him I told you, but...he was trying to shave."

Her mouth dropped open. "What?"

"Yeah."

She laughed a little. "Oh my God."

"It's alright. We discussed it. Someone at school told him he would grow hair if he shaved."

"Let me tell you, I don't know what I'm going to do with a boy...especially the older he gets."

"You'll do just fine. You certainly have up until this point. Just take one day at a time."

"I'm glad he didn't cut himself. Thank you for intervening. I guess I know I can't trust him to be alone in his room while I work in the yard."

I paused, unsure of whether to tell her the next thing that came to mind. "He said he remembered his dad shaving. I think that might have had something to do with why he wanted to do it."

Bridget sighed and nodded her head in thought. "He doesn't remember too many things about Ben very clearly, just odd things here and there. His dad worked a lot, so that didn't help. Of course, now *I'm* the one working all the time."

I leaned against the counter, moving in a bit closer to her. "My parents worked a lot, too. But I never blamed them for it. It just made me appreciate the time we had together more."

"What did your parents do?"

"Actually, my father's an ophthalmologist. He still has a practice in Leeds. My mother's a secondary school teacher."

"Wow. Did you have a good childhood?"

"I did. It was great up until a certain point."

She kept looking at me in a way that encouraged me to continue.

Tell her.

"I don't...I don't really talk about this. It's hard for me." Glancing out the window, I continued, "The other night you asked me why I wanted to become a doctor, and I told you it was because I wanted to save people..."

"Yeah...I figured there might have been something more to that."

"Yes." I nodded then took a deep breath in. "Calliope and I had a mutual friend named, Blake. We were like the Three Musketeers, and Blake was like a brother to me. We were on vacation at Calliope's parents' lake house in Scotland when we were sixteen. She'd invited us both along. We had the bright idea to take her father's small boat out in the middle of the night. There were only two life jackets. We agreed that Calliope should get one. Blake insisted that he was the better swimmer and told me to just take the other one. I don't know why I agreed. I shouldn't have let him get on the boat without a life jacket. We got pretty far out, the water was choppy...and we capsized. Blake went under, and I tried everything to find him. But it was dark and murky." I stopped to close my eyes for a moment before saying, "They didn't find him for three days." I was starting to choke up but managed to control it.

"Here I was thinking that you knew nothing about loss," she whispered.

"It's not exactly the same as your situation, of course, but it's certainly shaped my life. Becoming a doctor was my way of trying to make up for not being able to save him. Not a day goes by when I don't think about what he would be like now, and not a day goes by where I don't blame myself for letting him get on the boat like that."

"I'm so sorry."

Without hesitation, she reached for me and pulled me into an embrace. I could feel her heart beating against mine. Her ample tits felt so good pressed against my chest. In fact, it felt better than anything I could remember. My hands slid down her back and stopped short of her ass—as much as I wanted to touch it. I felt my erection growing by the second.

She looked up. *God...the way she was looking at me.* Her eyes were begging for more. No longer giving a fuck about any consequences, I slowly leaned in, readying to taste her lips.

The pitter-patter of footsteps coming down the hall stopped me in my tracks. I quickly turned toward the sink, pretending to wash the dishes as Brendan entered the room.

"Mom, can we have tater tots tonight?"

Bridget was out of breath. "Sure. Yeah, honey. Yup. Anything you want."

"Cool."

Brendan ran back down the hall.

Bridget looked dazed, almost embarrassed about what nearly took place between us. My hard-on had barely gone down. I didn't know what the fuck to do next. All I knew was I wanted her. I knew it was all wrong, but I didn't know how to change how I felt.

Frustrated, I went back to my space to be alone and spent a good portion of that evening lost in thought.

Grabbing a pen, I started to just write down my thoughts—what I wanted to say to her if I had the guts. I never planned to actually give her the letter.

Except, later that night, as my restlessness grew, I took a chance and impulsively slipped it under her bedroom door.

Chapter 12
Bridget

This was not good.

Simon almost kissed me.

His hand nearly touched my ass.

He was hard.

I could feel his erection against me.

It shouldn't have happened, and yet I couldn't turn my body off tonight, couldn't stop thinking about him, couldn't stop wondering what would have happened if Brendan hadn't come into the kitchen.

I never kept any pictures of Ben laying out. It was just too painful to look at him. I did, however, keep a photo of my late husband in my bedside drawer. Sometimes, I would take it out and look at it when I felt like I needed his guidance to get through a particularly rough day. Tonight, I took the photo out for an entirely different reason. It was out of guilt, because I knew without a shadow of a doubt that for the first time since Ben's death, I was really developing feelings for someone else. I was starting to move on.

The only problem was, I simply *couldn't* move on with Simon. His plans were to go back to the UK, and a future with him therefore wasn't an option. Even though he and I had never discussed it, Calliope also told me he didn't want kids. While he was great with Brendan, there was a big difference between developing a friendship with a child and taking on the role of parent. Anyone I would eventually end up with would have to accept the father role.

There were just so many reasons why we weren't a good match. So, this attraction would have to be ignored for my overall well-being. As I lay in bed trying to do just that, the urge to masturbate to memories of Simon reading me my novel replaced my good intentions.

Readying to do just that, I got up to shut off the light when I noticed a folded piece of paper by my door.

Bending down, I picked it up and started to read it.

It was the last thing I ever expected.

Dear Bridget,

It's highly doubtful I'll ever garner the courage to say this to your face. Don't feel you need to acknowledge this note the next time we see each other, either. In fact, I'd prefer it if you didn't. I promise to play dumb. I know you, and what I'm about to say would be awkward for us to talk about face to face.

So, here goes.

We're totally wrong for each other. We both know it. You're probably the last woman on Earth I should want and vice versa. You're the proper mum with a good head on her shoulders, who will always need to put her son first. I fully understand. I'm just the carefree, cheeky resident passing through town and temporarily living in your house.

But, here's the thing...what they say about wanting what you can't have is apparently true. For some bloody reason, I can't stop thinking about you in very inappropriate ways.

I want you.

Wrong as it may be...more specifically, I want to make you come. Hard. I want you to get lost in me, and I want to hear you say my name over and over while we fuck. I get stiff just imagining what that would feel like, given that you haven't been with a man for so long.

And these thoughts are making me insane. I've stopped fantasizing about anyone else and haven't been interested in seeing anyone, either.

The only reason I'm even admitting all of this to you right now is because I don't believe it's one-sided. I notice your eyes when you look at me, too. You probably don't think I can see the need written all over your face as clear as the days of the week on your knickers...but I can. Maybe I recognize it so easily because I'm feeling the exact same way. And as crass as I appear when we're joking around about sex, my attraction to you is not a joke.

So, what's the purpose of this note? I guess it's a reminder that we're adults, that sex is healthy and natural, and that you can find me just through the door past the kitchen. More specifically, it's to let you know that I'm leaving said door cracked open from now on in case you'd like to visit me in the middle of the night sometime. I'd love nothing more than to give you the best orgasm of your life. No questions asked. Just unbridled sex.

Maybe the way I've worded this has got you convinced that I think I'd be doing you a favor, but make no mistake about it, the pleasure would be all mine. Ultimately, this proposition is coming from a place of selfish desire. And I can't seem to shake it.

Think about it.

Or don't.

Whatever you choose.

It's doubtful I'll even end up sliding this under your door anyway.

—Simon

Every time I considered leaving my room, I would grab the framed picture of Ben and stare at it. The urge to go to Simon was so strong; I basically hadn't put down the framed photo of my deceased husband in an hour. I was lying in my bed, holding a picture of a dead man while fantasizing about one who was very much alive and in the other room. *With the door cracked open waiting for me.* There was one part of Simon's note that I just kept reading over and over.

I want to make you come. Hard. I want you to get lost in me and I want to hear you say my name over and over while we fuck.

While we fuck.

While we fuck.

I was pretty sure that Ben had never used the word fuck like that before. Did we even *fuck*? We made love, sure. Our sex life was normal—at least, I think it was normal. Don't get me wrong, the passion wasn't the same as when we first got together. But after ten years, both of us working full time and raising a child, it was normal to have some of the desire dwindle, wasn't it?

While we fuck.

I looked at the picture of my husband and sighed. We didn't fuck. Not even in the beginning. And I felt guilty for that now. Maybe we should have been fucking. I certainly didn't do anything to entice him to want me the last few years. Was it my fault our sex life had gotten boring? I rested the picture of Ben over my heart and laid my hand over it. I could feel my heart beating out of control beneath my fingers.

Shutting my eyes, I tried to force thoughts of Simon from my mind. But it was no use. Visions of his hard, sculpted body hovering over me had infiltrated my brain. So, here I was, a thirty-three-year-old, single mother lying in my bed all alone with a picture of my dead husband held to my heart while I visualized fucking another man.

Fucking.

Not making love.

I needed my head examined.

After two hours and no sleep in sight, I decided the only way I was going to be able to get any rest was if I got everything I was feeling off of my chest. Flicking on the light, I carefully set the framed photo of my beloved Ben on my nightstand and then opened the drawer and dug out a pen and piece of pretty stationery. I would write down my thoughts to clear my mind. I had no intention of actually giving the letter to Simon, so there was no reason to filter anything I said.

Dear Simon,

In your letter you said that you noticed my eyes when I looked at you and thought I might be attracted to you. Well, there has never been a more true statement. From the first time I saw you in the emergency room, I was drawn to you. While you were busy digging a fish hook from my ass, I was relishing the

*feeling of your big hand touching me and
imagining what it might feel like for you
to...*

I stopped and sucked on the top of my pen, rereading what I'd written down. I knew exactly what I'd imagined that day, but yet I was too much of a prude to pen the words. How could I, a woman who was too prudish to even *write down* my sexual fantasies, possibly *fuck* a man like Simon? I gave myself an imaginary smack in the head and forced myself to continue. If writing this letter was going to be cathartic and allow me to get some rest, I had to at least be honest. So I continued.

*While you were busy digging a fish
hook from my ass, I was relishing the
feeling of your big hand touching me and
imagining what it might feel like for you
to fuck me from behind while I was bent
over the exam table. I also imagined your
finger in my ass. Which is actually pretty
strange for me, since I've never done any
sort of anal play. But there, I said it. That
was my first thought of you. Basically, in
the first ten minutes of seeing you, I was
imagining your dick inside of me and
your finger in my ass.*

I laughed after writing that last sentence. Never in my life did I talk like that, but it was definitely fun writing it down. It was freeing to say these things, even if I'd never have the nerve to say them out loud or give the note to Simon. I thought he should know that, too.

By the way, Sexy Simon, as long as I'm telling you my innermost thoughts that I'd never have the nerve to actually share with you—random thought: Did you notice that never and nerve have all the same letters? That's pretty interesting since nerves probably lead to a lot of nevers. But anyway, back to you, my Sexy Simon. After that first encounter in the emergency room, I came home and masturbated to thoughts of you. It had been the first time I'd used my vibrator in years—since my husband died. You awoke something inside of me that I'd thought was dead.

So, yes, I'm attracted to you. In fact, attracted just doesn't seem to be a strong enough word to describe what I feel when I'm around you. There is nothing more that I would like than to come to your room right now. But there are just so many reasons I can't. And all those reasons lead back to one thing: I'm scared.

Scared you won't want me once you see my body. I'm not twenty-two anymore, Simon. I've given birth. Gravity has started to show me who's boss. I don't spend hours doing yoga or at the gym like I probably should.

Scared that I don't know how to fuck. I know that probably sounds ridiculous. But it's true. I've had sex and made love— but fucking is a whole different ball game. What if I get nervous and turn into a starfish? How will I ever be able to face you again?

Scared my son will walk in. Yes, I know, there are locks on doors. My fears aren't necessary rational, Simon.

Scared that I'll be cheating. (See above ^^ statement on rational.)

Scared that I'll grow attached to you and you'll leave. Even though, deep down in my heart, I know this has already started to happen, I fear that moving things into an intimate relationship will only make it harder when you leave.

So there, that's my truth—the good, the bad, and the ugly. I've never been so honored or felt so beautiful because you want me. But I'm afraid it can never happen.

—Bridget

Wow, I hadn't expected that to be so therapeutic. I reread my letter twice and then took a matching envelope from my stationery set out from my drawer and folded the paper inside. For good measure, I even got up from bed and spritzed a little perfume on it. Then, I turned out the light and settled back into my bed. I was a heck of a lot more relaxed than I'd been before writing it. Except...I had one more thing I wanted to say.

Sitting up, I flicked the light back on and grabbed my pen.

> *P.S. While I won't be able to join you in your room, I'd really appreciate it if you could video yourself jerking off. It's my most recent fantasy that I pleasure myself to, and things would go a lot quicker if I could just have a video of you doing that instead of having to imagine what that looks like in my head. Thanks!*

I was cracking up as I folded the letter back into the envelope and sealed it. Then I wrote Simon's name across the front with a big girly heart as the dot over the i. Sleep came easier after that. In fact, I'd fallen into such a deep sleep that I overslept. *Again.*

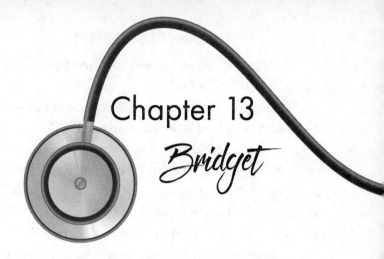

Chapter 13

Bridget

"**M**om."

"Mom."

"*Mom!*" Brendan shook my shoulder to wake me. I was in a fog and confused when my eyes flickered opened.

"What time is it?"

"It's eight-thirty. I'm going to be late for school. *Again.*"

"Shit!" I jumped out of bed.

"That'll be a quarter in the jar," Brendan grumbled on his way out of my room.

"Go brush your teeth! Get dressed!" I barked after him as I ran to my bathroom.

I grabbed my toothbrush and brushed my teeth while I took my morning pee. Spitting out the paste, I cupped a handful of water into my mouth and used it to gargle as I reached for my hairbrush and did a half-ass job of tying my hair into a pony tail.

"You almost ready?" I yelled while pulling on scrubs. Thank God I wore a uniform.

"I'm hungry," Brendan whined back from his room across the hall.

"I'll pop you in a Toaster Strudel as soon as I'm finished dressing. You can eat it on the ride to school."

After I was all dressed, I quickly ran around my bed, haphazardly making it. In my rush, I banged my knee into the open nightstand drawer, hitting it at that place that hurts so bad it took my breath away for a minute. "Damn it!" I slammed the drawer shut when I finally found my voice. Everything on top rattled around and then a pen fell to the floor. *Screw it, I'll get that later.* I'd made it to almost my bedroom door when I remembered last night. The pen must've reminded me of the letter. Where the hell did I put that thing?

I must have fallen asleep with it in my hands. Searching, I ripped apart the bed in a fury. Panic set in when I couldn't find it. I dropped to my knees, looked under the bed, and then opened the nightstand drawer and ripped everything out of it looking. I even went around to the other nightstand, which I was certain I hadn't opened in at least a year, and tore out the contents of that one, too. *No letter.* A sinking sensation hit my stomach.

"Brendan?" I ran to my son's room. He was putting on his backpack.

"Did you happen to see a letter in my room this morning?"

"You mean the one to Simon?"

My eyes went wide. "Yes, the one that said Simon on the outside of it."

"It was on your floor the first time I came in to wake you up. You were really out cold."

"Where did you put it?"

Unaware he'd done anything wrong, Brendan shrugged. "I gave it to Simon for you."

Maybe he hadn't read it.

Simon's car was already gone by the time I caught my breath enough to be able to leave my room. I told Brendan that I'd forgotten something in the house and instructed him to get in the car and buckle himself in while I went back inside and snuck into Simon's room. His room was pretty neat. A quick scan found no evidence of the envelope—neither read nor unread—so I walked over to his desk that was in the corner. He had a laptop, a notepad—which had paper frayed at the top from where he'd ripped out pages—a few pens, and a stack of medical books. *No letter.* It felt like I was violating his privacy when I opened the drawers, but there was no time for guilt. There was also *no letter*.

Looking over my shoulder to make sure no one was coming, I went to the first of his bedside tables and slipped it open. A large stash of condoms greeted me. *Trojan Magnum XL.* I stared at the box. *Extra large?* Oh, my God. My mind was about to start fantasizing when I was supposed to be on a search and rescue mission. I shook my head. "What the fuck is wrong with you, Bridget?" I grumbled. Lifting the condom box to check underneath, I found no letter—lube, *Men's Health,* some keys, and a thick envelope of papers that were from an attorney—but no damn letter. I attempted to put everything back in the rightful place I'd found them, but I was getting more and more freaked out by the moment, and my hands were shaking.

The room was pretty sparse of personal belongings, and there weren't many other places to look, except the other nightstand. Walking around to the other side of the bed, I took a deep breath and opened the drawer, praying it was there. I almost cried from relief when I saw the envelope. Until I picked it up and realized the envelope had been opened. And the letter that I'd tucked inside... *was gone.*

———

The emergency room was a madhouse. *Thank God.* I'd been successful at avoiding Simon almost the entire day. Every time I saw him walking in the direction of the nurses' station, I'd bolt the other way. When he'd walked into the front entrance of the cafeteria while I was getting coffee, I walked out the back door—effectively stealing my morning coffee. Tomorrow I'd have to pay double. But I'd succeeded in not coming face to face with the man for the first six hours of my shift. Until Mrs. Piedmont came in. I'd taken her vitals and called up to the maternity ward to ask that Dr. Evans come down to examine her. But instead, Dr. Hogue walked into the room.

He grinned at me. "Nurse Valentine. I was beginning to think you were avoiding me today." Of course, Simon knew what I was doing. The man was smart to begin with, no less he seemed to have a sixth sense when it came to figuring me out.

"Just busy, Dr. Hogue. But I actually called up to the Obstetrics Unit to have Dr. Evans come down to see Mrs. Piedmont. So, I think we're all good here. Thanks anyway."

Ignoring me, Simon opened a drawer and took out a pair of gloves from the assortment of disposables. When my eyes landed on the box that he'd taken them from, I felt the blush grow on my face. *Extra large.* Apparently he wore the same size in *all gloves.*

"Dr. Evans just got called into an emergency, so he asked me to see to Mrs. Piedmont, here. He'll come down after he's done." Simon snapped on the gloves and spoke to the patient. "You're six months along and having some pain in your back, is that right?"

"Yes. It comes and goes. But it's my lower back."

"And how long ago did it start?"

"It started yesterday afternoon. It's worse today, so I thought I should come in and get checked out, just to be safe. My regular doctor is in Europe on vacation, and his partner is delivering a baby."

"Have you lifted anything heavy lately?"

The patient smiled. "I have an eighteen month old at home. She's a little butterball and spends half the day on my hip."

Simon placed his hand on her shoulder. "Well, I'm sure that's it. You're probably straining a bit too much going into the third trimester. But let's take a look to make sure. I'd like to do an ultrasound to check in on the little guy, if that's okay."

"Sure. Of course."

"I'll go grab the portable ultrasound machine," I said, grateful to get even a short reprieve away from Simon.

While I went in search of the equipment, I debated sending another nurse back to the examining room to assist. But I was going to have to deal with Dr. Hogue a lot more than this, considering the fact that he lived in my house. After giving myself a good pep talk about how I was a professional, I wheeled the machine back to the exam room with my head held high.

Simon was apparently not as professional.

"Have you ever done a sonogram, Nurse Valentine?"

"No."

He looked at the patient. "This is a teaching hospital. I hope you don't mind if we do some of that today."

She smiled. "I don't mind at all."

Of course, the woman had no reason to suspect anything unusual. However, in a teaching hospital, doctors taught med students and other new doctors—*not nurses*. What was he up to?

I was standing behind Simon, so he could turn around without the patient seeing the way he was looking at me. Which was a damn good thing because the gleam in his eye and that sinister, sexy smile would have tipped anyone off that he was up to no good. "Can you pass me the *lubricant*, Nurse Valentine?"

Oh my God. He's such an asshole! "Sure."

He continued to face me as he carefully gave instructions so that they appeared to sound like true medical teachings. But we both knew what he was doing. "Some people like to just apply a thin layer to the belly, but I like to also apply some lubricant to the probe so that it glides nice and easy." He took the sonogram wand, squirted on the clear substance, and then looked at me while he rubbed it onto the tip. Grinning, he said, "Why don't you come around to my side, and I'll let you take control of my probe."

What I wanted to do was run out of the room and tell him to stick the probe up his ass. I was so pissed he was going to play games while a patient was with us. But instead, I gave him an overtly fake smile. "Sure."

Simon flicked on the machine and them came to stand directly behind me as I touched the probe to her belly. The screen illuminated and the patient's attention was completely redirected to the heartbeat and image of her baby. The good Dr. Hogue took complete advantage of that. He stepped closer to me, so that I could feel his body against mine and then leaned forward, covering my hand with his. His breath tickled my neck. "You don't mind if I show you how to guide the probe do you?"

I could barely speak. "Of course."

The sonogram lasted about five minutes and then Simon jumped right back into doctor mode when we flipped off the machine. I, on the other hand, was as useless as the shit he squirted out of the tube that the patient was currently cleaning off her belly.

Simon listened to the patient's breathing, took her blood pressure again, and then felt around her abdomen. "Everything looks really good. It's probably just a little muscle strain. But I'm going to ask the lab to come down and draw some blood as a precaution. This isn't an emergent situation, so I'll wait on Dr. Evans to decide if he'd like to do an internal examination. That way we don't have to make you uncomfortable twice for no reason."

The woman looked relieved. "Okay. Thank you."

Simon wrote some notes in her chart and then took out his prescription pad and wrote some more. Ripping the script from the pad with a loud tearing sound, he smiled warmly at the patient. "Do you have any questions?"

"No. I feel better already."

He nodded. "It will probably take Dr. Evans an hour or so to get down here. So, why don't you try to lie back and relax. I'll come check back on you in a bit."

"Okay."

Simon turned to me and handed me the chart. Then he handed me the prescription he'd written. "This is for the patient with the elevated heart rate."

I furrowed my brows. "Elevated heart rate?"

"Yes. This should help her to relax a bit." Simon winked, opened the door, and walked out.

I tucked the script into my scrub pocket and waited until I was alone before taking it out again. Which was a really good thing since I almost passed out reading what he'd written.

Eleven p.m. tonight, sharp. Why watch a video when you can see the action live? I'll leave my door open enough so you can watch.

Chapter 14
Bridget

I'd spent the last eight hours debating what I was going to do. I knew without a shadow of a doubt that Simon wasn't kidding when he'd written that note. He'd read my letter and decided that since I'd declined to join him, he'd at least give me the *P.S.* I'd requested. It was 10:55—five minutes to show time.

I couldn't believe I was even considering going to watch. I'd never even watched Ben masturbate. But the thought of getting to witness Simon pleasure himself live, in the flesh, was way too erotic to not give it serious consideration. *Maybe I can just sneak a peek, and he wouldn't even know it?*

Shocking even myself, at 10:59 I left my room. I listened at Brendan's door to make sure he was sleeping and then headed to the kitchen. Opening the fridge, I looked around and then pretended I'd been searching for a bottle of water. Who was I even trying to kid? The door leading to the converted garage was open, and I could see light streaming down the hall from where Simon's room was illuminated.

My heart was hammering inside the wall of my chest as I creaked the door open and stepped into the hall. It was probably only ten feet to Simon's room. Panicking, I realized I might be throwing off a shadow that he could see, so I leaned my back against the wall in a stealth move to conceal I was there. Blood whished around in my ears from my accelerated heartbeat, making it difficult to hear. I held my breath to listen for any sounds of life coming from Simon's room and then shimmied along the wall to get closer.

The sound of deep, heavy breaths made me freeze.

Oh my God.

Simon was really doing this.

Only a couple of feet separated me from watching Simon masturbate.

And he wanted me to watch him.

He'd invited me to come.

His panting was getting louder and louder and making me lose my mind. Which would explain how I summoned the courage to go closer—I'd most definitely lost my mind.

Just as Simon had said in his note, the door was left open a crack—enough for me to look through. So, I did. Disregarding all of the warning bells that were going off in my head that this wasn't a good idea, I tip-toed to his door and peeked inside.

My knees nearly buckled at the sight. Simon was completely naked, lying back on his bed. His right hand was wrapped around his ridiculously thick cock, and he was slowly stroking himself up and down.

Jesus.

I thought I might come before he did. Thank God fear had frozen me in place, or I might have done something even crazier like walk in and climb on top of him. The urge to do that was stronger than any urge I'd ever had in my entire life. I wanted to ride him more than I wanted to take my next breath. And this was coming from a woman who'd always preferred the missionary position.

The speed of his pumping increased, and I wondered if he knew I was watching. I couldn't actually know, because I was completely unable to take my eyes off his hand. As the intensity of his strokes increased, his grip around the long shaft seemed to tighten. His breathing became louder and he let out a few groans, which forced my eyes to dislodge from his hand and finally look at Simon's face. *God, he's beautiful.* His eyes were closed, and his lips were parted letting in and out deep breaths as his chest heaved in unison. Then he spoke. His words were hoarse gasps of air, but I heard every one of them.

"Bridget. Fuck. Bridget."

The hand that wasn't furiously fisting his cock, reached down and cupped his balls. Everything else in the world seemed to fade away as I watched the most amazingly erotic thing I'd ever witnessed in my life. My eyes were darting back and forth between watching his face and watching his hands. I felt the wetness between my own legs, and for a second, I thought I might be able to come without ever even touching myself.

The sound of his breathing became even more jagged as he pumped faster and faster. I was captivated when spurts of cum shot from his cock while he murmured my name over and over again. It was the most spectacular thing, and I was literally on the edge of my own orgasm. I knew that if I'd just reached down and touched my own clit, it would set me off. My body was literally vibrating— the human equivalent of a hum.

I had no idea how long I stood there and watched. The world around me ceased to exist. I was quite literally in a fog. It wasn't until I heard the sound of Simon's gravelly voice that I finally snapped out of it.

"Hello, luv."

Chapter 15

Simon

You've heard the term, *"You had me at hello?"* Well, I *lost* her at hello.

I was finding that what happens in my bedroom definitely stays in my bedroom. Bridget was making that quite clear as she attempted to go about the following week pretending that our little peep show never happened.

Every time I thought back to that night, it left me absolutely gobsmacked. Only a small part of me really expected her to actually take me up on the offer to watch me masturbate.

I didn't think she'd go through with it, but you bet your bottom dollar, I left that door open anyway. And apparently, it was a darn good thing I did.

As soon as I'd heard her at the doorway, I knew that was my cue, whether I was ready or not. I just started to stroke myself, trying to seem calm and collected when the truth was I had never wanked in front of a woman before. Simon Hogue had done a lot of things—but never that.

It was easier than I imagined, because once I could see how into watching me she was, that was all the motivation I needed to continue.

As I shot my load while calling out her name, it was probably one of the most intense orgasms I'd ever had in my life. She'd watched every last bit of it as I came. And then I said, 'hello' and she freaked out. Just like that, as if my cock was going to turn into a pumpkin at the stroke of midnight, Bridget disappeared.

I wasn't going to follow her back to her room, because if she'd wanted to join in, she would have. I knew I needed to be careful with her, and to be honest, I was certain that her trepidation about being with me was founded.

That letter had floored me, though. Once I got a look at what was inside, I figured out that there was no way she could've meant for me to see it. It was too raw. And her words continued to haunt me every day.

When Brendan handed the envelope to me—thankfully, still sealed—I'd asked where he'd gotten it. He told me he found it on the floor next to where Bridget was sleeping.

After he left my room, I read the entire thing with my mouth hanging open and my cock painfully hard. Bridget had a dirty, little mind and knowing her innermost desires made my predicament ten times worse.

Now that we'd crossed the line a bit, I really didn't know where to go next. Bridget seemed to be dipping her toes into the water, but I really didn't think she ever intended to go for a full swim. She admitted it herself; she was too scared.

So, now...she was avoiding me again.

The hospital, however, was the only place where she couldn't pretend I didn't exist.

And being the dick that I am, I really couldn't help playing around with Bridget at work. If I couldn't get off on her in other ways, I was certainly getting off on making her blush. I quite liked it. It was the only attention she would grant me, and I would take what I could get.

One afternoon, a little autistic boy with suspected strep throat had been admitted. He was terrified to let me merely touch him, let alone examine his throat so that I could properly swab him for diagnosis.

As I held the long swab in my hand, he kept squirming under me, refusing to sit still. He even kicked me in the nuts pretty badly.

I turned to his mother. "Does he ever cooperate for rewards?"

"Sometimes. But in this case, he thinks you're going to hurt him, so it's going to be a tough sell to try to get him to go along with it. He doesn't understand."

"There really is no other way to test him for strep. I'm wondering if there's a way that we could show him there's really no harm to it."

Knowing Bridget was just outside the examination room, I had a bright idea.

I stuck my head outside the curtain. "Nurse Valentine, I need your assistance."

"Yes, Dr. Hogue?"

I loved when Bridget called me Doctor, because her exaggeratedly submissive tone was always contradicted by the *fuck you* look in her eyes.

My mouth curved into a smile. "Are you available?"

"Yes. What do you need?"

I walked a bit closer to her and spoke low, "I need you to open wide while I stick something down your throat."

Her eyes widened. "Excuse me?"

I smirked. "I need to conduct a strep test for a little boy who won't let me near him. I'd like to demonstrate it on you first so that he knows it's nothing to be afraid of."

Bridget nodded in understanding. "Okay...I guess there's no harm in that."

Lifting my brow, I said, "I'll try not to make you gag."

Oh, yes. Watching Bridget Valentine lighting up red was perhaps my favorite pastime.

"Meet me in there," I said. "I have to grab something."

I made my way over to a desk drawer where I kept my stash of extra special reinforcements for particularly resistant patients of the younger variety.

Returning to the room, I noticed that Bridget was working to calm the boy's nerves.

His mother looked skeptical as I held up the swab. "There is no way he's going to let you near him with that thing," his mother said.

Bridget bit her lip. Perhaps she could relate to that scenario when it came to me in a different sense.

"Okay, Chaz...I see you've already met my friend, Bridget. I'm gonna show you how this works. She's gonna open her mouth and say 'Ah' and then afterwards, she's gonna get a big, swirly rainbow lollipop to suck on. I happen to have one for you, too."

Stifling my laughter, I turned to her. "Okay, Bridget... open wide and say 'Ah'."

She did as I said, sticking her tongue way out. "Ahhh."

I stuck the swab deep in her mouth, without actually culturing her throat, although for a split second I was tempted to catch her off guard and do it just so I could see her gag.

Turning to Chaz, I said, "See? That wasn't bad at all. Now, Bridget gets her lollipop." I took the plastic wrapper off and handed it to her.

Bridget took an exaggerated lick. "Mmm."

My cock twitched.

Fuck. Quick. Think about Nana.

Opening a new swab, I turned to the boy. "Alright, Chaz, your turn for a lollipop."

With tears in his eyes, he reluctantly opened his mouth and allowed me to swab him. I handed him the lollipop along with a pat on the head.

His mother was amazed that he'd cooperated. "Wow. Props to you, Doc."

"Well, I couldn't have done it without Nurse Valentine." I winked at Bridget.

"Anytime, Dr. Hogue."

Translation: "Fuck you, Dr. Hogue."

"Someone will be back with the results in about fifteen minutes. Hang tight," I said to them before exiting the room.

Bridget followed behind me.

I turned around and walked backwards, smiling. "I'll let you know if we find any streptococcus in your sample."

Of course, I put the emphasis on *cock*.

A few days later, it was early evening at Bridget's house. I was minding my business when I heard screaming coming from the kitchen. Soon after, the smoke detectors started to go off.

What the fuck?

Bridget was running frantically around the stove while flames shot out around the pan she'd been frying something in.

"Run outside, Brendan!" she screamed.

Having to think fast, I reached past the flames and turned off the heat, which she hadn't done.

"Do you have baking soda?" I yelled through the chaos.

She pointed to the refrigerator in a panic.

I found it in the back of the first shelf. Dumping the entire box over the flames, I was able to douse them.

She was shaking uncontrollably.

Instinctively grabbing her and pulling her close, I rubbed her hair and tried to calm her down. "It's okay. Everything is fine. You're fine. It's out."

Tears were streaming down her cheeks as she looked up at me. "Oh my God. I didn't know what to do. I seemed to remember that I wasn't supposed to use water but I just...froze."

"It's alright, Bridget. It was a small grease fire."

"What if you weren't here?"

"Then you would've run out and called the fire department."

"While my house burned to the ground? That's all we need."

"It's okay. That didn't happen."

We went outside to check on Brendan who was patiently waiting on the front lawn with the neighbor.

"Are you okay, Mommy?"

"Thank you for listening to me and running outside," she said.

"I ran over to Mrs. Savage's house. She called the firemen."

"Thank you, my big boy. You did the right thing, but everything's under control because Simon acted really fast."

Sirens were blaring in the distance.

I turned to Bridget. "Why don't you take Brendan out of the house for a bit. I'll talk to the fire department. Then, I'll air everything out and clean up in there."

"You shouldn't have to do that."

"It's fine. He shouldn't be breathing in the smoke. Neither should you. I'll text you when it's okay to come back."

Even with all of the windows open in the house, it still reeked of smoke.

Bridget and Brendan never ended up coming home that night. I reserved them a hotel room at the local Hampton Inn, since the house was in no shape for them.

It was a longer night than I ever could have imagined. For a quickie fire, it sure wreaked a fuck ton of havoc.

Everything in the kitchen was covered in soot residue. I ran to the local home improvement store in town just before they were closing to purchase rubber gloves, chemicals, and other supplies that I'd read about on the Internet for remedying this sort of situation.

Using a mixture of trisodium phosphate and water, I cleaned all of the surfaces. The cabinets had to be emptied completely. After I fully cleaned the shelves, I inspected everything in the kitchen for damage. It didn't end there. After I removed all of the soot, I used a special citrus cleaner to go over everything all over again.

I'd also read online that leaving open bowls of vinegar throughout the house would help absorb the smell, along with sprinkling baking soda on the carpets in the adjacent room before vacuuming.

Even though it was quite cold, I kept all of the windows open in the house. It was going to be a long night.

———

When Bridget returned the next afternoon, I'd just finished getting the place looking presentable again. She was likely going to need to repaint in some areas, but at least a good majority of the mess from the fire was eliminated.

Brendan was ecstatic to get back to his room after being away.

Bridget looked around in amazement.

"I can't believe this. It looks almost normal in here. Did you even sleep?"

My hair was disheveled, and I must have looked like death warmed over.

"I managed a couple of hours."

She looked flabbergasted. "Simon, I don't know what to say. This is beyond what I would ever expect..."

"It's fine. It had to be done."

"Yeah, but I could've hired someone."

"You were freaked out. I didn't want you to have to wait and worry about it."

She was starting to get teary-eyed as she approached me and did something she'd never done before. Bridget rarely touched me; she avoided it at all costs. But she gently brushed my hair to the side with her fingers.

It felt so fucking good.

"Jesus, have you even eaten anything?" she asked.

"I need sleep more than food right now. I'll grab a bite after I wake up before my shift tonight."

"After all that work...you have a shift tonight? Simon, I can't thank you enough for this."

"Anything for you, luv."

"I've heard you say that to an old lady before, but honestly I do believe you mean it. You're a good guy, Simon."

If this were a movie, she might've leaned in and kissed me at that moment. But when Bridget Valentine was the star of the show, things were never that simple.

Chapter 16
Bridget

I'd decided to do something I'd been putting off for a very long time.

Dr. Laura Englender came highly recommended. It was my third appointment, and I'd filled her in on pretty much everything that happened with me since Ben's death.

Her office was conveniently located in Providence. A nice view of the river could be found just outside her window, so I liked to gaze at the water as I poured my soul out to her.

We'd spent a good portion of the first two visits discussing lingering issues having to do with my late husband. The most recent visit, however, was exclusively focused on my situation with Simon. It wasn't easy, but I opened up to her about the sexual stuff that had been going on without getting too graphic.

"So...you can see why I'm so conflicted," I said.

Dr. Englender straightened in her seat. "Sure, I mean, a hot, kind-hearted doctor who's great with your son moves in with you, wants to give you intense orgasms while talking dirty to you in a British accent...it's really a difficult decision."

My mouth dropped. "Are you mocking me?"

"Even therapists can joke a bit, can't we?"

"Oh, I guess. Okay."

She scribbled something in her notebook—probably *"can't take a joke"*—then looked up at me. "So, let me ask you something, Bridget...what is the worst that could happen if you gave into your physical attraction to him?"

Blowing out a breath, I really tried to think on that.

"The worst is that I could become even more attached to him than I already am."

She tapped her pen. "Listen to your words—*more attached than you already are*. On a scale of one to ten, rate your current obsession with this man. How often do you think of him on a daily basis, ten being the most."

"Nine."

She adjusted her glasses. "Nine..."

"Yes."

"So, essentially, if you sleep with him, your obsession may then move to ten."

Is she mocking me again? I think she is.

"Yes. Most certainly, it would," I said.

"So, you're depriving yourself of something that you greatly want on many levels, when really, I would say your worst fear has basically already happened. You've already concluded that he's leaving—yet you're attached anyway, thinking of him all of the time. Knowing that he's leaving has not stopped you from focusing on him."

What is she getting at?

"You think I should give in to my desires despite the consequences?"

She shook her head. "That's not my decision to make. I do, however, think that you should probably realize that the attachment you fear has already happened."

Sweat was permeating my forehead. "This is not exactly what I wanted to hear."

"Do you disagree?"

"I'm not sure."

"Look, Bridget, there's a certain amount of risk in everything. We take chances every day. The only thing we can control is what happens today. As an adult woman, you shouldn't be depriving yourself of something that you clearly want. You've admitted that you want him and that it's been a struggle to resist."

"Okay, but that's selfish, isn't it? What about Brendan?"

"What *about* Brendan? Your son already seems to be enamored with Simon. Your choosing a physical relationship with this man is not going to make a difference from Brendan's perspective, as long as you choose to keep things discreet."

It seemed no matter what I said, my therapist was making a case for my taking the plunge with Simon, and it was making me very uneasy. I needed someone to talk me out of it at this point, not talk me *into* it.

I was getting defensive. "I don't agree with you—on all of this. I really feel like giving in would be an emotional disaster waiting to happen."

"Ultimately, you need to do what you're comfortable with. My job is just to help you identify your feelings. You may still choose to make the decisions that you deem right by some internal court of law in your mind. No decision is the wrong one, necessarily."

When I stayed lost in thought, she continued.

"You've been thinking with your head for a very long time. While that makes for a very safe existence, we sometimes inadvertently inhibit our true happiness when we do this. Life choices shouldn't always be about the end result. People fail to realize that the small adventures in the middle are sometimes more important. When you're old, you're going to reflect on your life and everything is just going to be one big ball of memories anyway. Why not have something worthwhile to look back at?"

I hated that this bitch was making a point.

Simon snuck up on me at the nurses' station. "So, when were you gonna tell me it's your birthday?"

A chill ran down my spine at the sound of his voice.

"How did you know that?"

"Brendan told me."

"Well, when you get to a certain age, it's not exactly something to celebrate anymore."

"That's utter tosh, Nurse Valentine."

"Tosh?"

"Rubbish."

"Oh."

"What are you plans tonight, birthday girl?"

"Brendan and I have a tradition on my birthday that started last year. We go to this fancy Chinese restaurant and gorge ourselves."

"You have room for one more?"

"You want to join?"

"No, I was going to send Alex Lard to cough on your food," he teased. "Of course, I want to join."

I hated that I was starting to feel giddy. "Oh...sure, yeah," I said nonchalantly, even though my heart was pounding.

"Okay. I get off a bit later than you. I could meet you guys there around eight?"

"That sounds great. I'll text you the address."

Later that night, Brendan and I snagged a corner booth at Willie Chen's Asian Bistro. The restaurant was known for their amazing moo shu, live music, and exotic drinks. Of course, there would be no drinking for me tonight since I would be driving home.

Brendan was playing with the chopsticks while we waited for our appetizer. I kept glancing back toward the door, checking for Simon.

It wasn't until I stopped looking for five minutes that I smelled his delicious scent behind me.

He looked gorgeous. His sky blue sweater fit him like a glove. He wore a white collared shirt underneath it and donned a chunky watch I'd never noticed before that accentuated his massive hands.

His eyes fell to my breasts. I might've let a little more cleavage than normal peek out tonight.

"The birthday girl looks amazing," he said, taking a seat next to Brendan across from me.

"Thank you."

He looked down at Brendan, and I braced for Simon's reaction.

"Wow, buddy...your hair. It looks..."

"Like yours," I reluctantly admitted. "Now that he's grown it out long enough, he's taken it upon himself to brush the front forward to match your unique style."

It made me a bit uncomfortable that my son had done that, but I didn't have the heart to make him change it, because it was truly adorable.

Simon looked really amused. "I'm flattered. It looks great on you."

Brendan smiled. "Thanks."

Simon's smile lingered on Brendan. Then, he grabbed a menu. "So, what's good here?"

I pointed to a certain section. "We love the moo shu pork, and we get the poo poo platter for an appetizer because it has a little of everything if you like the fried stuff, but really anything on the menu is a sure bet. They have really good food."

When the waitress came by, Simon ordered a beer. After I declined a drink, he looked at me like I was crazy.

"It's your birthday. Have a drink!"

"No, I don't drink when I drive, especially when I have him in the car."

"I'll drive us home. You get a drink and unwind. You only have one birthday. We'll come get your car tomorrow."

That sounded really tempting. "Okay, I'll have a mai tai."

When the waitress lit the flame in the middle of our poo poo platter, Simon joked, "Don't get too close, Bridget, I've had my share of putting out fires for a while."

I squinted my eyes at him. "Very funny...but true."

We shared a silent moment, just staring at each other.

Our meal came, and Simon noticed Brendan struggling to use the chopsticks.

He put down his own and took Brendan's from his grasp. "Like this." Simon spent the next five minutes showing him how to use them properly.

My heart was definitely pitter-pattering even more than usual tonight.

At one point, Simon got up to use the restroom, and I let out a deep breath. It made me realize that having him here was actually making me a bit nervous, not in a bad way, but in the butterflies in your stomach kind of way.

Once he returned a few minutes later, a waitress came to the table with a piece of birthday cake and a candle.

Brendan looked so excited. The waitress addressed him, "Your daddy told me it was your mother's birthday!" She placed the cake in the center of the table along with a second mai tai in front of me.

I was going to need that drink after I heard Brendan tell her, "Oh, Simon's not my dad. My dad's dead."

A few seconds of awkward silence passed.

The waitress looked mortified. "Oh, I'm sorry. I just assumed..."

My son grinned. "That's okay. He's my good friend and sometimes uncle."

Simon fist-bumped Brendan. "Good answer."

Relieved that the moment of sadness had passed, I took a long sip of my drink.

Simon watched me. "Better drink up, Mummy. Only one beer for me. I'm the designated driver so you can enjoy it. Take advantage of me."

God, I'd like to take advantage of you tonight.

The rest of the evening turned into a really fun time. The second mai tai certainly helped with that. Simon told Brendan lots of stories about his childhood in England. In the meantime, a third mai tai magically appeared, and I knew Simon had told the waitress to just keep bringing them to me.

Brendan was in his glory having Simon's full attention, and I was honestly in my glory, too, watching them interact. I was also completely buzzed, which seemed to drown out all of the negative thoughts normally ruining precious moments like this.

At the end of the night, the waitress brought out three fortune cookies, and we each took one.

Brendan opened his and handed me his fortune.

I read it aloud, "*Land is always on the mind of a flying bird.*"

"What's yours say, Mom?"

I opened mine and read it aloud. "*The Wheel of Good Fortune is finally turning in your direction.* Well, that's nice to know," I said, taking a bite of the cookie.

Simon discreetly read his fortune, but I noticed him slipping it into his back pocket.

"Aren't you gonna read yours, Simon?" Brendan asked.

"I'm gonna save it, actually." He winked.

Brendan was practically asleep on the ride home. It had been a late night for him.

I tucked my son into bed as soon as we got back to the house.

While I was with Brendan, Simon had cracked open a bottle of wine and was sipping it in the kitchen when I made my way over to him.

I grabbed the glass from him and took a long sip then licked my lips. His gaze was fixated on my mouth.

Our eyes locked.

I wanted him.

The alcohol I'd consumed was making the need worse.

"Your being there tonight really meant a lot to me, Simon. And you shouldn't have insisted on paying for dinner."

Simon took the wine from me. "It was the least I could do. I hadn't had a chance to get you a present, seeing as though *someone* was trying to hide her birthday from me."

"Well, I'm no spring chicken anymore. I don't advertise this day."

He took a sip. "You're thirty-four. That's not old. In fact, I find the slightly older woman thing to be quite a fucking turn-on."

The last time my kitchen felt this hot, there was an actual fire.

He moved closer to me to the point where I could feel his words while he spoke and could smell the wine on his breath. "In your letter, you mentioned—among other things that shall not be named—that you were scared I wouldn't want you once I saw your body. You're forgetting that I *have* seen you, more than you probably realize. I got quite an eyeful that first day I walked in on you on the bathroom floor. All the things that you probably think are negatives are actually the things that I find the most sexually arousing: your luscious, plump arse, the slight feminine curve of your stomach, your soft, natural tits. And on top of those things... your eyes—they slay me. Despite everything you've been through, they still shine with hope and wonder, whether you realize it or not. You're beautiful, Bridget. Absolutely fucking beautiful and don't ever believe otherwise."

I wasn't even sure if I had any breath left in my body. It felt like he'd taken it all with those words. But he hadn't, because all of the air within me only became depleted the moment he looked down at the floor then back up at me and whispered, "I wasn't expecting you, either, you know."

Simon placed his wine glass down on the counter and took something out of his back pocket.

It was his fortune from tonight. He smacked it down on the granite then said, "Happy birthday."

I stood there and watched as he then left to go back to his room.

The small strip of paper was taunting me. I picked it up and read it.

The greatest risk is not taking one.

Chapter 17

Simon

I'd just taken off my shirt to get ready for bed. When I turned around, the sight of Bridget leaning in my doorway was completely unexpected. Her eyes were fixated on my naked torso, and I noticed she had my fortune in her hand. She swallowed before speaking.

"I might not have wanted you to read my letter, but I meant everything I wrote in it."

I took a few tentative steps toward her. "Like wanting me?" I didn't need to hear her say the words to know—I was certain she wanted me. Her eyes and body language had told me that from the first time I met her. Yet I wanted to hear her say them aloud—to accept that it was okay for her to want me.

She looked down. A pink blush tinted her beautiful skin when she looked up. "Yes. I want you more than anything that I've ever wanted in my life. Honestly, it scares me how much I'm attracted to you."

Those words were exactly what I wanted to hear, yet I knew there was a *but* coming. "Can we just stop there, and I'll tell you the feeling is mutual? Because I have a feeling whatever you say from this point on, I'm not going to like as much."

She smiled sadly. "What happens when your residency is over, Simon? Where will you go?"

I nodded, knowing what she was getting at. "Back to England. It's my home, Bridget. Living here has never felt anything but temporary for me."

"And do you want to have a family someday?"

I looked down and shook my head. "No. I don't"

"It's true that the greatest risk may be not taking one. But a risk is taking a chance when you have the potential to gain or lose something in the future. When that future is certain that you're going to lose that something—it's not taking a risk, Simon. It's jumping out of a plane without a parachute and expecting to land on your feet anyway."

Of course, she was right. As much as I didn't want to hear it, deep down, I knew she was doing the right thing—for both of us. I wanted her so badly that I couldn't focus—but it wouldn't just be sex with us. Even I knew that much. "I understand."

Bridget hesitated at my door for a while, looking torn. Finally, she said, "Can I just lie with you for a little while? I'm not ready to be alone, and it's been a really long time since anyone has held me."

She mistook my delayed response as a no.

Turning before I could answer, she shook her head and started to walk out of my room. "I'm sorry. I shouldn't have asked you that. It's not appropriate or fair."

"Bridget, wait!"

She froze with her back to me. I walked over and stood so close that I felt her body shaking. "I want to lie with you. There's nothing more that I would like right now. It's just..." I couldn't believe I was embarrassed to say anything to her after the show I'd put on last week. But I was. "...it's just that I'm already hard from just being around you, and there's no way in the world that's going to change if you get into my bed. If that won't upset you...if you don't mind, I'd love it if you would join me in my bed. Maybe I could put a pillow between us so we can spoon without you getting forked."

She smiled. "I'd love that. Just for a little while."

I took Bridget's hand and led her to my bed. Once she got in, I slipped in behind her, put a pillow over my groin, and wrapped my arms around her waist. I pulled her flush against me and held her as if my life depended on it. My hard-on was excruciatingly painful, and I had the strongest urge to thrust back and forth against her soft ass—pillow or not. I could've probably come just from dry humping her fully clothed. But I didn't even attempt to move. Instead, I focused on listening to the sound of her breathing. It was jagged for a long time, but eventually it smoothed out, and I could feel that her body had also relaxed.

There was no way in the world that I could sleep with her pressed up against me. At least not without a quick trip to the bathroom to give myself a good wank so that my cock might deflate a little. But that would have meant letting go of her, and I wasn't ready to do that because as good as it felt, I knew that this would most likely be the first and only time that we did this. Bridget would begin to distance herself again in the morning, and I wasn't about to miss a minute of what she was allowing me to have tonight.

After about forty minutes, her breaths slowed even more and her shoulders fully relaxed. Bridget had fallen asleep in my arms.

Hours later, when she stirred, I was still awake, but I pretended not to be for her own sake. She turned to face me, and then I felt her soft lips on my cheek before she whispered. "Thank you, Simon." And then she was gone.

I had long shifts over the next few days. Since Bridget was off, I hadn't seen her since she crept out of my bed, and I was feeling some sort of depressing withdrawal. During a particularly slow overnight shift, Brianna, the nurse I'd dated a few times, propositioned me for a quickie in the supply room. Even though it would have probably been the smartest thing for me to do—screw Bridget right out of my head—I doubted if I could even get it up for anyone else at that point.

When my lunch break rolled around, I decided I needed to get some fresh air and headed over to Calliope's studio for a much-needed pick me up. My friend was always a bright ray of happiness.

As usual, she was teaching a class when I walked in. So, I took my regular position in the back of the room for a session of arse watching while I drank my protein shake. Not even that did anything for me. A bunch of skinny, boyish-shaped arses on women who dressed up in expensive yoga outfits that matched their sneakers couldn't hold a candle to Bridget in a pair of sweatpants bending over and unloading the dishwasher.

Christ, I'm fucked.

I'd rather be at home watching a mum who was never going to be with me unload her dishes, than checking out a line of twenty-five-year-old arses. This shit is depressing.

Class ended, and I made me way up to the front, genuinely happy to see my friend. "Calli...I'm always dropping by to see you at work. I'm feeling neglected that you don't at least make an effort to break an arm or need some stitches."

"Someone might need stitches in the ER, but it won't be me, you jerk."

My brows furrowed. What the hell? Where had my ray of sunshine gone? I smiled wide. "Did someone accidentally put two scoops of bitchy in her bowl of grumpy this morning?"

Calli's hands went to her hips. "I told you not to screw with my friend."

"What are you talking about?"

"Don't play innocent with me, Simon Hogue. I know you did something."

I folded my arms over my chest. "Well then, if you know, fill me in, because I've no fucking clue what you're rattling on about."

Calliope squinted at me. "What did you do to Bridget?"

"Let's see. I cleaned up her entire house after a grease fire and then I took her out to dinner on her birthday. Oh, wait, that's not it. Might it be because I was a perfect gentleman when she rubbed her ass up against my dick half the night?"

"If you didn't do something, then why is she leaving?"

A sudden panic came over me. "Leaving? What are you talking about?"

"She came in for a class this morning and looked like she'd lost her best friend. When I asked her what was wrong, she said nothing, and then told me she had just booked a trip down to Florida."

"Okay..."

"So I know you did something."

"I didn't do anything."

"So why does she look so sad, and she's running down to Florida all of a sudden because she *needs to get away*."

I took a deep breath and exhaled audibly. "It's not what you think."

"Really? What is it, then?"

"Bridget and I..." I searched for words to explain what the hell was going on, but since I didn't understand what we had myself, it wasn't easy. "...it's complicated, Calliope."

Suddenly, my friend's face changed. Her anger morphed into wide-eyed shock. "You have actual feelings for her?"

"I like her. Yes. She's a good person."

"Of course, she is. I'm not friends with assholes."

"I'll take that as a compliment."

"You're falling in love with her."

"No, I'm not." I'd answered so fast, it made me even question if I was lying. *Was I* falling in love with Bridget? The thought seemed ludicrous. "I can't be falling for her."

"Why not?"

"Because that can't happen."

A huge smile grew on Calliope's face. "Not wanting love to happen doesn't make it not happen, Simon."

I'd have to think on that one later. There were more important things to discuss. "When is she going to Florida?"

"Tomorrow morning. Brendan is off of school next week for break so she booked a last-minute flight for tomorrow morning. She's taking him out of class for a day and was able to get the week off by switching shifts with some other nurses."

Was she even going to tell me? "I gotta go." I leaned down, pecked my friend on the cheek, and headed for the door.

She yelled after me. "Don't hurt her, Simon!"

I was starting to think her warning should have been the other way around.

Chapter 18
Bridget

"**G**oing somewhere?"

I jumped hearing Simon's voice at six in the morning. He wasn't supposed to be off shift until hours after we were gone. I had been so lost in thought as I packed, I didn't even hear him come in.

"What are you doing here?"

He smirked. "I live here, remember?"

Simon walked into my room and sat down on the bed next to my open suitcase. "Taking a trip somewhere?"

I busied myself folding some shirts, trying to seem nonchalant about the whole trip. As if it was everyday I made rash decisions to fly down to Florida. "Brendan and I are going to go down to Florida to visit my mom. I'm sorry I forgot to mention it. I guess it slipped my mind."

Simon looked like he didn't believe a word I was saying, although he didn't call me out on it. "How long will you be gone for?"

"A week."

He said nothing, preferring to wait until I looked up at him. When I did, he spoke into my eyes. "Should I move, Bridget? Will that make things easier for you?"

I sighed. "I don't know, Simon. My head is really confused right now. I know I don't want you to leave. I really enjoy you being here. But would it make things easier for me in the long run? Maybe? Would it make things easier on you if you moved?"

Unlike mine, Simon's answer was unqualified. "No. It wouldn't make it easier if I lived somewhere else. But I'll go if that's what you want."

"It's not what I want."

"Is it what you need?"

My shoulders slumped. "I don't know the answer to that, Simon. I wish I were as certain of things that I wanted and needed as you seem to be. But I'm not. So, if I'm being honest, that's the reason I'm taking this trip. The one thing I am sure of is that I need some time to think about things."

"You shouldn't have to leave your own house to do that."

I forced a smile but knew it came out as sad. "Yes, I do, Simon. And although my confusion over you is a big part of my uncertainty right now, this house has a lot of memories that I need to get away from to clear my head."

He looked sad. "I understand."

"You do?"

Simon nodded. "One of the reasons I came to the US was because of Blake. After he died, I was stuck in place for a long time. So much reminded me of him. I felt guilty when I forced myself to not think about our memories, and I felt sad when I allowed myself to think about them. It was a no-win situation. I applied to college here on a whim. Hadn't even spoken to my parents about it because I didn't want anyone to analyze my decision for what it was."

I sat down on the other side of the suitcase. "I guess you understand a lot more than I thought you would."

We looked into each other's eyes. "Were you even going to leave me a note?"

"I was. That's why I'm up so early. I tried to write it last night a half dozen times, but couldn't figure out what I wanted to say."

Simon gave me that sexy, half smile I loved so much. "You should have just gone with whatever was on your mind. The last time you did that was quite memorable."

We laughed together, and it seemed to have broken the tension a bit. "I'll be back in a week."

Simon stood. "Think about things while you're gone. If you decide that it's best that I find somewhere else to live—no hard feelings."

"Okay."

"Have a good time with Brendan." He pointed to my suitcase with his chin. "And get rid of that one-piece suit you have packed on top. Go out and get yourself a bikini. You can totally rock it, Bridge."

Fort Lauderdale weather was beautiful this time of the year. My mom had taken Brendan down to the fishing pier to pick up some bait, while I went to the mall to pick him up a new bathing suit. I was shocked when he couldn't fit into the one from last year. Obviously he was growing, but I guess I hadn't realized how much he'd sprouted. Seeing last year's baggy bathing suit that had reached his knees turn into tight, hot shorts was really an eye opener as to how big he was getting.

Tommy Bahama was generally out of my price range, but the front of the store had a huge fifty-percent-off sale that caught my eye, so I wandered in. There wasn't a kid's section, but I was able to pick Brendan up a pair of Hawaiian-looking swim trunks in a men's extra small that looked like it would fit. On my way to the register, I passed a rack with colorful bikinis all priced at under twenty dollars. *What the hell?* Remembering what Simon had said, I decided to try one on just for fun. It had been a good ten years since my stomach had seen daylight, but trying one on wouldn't hurt.

I was amazed that it actually looked pretty good. I wasn't eighteen years old and stick thin anymore, but Simon was right—I could totally rock this suit. My curves didn't look half bad in a bright, floral-colored two-piece— and it coordinated with Brendan's. If only I had the nerve to wear it out in public. As if on schedule, my phone buzzed from inside my purse. Before changing, I dug it out. Seeing Simon's name on the screen had my heart pounding in my chest.

Simon: Get yourself a new suit while you're out.

What? How could he have possibly known I was out buying a bathing suit?

Bridget: How the heck do you know I'm out shopping?

Simon: Brendan texted me to show me the worms he was buying and said you were out getting him swim trunks because his didn't fit.

I hadn't known Brendan even knew Simon's number.

Bridget: Does he text you often?

Simon: Mostly it's just pictures of what you guys are doing.

Wow. I had no idea.

Bridget: Well then I'm glad he's not here right now to take a picture.

Simon: Why? What are you doing?

Bridget: I'm standing in the fitting room at Tommy Bahama. My plan was to pop into Target and pick up Brendan a suit but instead I'm in Galleria Mall trying on a bikini. My stomach is whiter than milk.

The dots started to bounce around and then stopped. Then started again.

Simon: Send me a pic.

There was no way I was sending him a picture. My selfie skills were pretty weak, and while I didn't look horrible, it wasn't Simon worthy. Before I could respond back, Simon texted again.

Simon: Stop thinking about it, luv. Send me a shot. I won't let anyone else see it.

Against my better judgment, I snapped a pic in the mirror. It wasn't half bad. Another text from Simon came in.

**Simon: I know you just took one. Now stop
analyzing it and send it to me.**

I giggled in the dressing room. It dawned on me that
it was the first time I'd laughed since I'd arrived in Florida
yesterday. But I still wasn't sending him the picture.
Although...

I reached into the cup of the bikini top and lifted my
boobs so that they were perked up. Then I raised the sides
of the bottoms so that it gave the appearance of longer
legs. Smiling, I put one hand on my hip and posed for a
selfie in the mirror.

Well I'll be. No wonder all the teens did this hand on
the hip thing. I looked ten pounds lighter. And the boob
fluff up I'd done made my naturally full breasts look perky
as hell.

Simon texted again.

**Simon: How about if I send you a selfie
first? Will that help?**

I chewed my fingernail.

Bridget: Maybe...

Less than a minute later, my phone pinged indicating
a photo had arrived. Of course, he'd done it. I started to
crack up when I opened the picture. Simon was at work,
but must've stepped into the supply closet. He was wearing
blue scrubs and had a big goofy smile on his face.

**Bridget: Ummm. Cute. But if you expect a
bikini shot, you're going to have to put up
more skin than that, Hogue.**

Again, a minute later, my phone pinged. Simon was
still standing in the supply closet but was lifting his shirt
so that I could see his abs and had let his scrubs fall to

his knees. His tight boxers showcased his thick thighs and the V north of the good stuff. I also knew firsthand that the big bulge he was sporting was not the result of a good camera angle or any fluffing.

I stood in the dressing room for a few minutes and debated sending him my selfie in return. Eventually, my phone pinged again.

Simon: You owe me BIG now.

Bridget: Why?

Simon: Nurse Hamilton walked in on me. Apparently, I hadn't locked the door like I thought I did. I think she thought I was masturbating.

I covered my mouth laughing. Nurse Hamilton was probably close to seventy. She was also extremely proper. I supposed I couldn't hold out on him after that. Calling up the picture I'd taken on my phone...I let my finger hover over the button for a good three minutes. Then I held my breath and pressed send.

It took a few minutes before my phone pinged again. But then...

Simon: Nurse Hamilton might not have been so wrong, after all. *Fuck, Bridget*. You're gorgeous.

I was never very good at accepting compliments. While I didn't think I looked gorgeous, oddly, I believed that Simon thought I did. He had rose-colored glasses when it came to me for some unknown reason.

Bridget: Thank you, Simon. You've made my day.

My phone went quiet after that. I changed back into my clothes and spent a few minutes trying to figure out how to get the suit to display on the hanger the pretty way it had been when I'd found it. I left the fitting room feeling good about myself. Although there was no way in hell I was actually wearing a bikini in public, it was fun to pretend. A salesgirl was hovering close to the room I changed in.

"Is there anything else I can get you?"

"No, thank you. But can I give you this?" I held out the bikini and hanger. "I couldn't figure out how to hang it up properly."

"Sure. Are you ready to check out?"

"Yes. Thank you."

I took Brendan's suit up to the register, following the young girl who carried the suit. When she rang it up, the total was $43.21.

"I thought the men's suit was on sale for $19.99?"

"It is. And so is this one." She lifted the bikini I'd tried on.

"Oh. I won't be buying that today. I'm just taking the men's suit."

The young girl smiled. "The gentleman said you would say that."

"The gentleman?"

She continued to wrap up the bikini in tissue paper, even though I'd told her I wasn't buying it. "A man called while you were in the fitting room. He bought a $200 gift certificate over the phone and told me to use it to pay for your purchases. Said to include the bikini you came out with, whether you wanted it or not."

146

I was dumbfounded. "Can I assume he had a British accent?"

The girl placed my items in a bag. "Sure did. Sounded kind of hot. You're a lucky lady." She handed me a gift card along with my bag. "You have a balance of $156.79 on your card."

I walked out of the store still shaking my head. *I am a lucky lady, aren't I?*

Once I was at my car, I started it and dug my phone back out of my purse. I typed and erased a half dozen messages to Simon before going with a simple one.

Bridget: I can't believe you did that. Thank you, Simon.

Simon: Did you buy the suit?

Bridget: How could I not when you were so sweet?

Simon: Good. Enjoy it and wear it. Have a great vacation. I expect to see tan lines when you get home. P.S. My thoughts of you when I look at that picture are anything but sweet.

The rest of the afternoon, I did exactly what the doctor had ordered. I wore my new suit and enjoyed myself. After an evening swim with my son in the warm, ocean water, I took a stroll along the beach with my mom and Brendan. The sun was beginning to set and lit the sky in vivid shades of purple and deep orange.

"Wow. It's beautiful," I said to Mom.

"Isn't it?"

I found myself thinking that Simon would probably enjoy a beautiful sunset. So, I snapped a few pictures intending to send them to him later. I might have even encouraged Mom to take a picture of Brendan and me on Brendan's phone with the sunset in the background as we stood on the beach wearing our matching suits. I secretly hoped my son might send it to a certain someone.

When it got dark, we headed back up to Mom's. I took a quick shower and then Brendan went to take a bath. Mom poured us each a glass of wine in the kitchen. She smiled warmly at me. "You seem better now, Bridget?"

"Better?"

"Happier. The last time you came down to visit, I was really worried when you left. You weren't yourself. Actually, it's been quite a few years since I saw the real Bridget."

I sipped my wine. "Well, my husband died, Mom."

She hesitated for a moment. "Yes, of course. But I meant it had been a few years even before Ben died since I saw you smiling like you did today."

"What do you mean? Ben and I were happy."

"I didn't mean that you weren't. You just…I don't know, dear. I suppose the best way to describe it is sometimes we lose our spark. It doesn't mean we're not happy. There are just certain times in life when, for whatever reason, we go through the motions without feeling the zest for life. You know? Think about it, when was the last time you enjoyed a sunset like you did tonight? You were absolutely radiant watching it this evening."

I hated to admit it, but she was right. I'd been coming down here every year for the last ten years, and I couldn't remember the last time I took notice of a beautiful sunset. But that didn't mean I wasn't happy with Ben, did it? "I don't think we usually stay out on the beach that late, Mom."

She smiled. "We allow ourselves to see what we're looking for."

My brows drew down. "How many glasses of wine did you have while I was in the shower? You sound a little Maya Angelou-ish to be my mother."

We both laughed. Finishing off my wine, I caught the time on the wall clock—it was almost eight. "We should order some dinner. I haven't fed Brendan since lunch. He must be starving."

"There's a new little Greek place down the block. How about that?"

"Sure. That sounds perfect. Do you have a menu?"

Mom dug it out from her packed menu drawer and handed it to me. "I'm going to take a shower. Add four chicken kabobs and some hummus and chips to whatever you and Brendan want."

"Four chicken kabobs? You must be starving, Mom."

She smiled. "Did I forget to tell you that we're having company in a little while?"

"Company? Who?"

"My new neighbor, Jonathan. He's a few years older than you and widowed. He's also extremely handsome. I've told him all about you, and he can't wait to meet you."

Oh, goodness. I could see where this was going.

"You're trying to set me up with him?"

"I didn't say that. I just thought it would be nice to introduce you two."

"Great."

A half-hour later, Jonathan Leopold joined us for dinner in the screened-in Florida room. We enjoyed the Mediterranean food while a warm, evening breeze blew in. You could see Jonathan's house from my mother's; it was just a stone's throw away. It made me happy to know that he looked out for her often.

He seemed like a great guy. We'd all gotten a good laugh when he ran around trying to help Brendan catch a small lizard that was hopping around the room.

Jonathan was a real estate agent who'd lost his wife to cystic fibrosis five years ago. They'd never had kids. He was smart, charismatic, and darkly handsome—everything you could want in a man, really. The only problem was that Simon was infiltrating all of my thoughts. So, I wasn't giving Jonathan the attention he probably deserved.

Dinner was pleasant but ended on the early side.

Deciding to give it another go, I accepted Jonathan's invitation to lunch the following day. He ended up taking Brendan and me to his favorite restaurant by the beach, and we spent the afternoon frolicking by the water. Still...I felt nothing. My mind was too focused on Simon to really enjoy Jonathan's company. I pretty much ruled out anything happening between us after that. Not that it could have really worked out anyway, with my being in Rhode Island and Jonathan living down in Florida. But I suppose a fling couldn't have hurt me, under different circumstances. I just couldn't get myself to want that with him. Even though I knew focusing on Simon at this point was not helping me, I couldn't stop my feelings. Sadly, even masturbating to thoughts of Simon seemed more appealing than actual sex with Jonathan.

That night, while putting Brendan to bed, I decided to check his phone. What eight-year-old has a phone? One whose mother was trying to compensate for his lack of a father during Christmastime. My son assured me he would only make calls in an emergency. He used it to play with his apps and watch YouTube. He didn't have any social media accounts, of course, but he'd often take pictures and text them to me or Ben's mother. Brendan always used voice to text so that his messages didn't contain typos.

As of late, he'd been texting Simon—a lot.

In fact, he'd apparently sent Simon a photo diary of our entire day.

Shit.

There were picture texts of Jonathan and me walking on the beach, taken from behind. He caught another snapshot of me laughing at something that Jonathan was saying.

Shit!

Simon: Hey, buddy. Interesting pictures. Who's that guy?

Brendan: That's grandma's neighbor, Jonathan. He took us out to lunch. He looks at Mom like Miss Santoro looks at you. Yuck!

Simon: Wow, well keep an eye out on your mother for me, okay?

Brendan: Okay!

Shit. Shit. Shit.

Why did I even care if Simon saw these? But, I did. I knew enough to know from the brevity and tone of his response that Simon was upset. Don't tell me how I knew that from a simple sentence, but I did. I could only imagine what that would have felt like if Brendan had sent me the same photo of Simon and some woman.

We had two more days left here in Florida. It didn't feel like I could wait that long to explain this to Simon. I felt like we needed to talk about more than just Jonathan. I didn't even know what I would say. I just needed to see him, needed to clarify things once and for all and also make a decision about our living arrangement.

That night, while Brendan and my mother slept, I called the airline and changed our ticket.

We'd be flying home tomorrow.

Chapter 19
Simon

I emptied the drawer of all my boxers. Just the essentials for now. I would have to come back gradually for the rest of my things.

Calliope gave me shit when I told her I needed to crash with her and Nigel for a while. Mainly, she was mad because I wasn't being frank with her as to the exact reason why I was moving out of Bridget's. I assured her it would only be temporary until I could find another place. I already had two appointments to see apartments in Providence.

I still needed to decide how to address my moving out with Bridget and especially Brendan, but I knew I couldn't spend another night here. It wasn't fair to her, and quite honestly, given my reaction to seeing the photos that Brendan had sent, moving out would also be in my own best interest.

I fucking lost it, and it wasn't pretty. I'd been in the middle of a hectic shift and was barely able to function the rest of the day.

When she'd first arrived down to Florida, I was bloody loving flirting with her over text. And even though I knew

I should've been taking advantage of the separation more productively, I found myself counting the days until her return.

But when Brendan sent me those pictures from their day out, I was gutted. It had taken me several minutes to even respond to the poor kid.

Seeing her with that guy—it put me over the edge. He looked older, like someone ready to settle down. That was exactly what she needed. Yet, I couldn't get over my own selfish anger, which was irresponsible and unfair. I had an urge to get on a plane and interrupt whatever was going on.

So utterly disappointed in myself for even considering that, I came to the conclusion that the only option was to physically remove myself from this living situation. If I couldn't change my feelings, then I could, at the very least, change my environment.

It was now or never. Once she returned, I wouldn't ever have the bollocks to do it.

Zipping my suitcase, I heard a car door shut outside. I looked out the window, which was covered in droplets of rain.

It was Bridget. Fuck. What was she doing home?

The front door slammed shut, and then came the sound of her footsteps nearing my room.

My body went rigid as I braced for her arrival.

She appeared at the doorway, looking sunkissed and fucking gorgeous.

"Simon. You're here. We need to talk."

"What are you doing here, Bridget?"

She leaned her neck to see behind me and noticed the large black suitcase.

"What's going on? Why is there a suitcase?"

"I thought it would be easier if I—"

"Moved out before I came back? You weren't even going to discuss it with me?"

"Of course, I was going to tell you." I looked down at her neck and could see a bit of the tan line at her shoulder. "Shit, Bridget, I wasn't expecting you back today."

"Clearly."

"Where's Brendan?"

"I dropped him off at Ben's mother's for the night before heading home. I wanted the house quiet so I could talk to you. But apparently it was your intention not to be here when I came back."

"You came home a day early to talk to me?"

"Yes."

"Why?"

Her face was turning red in anger. "Stupidity, apparently."

"No." I walked toward her, despite my better judgment and demanded, "Tell me why."

"I saw that Brendan had sent you photos that made it look like something was going on with my mother's neighbor, Jonathan. I didn't want you to get the wrong idea. I know that shouldn't matter to me, but it does. I only took him up on his offer to take us out to lunch by the beach. That was it. There wasn't any chemistry, Simon. I haven't been able to feel anything for anyone but you. That's really scaring me."

I looked up at the ceiling and expelled a breath.

Fucking relief.

Nothing happened between them.

Relief consumed me. And that was not good, because it shouldn't have mattered so damn much.

"You were on the fucking beach in my bikini with him. I just assumed something was going on."

Her eyes widened. "*Your* bikini?"

Perhaps it was a Freudian slip, but I owned up to it.

"Yes. *My* fucking bikini."

In that moment, it was like my inhibitions just snapped. Running my thumb along the slightly burned skin below her neck, I said exactly what I was thinking.

"It's *my* bikini because every inch of the body inside of it belongs to me, whether you want that to be the case or not. I know how that struggle feels because it's no different for me. As much as I would give anything to want someone else right now, my body only wants *you*. And quite frankly, Bridget, it's not going to rest until it has you. I took her hand and placed it on my bare chest, sliding it down to my lower abs. "Feel this. You own this. Is that wrong? Maybe. But it's yours."

She leaned in and shocked the shit out of me when she just started softly kissing my chest. The longer it went on, the less I cared about consequences. She was running her tongue along my skin now. I had zero fucks left to give.

I dug my fingers into her hair, which was damp from the rain. "Let me fuck you, Bridget." I wasn't too proud to beg. "Please."

My chest was heaving, and my dick was painfully hard.

She was trembling as she whispered over my chest, "Just one time."

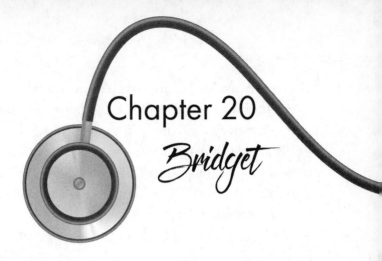

Chapter 20
Bridget

No sooner than the words exited my mouth, Simon let out the breath he'd been holding. He lowered his mouth to my neck and groaned, devouring my skin like an animal who'd found his prey. Except I was willing prey.

Feeling his mouth on my body for the first time was pure ecstasy. I worked to remove my damp jacket as fast as possible. Simon pulled at my shirt before slipping it over my head. He buried his mouth into my cleavage, tasting my tender skin and sucking so hard that I knew there would be marks tomorrow.

He stopped for a few seconds to remove my bra, and that small break where his lips weren't on me was torture. I just wanted his mouth back on me. His hazy stare landed on my bare breasts as he took them in, panting. Licking his lips, he lowered his head and began to teasingly flick his tongue at my nipple. The scruff of his chin felt like little pinpricks and only enhanced the sensation. The muscles between my legs tightened.

Simon suddenly began to suck on my nipples harder. It hurt a little but felt so incredibly good at the same time.

No man had ever been this rough with my body, and I didn't realize the level of arousal I'd been missing.

His thick hair felt like silk as I gripped the strands, pushing him deeper into my skin.

His breath suddenly hitched as he pulled back before frantically unbuckling his belt. He slid off his jeans. Just as I reached for the elastic of his underwear, he placed his hand on my wrist, locking it in place.

"You're on the pill, right? I saw them in your bathroom once."

I nodded.

"I can assure you I'm clean. If this is our one time, I'd like to feel you without a condom, if that's okay."

"Yes," I gasped.

He let go of my wrist. "Do what you were going to do."

I lowered the elastic band and slid Simon's boxer briefs down. My gaze stayed fixed on his beautiful cock. It was just as thick and hard as I'd remembered. Wrapping my hand around the warm, throbbing flesh, I began to jerk him off. I watched as his eyes rolled back and low grumbles of pleasure escaped him.

He stopped me before pulling me close. He took a moment to smell my hair then suddenly lifted me up and over him. Placing my hand back over his shaft, he said, "Jerk me off, then put me inside of you."

With my legs wrapped around his waist, I reached down and pumped him into my hand. My clit was aching with need. When I couldn't resist any longer, I stopped stroking him and placed his slick cock at my opening. He was looking down so that he could watch the moment that he entered me.

The feel of his thick crown stretching my entrance caused a pleasurable, burning sensation. Just as he'd begun to penetrate me, he very suddenly pushed all the way inside.

"Fuuuuck. I couldn't help it. I'm sorry," he said as he began to fuck me.

My hips moved over him.

"Oh, fuck, Bridget. That's it. Ride me," he breathed. "You feel so fucking good."

No longer able to form words, I grinded around his cock. With my arms wrapped around his neck, I rode him hard as he guided my movements with his hands on my ass.

"Ride me harder, Bridget. Ride me harder. Look at you. You're so fucking beautiful with me inside of you."

I'd never had sex from this angle. I moved my hips in a circular motion rubbing my ass against the root of his cock while he was balls deep inside of me.

"Slow down," he hissed. "I almost came. You feel too good."

Simon then carried me over to the bed. Pulling out of me, he placed me down flat on my back. He hovered over me on all fours, nudging my legs open with his knee. Letting out a deep sigh into my ear, he reentered me and began to kiss me passionately. The kiss actually made my heart break because it opened up a level of intimacy that hadn't been there moments ago. This was supposed to be hardcore sex, and I was trying to keep my emotions out of it.

I squeezed my muscles, tightening myself around him.

He moved his mouth away from my lips.

"Do that again. Squeeze your pussy around my cock. Swallow it up."

When I followed his command, he thrust into me with more force. He began to kiss down my neck before landing on my breasts. He took my nipple gently between his teeth and spoke huskily into my skin, "I love seeing my marks on you."

Every time he spoke dirty, I became even more revved up.

"Tell me what you want, Bridget."

"I want you to fuck me harder."

"Wrap your legs around my back."

After I did just that, I could feel him even deeper at this angle. I loved watching his perfect chest and abs as he moved in and out of me. His hair was a sexy, rustled mess, half-covering his smoldering eyes. In that moment, he truly had never looked hotter to me.

The slick sounds of our arousal and the slapping of our skin was all you could hear.

He spoke through his thrusts, "I want you to think about me tomorrow when you feel me between your legs."

I began to move my hips, encouraging him to go even rougher on me. He took the hint and sped up his thrusts. He returned his mouth to my lips, his kiss an attempt to soften the blow of his ramming into me.

As I savored the addicting taste of his tongue, I realized that I could never forget how this felt.

He stopped kissing and looked me in the eyes. I almost wished he hadn't. I could handle fucking him with my eyes half closed, but the connection was too painful.

I closed my eyes.

"Open your eyes, Bridget."

I opened them again and saw my reflection in his blue pupils.

"Look at me until you come. Don't close them again."

I finally let go of the hold that I had placed on my orgasm. My mouth opened into a silent scream as my pussy convulsed around him. Simon kept his eyes on me as the guttural sounds of his orgasm echoed through the room. The heat of his cum filled me. He kept moving in and out of me, gradually slowing his movements as he kissed me softly.

"You're amazing, Bridget. So goddamn amazing."

An enormous sadness suddenly replaced the euphoria of my orgasm. The empty feeling I knew would come was even stronger than I imagined—the fear stronger than I imagined. It was hard for me to admit to myself that even though I'd implied that it would be just one time, just sex—I wished it meant more.

I wished he would stay. And I wished he would love me.

Simon and I lay in his bed listening to the sound of the afternoon rainfall.

I did something I almost never do; I took a nap—in his arms. Around 6PM, Simon was still sleeping when I threw one of his T-shirts over me and made my way to the kitchen.

I poured a tall glass of water to quench my parched throat.

A few minutes later, chills ran through me when I felt him at my back. Knowing he was behind me, my body came alive. The need for him was ten times worse now.

He didn't say anything as he gathered my hair to the side and kissed my neck.

I was expecting him to say something, maybe talk more about his planned move or apologize for his plan to fuck and run.

Instead, I closed my eyes and relished the feel of his lips on my body again. My clit started to throb as if our fucking had installed a magic button of recognition inside of me that turned on the moment he touched me.

I could feel that his cock was fully rigid through his boxer briefs. He was rubbing against my ass.

"I thought we said just once," I muttered.

"I need you again. Please. Just one more time," he said against my neck as he pulled on my hair.

I closed my eyes, conceding to my body.

Still behind me, he lifted the T-shirt and soon I felt his fingers sink into my pussy.

"You're so wet right now. Or is that my cum still inside of you? So fucking hot, Bridget."

He pulled his fingers out of me and instead stuck one of them at the entrance to my ass. Using my own arousal as lubricant, he slowly pushed it inside, moving in and out ever so slowly.

The sensation was nothing like I'd ever felt before.

"Isn't this what you said you wanted? My finger in your ass..."

Panting, I answered, "Yes."

He spoke gruffly in my ear, "Actually, I believe what you wanted was my cock inside of your other orifice while I finger fucked your ass."

I could hear him sliding his underwear down. Within seconds, I felt the hot tip of his penis at my opening. He entered me in one swift movement. Fully inside, he began to fuck me in sync with the movement of his finger in my ass.

I leaned against the counter, gripping the granite for dear life as he took me doggy-style in the middle of my kitchen. Catching a glimpse of his face in the reflection of the window over the sink, I realized he was just as lost in lust as I was.

We both climaxed fast and furiously. As he came, he gripped my body, holding me in place while he slammed into me, once again filling me with his heat.

When he stopped moving, he whispered, "I'm fucking addicted to you. I'm sorry."

I didn't know whether he was apologizing for wanting me or apologizing for his impending desertion. Either way, I was screwed.

Chapter 21
Simon

Naked macaroni was now my very favorite meal. After fucking Bridget in the kitchen, we decided to make a quick dinner. She'd attempted to put her clothes back on, but I persuaded her to cook with me naked. Naked cooking led to naked eating, and I was beginning to think we should just stay naked forever. Naked with Bridget was fucking awesome.

We were sitting on the floor in the living room with our empty plates on the coffee table. I swiped two fingers across the remnants of sauce on her plate and used it to paint one of her nipples before I bent to lick it off.

"Mmm. This sauce is fucking fantastic."

She laughed. "You're a little insane, Simon."

"Come on, admit it. You just eyed the sauce on my plate and thought about painting my cock, didn't you?"

My beautiful, naked girl blushed. "We're already one over our agreement. Not sure a painting party would be a good way to ensure we kept to the terms."

Fuck the terms.

"About that. We agreed to have sex once only, right?"

"Well, clearly those terms were modified, but yes, that's what we agreed to."

I nodded. "Good. So there was no other agreement."

Bridget squinted. "What are you getting at? I can see the wheels spinning inside that mop-covered head of yours."

"Well, we agreed on sex, right?"

"Yes..."

"I'd like to point out that it was *your* former President who declared that sexual relations referred only to the act of having intercourse."

Bridget choked on the wine she was sipping. "You want to use President Clinton as your precedent so you can what...feel me up still?"

I nodded. "Amongst other things, yes."

"What type of other things?"

"Well, I'd like to refrain from making a conclusive list that can be held against me in the form of a second agreement. But I believe cunnilingus, fellatio, fingering, anal sex, heavy petting, handies, pillow pounding, and mutual self stimulation with visualization are all excluded from our deal."

"I got the first few." Her face was adorable when it scrunched up. "But what in the Lord's name is pillow pounding and mutual self stimulation with visualization?"

"*Ah.* I'm glad you asked." I reached over and grabbed both her breasts. (Have I mentioned I fucking love naked macaroni?) Squeezing those beauties together, I looked up at her and wiggled my brows. I'm going to stick my cock between these beautiful pillows—hence, pillow pounding."

Bridget's eyes bulged, so I took that as a sign I should keep talking.

"And mutual self stimulation with visualization? You're going to open these legs wide and show me your pretty pussy while you get yourself off with your vibrator. I'll be doing the five knuckle shuffle on my wood at the same time. Hence, the mutual part." I winked.

Bridget wanted to be appalled—she really did. But her wide eyes dilated and nipples pebbled telling me she really liked my dirty talk even if she didn't think she was supposed to. "Simon—we can't do any of that."

"And why not?"

"Let me ask you something serious for a minute?"

"I was being serious, but okay."

"Are you still planning on moving out?"

My heart sank. I never really wanted to move out to begin with. "Do you want me to move out?"

I saw the sadness in her face. "Do you think we can live together and keep our hands off of each other?"

Honesty isn't always the best policy. I'd learned that in third grade when Alison Eggert asked me if she looked plump in the dress she was wearing. Apparently, *yes* was unacceptable even if the stripes made her look a bit portly. She never spoke to me again. I put on my best serious face and responded to Bridget adamantly with a lie. "Yes, I do."

Bridget's brows jumped. "Yes? *You do?*"

"If that's what you need from me, yes."

She sighed. "God, Simon, why do we have to be in such different places in life and want such different things out of it when we obviously enjoy each other so much?"

I fucking hated that she was right. "I don't know, Bridget. But it seems a little cruel, doesn't it? You haven't had sex in two years, and I haven't wanted to be around a woman *after sex* in...I don't know...almost my entire adult life. Isn't there a way for us to live in the moment and enjoy what we have for just a little while longer?"

She looked back and forth between my eyes. "Where were you planning on moving?"

"I was going to stay with Calliope and Nigel for a few weeks while I found myself a new flat."

"Well, how about this. Why don't you do that? Go stay with Calliope for a week or two. But don't get a new place just yet. Let's keep some distance between us and see if we can be adults about it. Maybe our libidos will cool off, and we'll be able to resume cohabitating after a little while."

I fucking hated the thought of leaving her, even if she was right that it needed to happen. "If that's what you want, okay, I'll go stay with Calliope for a while. But I'd like to ask two things from you, first."

"What's that?"

"One. I'd like to amend our original agreement to one *day* of sex, twenty-four full hours, rather than one act. Because I want you in my bed tonight, and I plan to fuck you several more times."

She swallowed. "Okay. We can do that. What's the other condition?"

"I want you to agree to my definition of sexual relations. Because on the off-chance you beg me to make you come, I want to be clear on the methods I'm permitted to use."

Bridget laughed. "You've got a deal. But you should know, I've never begged anyone to make me come in my entire life. So no matter how handsome, well endowed, and witty you are, I doubt that will be happening, Simon."

I smiled from ear to ear—loving hearing that she'd never begged a man. But even more so, I couldn't wait to be the first for her.

My good mood had plummeted the first night I slept at Calliope's. I wanted to be back at home with Bridget in the worst way.

Back at *home* with Bridget.

What the fuck?

It wasn't my home. My home was in England.

Frustrated, I punched my pillow a few times to fluff it up and laid back down, staring at the ceiling in the dark. For the most part, I lived a very simple life. I didn't need fancy cars or money. I worked hard, yet didn't need to be the chief. But every once in a blue moon, something came along and lit a fire under my ass. My desires were limited, but when they struck—they were consuming.

There were no two ways about it, I desired Bridget Valentine.

I shouldn't.

We shouldn't.

But the woman was addicting.

At four-thirty in the morning, I still hadn't slept a wink, so I decided to go into the hospital early. Maybe the change of scenery would help, and I could catch some shuteye in the residents' lounge.

I was surprised to find Calliope in the kitchen standing in front of the coffeemaker.

"Does it brew faster when you stare at it?"

Calliope jumped. She turned clutching her chest. "You scared the fuck out of me, Simon."

"Sorry. I thought you heard me walk into the room."

"It's four-thirty in the morning, and I haven't had my coffee yet. My hearing is still sleeping."

"Why are you up so early?"

"This is what time I get up every day. I teach a 6AM, private, sunrise yoga class over on Gooseberry Beach."

"Damn. I didn't know that."

"Why are you up? I thought you said your shift didn't start until eight today?"

I ran my fingers through my hair. "I couldn't sleep."

Calliope nodded. The coffee pot beeped to indicate it'd finished brewing, and she grabbed two mugs from the cabinet above her head. "Still take your coffee the same way?"

"I do. I don't change good things."

Calliope fixed us both coffees, and together we sat at the kitchen table. "Is the bed in the guest room not comfortable?"

"No, it's fine."

She sipped her mug and watched me over the brim. "You look pathetic, Simon. Like someone just ran over your dog. When are you just going to give in?"

"Give in?"

"That you have feelings for Bridget, and you belong together."

I wouldn't even attempt to lie about the first part. "I do have feelings for her. But we don't belong together—we want very different things. That's the problem."

"What does she want that you don't?"

"A family, for starters."

"Why are you so adamant that you don't want a family to begin with? You're still so young. You'd make an incredible father. You shouldn't rule that out as a possibility."

"Look who's talking? I don't see your house filled with a bunch of little buggers running around. Tell me, Calliope, why is that? Because I'm pretty sure that our reasons aren't all that different."

Calliope looked away for a minute and then her eyes met mine. "Nigel and I have been trying for two years. I've had three early miscarriages."

"*Fuck.* I didn't know. I'm sorry."

"There's nothing to be sorry about. I didn't tell you to make you feel bad. I told you to prove a point." She reached out and took my hand. "I was there, too, Simon. I feel as responsible as you do. We were stupid kids when the three of us went out on that lake together. I think of Blake all the time. But I'm not punishing myself by not having children of my own."

"That's not what I'm doing."

"Really? Then what are you doing?"

"I don't know the first thing about having kids."

"Newsflash, buddy, no one does when they start off. You drop them a few times, pull their head out from between the stair balusters, and get scared when their poop turns hot pink to match the crayon they snuck and ate when you weren't looking. But you figure it out."

"Bridget has a kid. She knows what she's doing."

Calliope studied me for a moment. "Let me ask you something. What does Brendan want more than anything?"

I shrugged. "A new bike. Flat black with flames." *I wonder if they make one my size.*

"And is he allergic to anything?"

"Latex. What's your point?"

"Just go with it. How about his teacher? What's her name?"

"Miss Santoro. Cute, but doesn't hold a candle to Bridget."

"Favorite subject?"

"Science."

"And did you go to field day with him a few weeks ago where he smiled all that day and then for two more after?"

"Yes."

"Seems like you know what you're doing with Bridget's kid, too, Simon. So what other excuse you got?"

"Well, there's the little fact that my home is in England."

Calliope shook her head. "What's back there for you? A home isn't a bunch of bricks. A home is your happy place." She looked at the time on her watch. "I gotta get going. But think about it. If I told you to close your eyes right now and imagine being anywhere in the world you could, what would you see?"

I waited until my friend was out the door before I sat at the kitchen table and shut my eyes for a few minutes.

I wanted to conjure up pictures of an oceanfront hut in the Indian Ocean, or the top of the beautiful mountains of Snowdonia in Wales as my happy place. But when I closed my eyes, the only thing I was able to see was Bridget. She was my happy place.

Fuck. I was even more screwed than I thought.

Chapter 22

Simon

I woke up in a cold sweat and with my hand down my pants.

Lucky for me, no one else was in the residents' lounge. I'd finally fallen asleep for a bit, only to have the most intense dream I'd ever had in my entire life happen while at work. That was some serious shit. I sat up and blinked a few times. The vividness of it hadn't been dulled by my consciousness.

Bridget and I were in the supply room here at the hospital. Everything was in black and white—our clothes, our skin, the supplies—everything except her mouth. Her fucking lips were painted blood red—gorgeous, full, glossy, blood red. And those lips were wrapped tight around my cock.

I'd woken up with a hard-on and my hand around my cock. That shit could have been embarrassing. Checking the time on my phone, I still had a half-hour before my shift started, so I decided to take a shower—an ice cold one. When I was done, and no longer at risk for being arrested for public indecency due to the outline of my cock straining through my pants, I still had a few minutes to kill, so I decided to run out for coffee.

On my way back, a poster of a woman hanging in the window of the CVS caught my eye, and I wandered in. The next thing I knew, I had eight different shades of red lipstick tested on my hand.

"Is there a certain shade you're looking for?" The clerk smiled warmly.

"Actually—I like the one in the window. The brunette with the bright red lips, but I can't seem to find the right shade."

She ran her finger across a plastic dispenser full of at least a hundred different shades and tapped her nail on one. "Here it is. It's new. It's called Drama. The sample isn't out on display yet, that's why you couldn't find it, but I can open this one for you to try it out."

"Thanks."

She looked up at me. "It will really look bold with your fair skin and blue eyes."

What? "Uhhh...it's not for me."

"Oh. Okay." She gave me a look that said bullshit, and continued to open the packaging.

"No, really. It's not."

"It doesn't matter if it is. We all need things in life to make us feel beautiful."

What has my life turned into? This whole situation might have been comical had I not been totally freaked out that I didn't give a shit if anyone thought I wore lipstick or not, so long as I found that color. Packaging open, the clerk twisted the bottom of the tube and the reddest of reds color rose from the canister. It had a shimmery wet gloss to it that was almost exactly from my dream. Unfortunately, my body recognized it, too. *Shit.* "I'll take it. Thank you." I snatched it from her hands and began to walk toward the register before this got even more embarrassing.

"Wait!" She yelled after me as a hurried down the aisle. "Don't you want a sealed one?"

"Nope. This will do."

The Emergency Room was busy for most of the morning. So, lucky for me, my little dream had been put on the back burner. Until Bridget arrived for her shift. We'd stolen glimpses of each other across the ER, but it wasn't until I was finishing up suturing the knee of a woman who had taken a fall, that Bridget was on my side of the oversized room.

"Nurse Valentine?" I yelled as she was passing by.

"Yes?"

I cut the suture and tied the last stitch. "Would you mind bandaging up Ms. Axelrod? I need to go speak to Dr. Wong before he goes upstairs for rounds in a few minutes."

"Sure. Of course."

I looked at the patient. "You're in good hands. I'd let Nurse Valentine *take care of me* anytime."

Bridget tried to hide her smirk, but I caught it. On my way out of the treatment room, I turned back around. "When you're done, we're almost out of 3-0 and 4-0 sutures, as well as bandages and tape—if you wouldn't mind restocking."

Bridget's brow furrowed. "Really? I just restocked everything two days ago in this room."

I shrugged. "Must have been a run on cuts and bruises."

"Okay. Sure."

Leaving Bridget to finish with the patient, I quickly went to the supply room to empty my pockets of all the shit I'd swiped from the drawers. Then, I went to the nearest vacant treatment room where I could keep my eye on the supply closet and wait for Bridget to walk in.

———

"What are you doing, Simon?" Bridget was reaching up to the top shelf looking for supplies when I walked in and locked the supply closet door behind me. I walked to stand right behind her, effectively blocking her between the shelving and my body from behind. Then I caged her in by grabbing either side of the shelving around her.

"How was your night last night?" I asked to her back.

"Fine."

"Did you sleep well?" I ran a finger up and down her exposed arm. Her breath hitched and goosebumps prickled.

"What are you doing, Simon? We're at work."

"Aren't you going to ask me how I slept?"

"Will you back up and give me some space so I can turn around?"

I did, giving her maybe six inches. But my hands didn't let go of the shelves, so when she turned around, she was confined by my body surrounding her on three sides. "I slept like shit. I'm glad you asked." Of course, *she hadn't.*

"I'm sorry you didn't sleep well, Simon."

"I did manage to get an hour nap in this morning."

"I'm glad."

"But you screwed that up, too."

Her neck pulled back. "I screwed your nap up?"

I nodded slowly.

"How, exactly, did I screw up your nap?"

"You were in my dream, and you were wearing something very special."

She swallowed. "What was I wearing?"

I dug into my pocket. "This."

Rightly, she was confused. I was holding an unpackaged tube of women's lipstick. "Whose lipstick is that?"

"I went to the store and bought it this morning when I woke up. I opened it to make sure it was the exact color you needed."

Her breathing grew heavier. "You bought me the lipstick I was wearing in your dream?"

"Did you ever dream in black and white before?"

She shook her head.

"Everything in my dream was black and white..." I rubbed my thumb over her lips. "...except for this."

Her mouth parted, and I knew if I'd dipped my head down and crushed my lips to hers, she wouldn't stop me. My eyes dropped down to her breasts. Bridget's nipples were swollen and pointing from under her shirt as her chest rose and fell with deep breaths. *God, she's fucking amazing.*

I opened the palm of her hand and folded the lipstick into it. "I can't wait to see you wear this for me."

Somehow, I managed to rein myself in enough to step back. As much as I wanted her, as much as it physically pained me to put distance between us, it wasn't going to be here in the supply closet at work. Because once I got started touching her again, there would be no way I could fucking stop. Plus, Bridget needed to be the one to initiate things so she couldn't hold it against me.

My girl seemed too stunned to focus on anything so I grabbed the supplies that were needed in the treatment room. "I'll take care of restocking room three."

As I reached for the door, her hoarse voice stopped me from opening. "Simon?"

"Yes, luv?"

"What were we doing in your dream that I was wearing this red lipstick?"

I smiled broadly, thrilled that she'd asked. "Your beautiful red lips were wrapped around my cock."

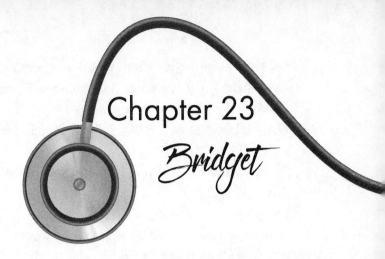

Chapter 23
Bridget

Simon and I had somehow ended up working opposite shifts over the next several days.

The break was both good and bad. While I'd definitely missed the excitement of seeing him, when he wasn't working the ER, I didn't have to worry about any distractions.

I was in the middle of another Simon-less shift—or so I thought—when I heard his voice behind me.

"Thought you'd get lucky another day without me, eh?"

"What are you doing here?"

"Well, this an emergency room. And I'm a doctor, so..."

"I know, but you weren't supposed to be on this shift."

"I switched with Dr. Boyd. He had an obligation."

"I see."

"And I missed you. So, I took advantage of the opportunity, even if it's just working alongside you. It's the only way I get to see you these days."

"It *has* seemed like a while. How are things over at Calliope's?"

"She's pretty sick of my smart mouth in the morning. I've been interrupting her quiet time. She needs lots of coffee before she can deal with me, apparently. I think she's ready to be rid of me. Luckily, I think I found a place."

"You did?"

"Yeah. A small apartment in Wayland Square with no lease."

I pretended to be happy for him. "That's great."

A part of me was sort of hoping that he wouldn't be able to find anything, that he would decide to come back to my house. That was stupid, but nevertheless, I had hoped. His moving into a new place seemed like the first step toward his leaving my life altogether.

"Yeah, it'll do," he said. "It's small, but it will only be temporary."

Temporary. Right. Because you're leaving. Get that in your head, Bridget.

Simon was staring at my lips then his eyes travelled down to my breasts. I changed the subject.

"Brendan told me you've been keeping in contact with him."

"We text back and forth, yeah. I don't want him to feel like I can't be there for him just because I've moved out. I've told him I'm just a phone call or text away anytime he needs to talk."

"That's very nice of you. I know he appreciates your friendship."

I know now that's all it will ever be—a friendship. That's for the best.

"He's a special boy. I'd like to always keep in touch with him."

That thought didn't exactly sit well with me. There would be a time when Simon was back in England moving on with his life. If he was keeping in touch with Brendan, I didn't know that I would want to know certain things, like if he'd moved on or ended up getting married someday. I didn't know if I was strong enough to handle that. Even thinking about it gave me a pain in my chest. I guess I had to respect my son and his wish to remain close to Simon. I wasn't sure if I really had a say in the matter.

———

I couldn't get thoughts of Simon moving on out of my head most of that morning. Even though he was on duty, we hadn't crossed paths much. Despite that, his presence weighed heavily on my mind.

During a bathroom break, I opened my purse and saw the red lipstick that he'd purchased for me. I'd never put it on, but for some reason, I decided to open the tube and try it on.

It was extremely...red. I guess, that was the point.

It was amazing how many of my co-workers commented on my lips. One little thing like a pop of color definitely got you loads of attention. Unfortunately, it wasn't their attention I was looking for. I was dying to see Simon's reaction. The fact that I was craving his attention right now was definitely a bit troublesome.

Finally, I was called into the room where he was examining a patient, who'd been taking up a good deal of his time all afternoon.

Simon turned around to look at me. "Nurse Valentine, if you could..." he hesitated then smiled once he got a look at my lips. He blinked a few times, then continued, "If you could prepare an IV drip for Mr. Norton. I'm going to keep him here for a bit."

I licked my lips. "Of course, Dr. Hogue."

Simon abruptly left the room, and I didn't see him for a while again.

About a half-hour later, I flinched when I felt his hand on the small of my back as he walked to keep up with me.

"Are you due for your break, Bridget?"

"Not for another hour."

"How long do you get again?"

"Thirty minutes."

"Meet me by the elevator in an hour."

He zipped past me so fast that there wasn't any time for me to respond.

When it came time for my break, I found myself waiting by the elevator alone. Just as I was about to leave, Simon came running down the hall in his scrubs. His hair was disheveled. He didn't say anything as he pushed the up button.

We entered the packed elevator together. While he glanced over at me, he still wasn't saying anything. The doors opened, and we made our way up to the third floor.

"Where are we going?" I finally asked.

Without answering me directly, he said, "Follow me." He then led me down a side hallway.

There was a one-stall family bathroom. He looked around, and when there was no one in sight, he pulled me inside and locked the door behind us.

My heart was beating rapidly.

He placed both of his arms around me, locking me in.

"Why did you put that lipstick on at work?"

"Didn't you buy it so that I could wear it?"

"Not here. Do you realize that scrubs do absolutely nothing to hide an erection?"

"I—"

"You think it's funny that I had to run to the bathroom the minute you walked in with those lips?" He leaned in, and I could feel his breath.

There was only one answer. "I do."

"You put it on for one reason and one reason alone. And that was to drive me mad. Am I right?"

"Maybe."

"Does it please you to know that you have this kind of sexual power over me, Bridget? Look down."

Simon's erection was practically vertical, and there was a huge wet spot that had seeped through the thin material of his blue scrubs.

He pointed down. "You think I can go back to work like this?"

"No, I don't think you can, actually." I laughed.

Simon's arms were trembling as they continued to lock me in against the wall. I was making light of this, but clearly I'd gotten him all worked up.

He started to kiss my neck, and I could feel my underwear getting wetter by the second.

I knew what he fantasized about. But I also knew that he wasn't going to come out and ask me for it, because by nature, he was a giver, not a receiver. As much of a dirty talker as he was, I couldn't picture him asking me to get on my knees and suck his dick. Although, that was exactly what he wanted.

If I was being truly honest with myself, it was the real reason I wore this damn lipstick. I wanted to live out his little dream from the moment he told me about it. I wanted him in my mouth, to taste him. I just wanted to drive him a little crazy first. And it seemed it was time for me to put him out of his misery.

I dropped to my knees and pulled his scrubs down slowly. His breathing became labored as I wrapped my hands around his throbbing cock. A string of pre-cum dripped down, and I caught it with my mouth. Simon moaned as I licked the rest off of his tip.

I looked up at him, and he was just on another planet. His eyes rolled back as he buried his fingers in my hair.

I waited for him to look at me again before I took him all the way down my throat, sucking him as I stroked the slick and silky skin of his thick shaft.

"Fuck, yes. Just like that, Bridget. I've always wanted to feel this beautiful mouth around my cock. You have no idea...how good...this feels..."

He kept tightening his abs to keep from coming. I started to suck harder and move my hand faster.

His body began to shake. "I'm coming. You'd better—"

Ignoring his warning, I felt streams of hot cum exploding out of him and into my mouth. I swallowed all of it, something I hadn't ever done—not even with Ben.

Simon's abs were moving in and out as he continued to pant. His hair was all fucked-up, and he looked like all of the wind had been knocked out of him.

"God, you give good head, baby." He still looked dazed. "That was..."

I stood up. "We'd better go."

"You think I'm going to let you go, just like that? We still have ten minutes. I'm not wasting it."

He pulled up his pants then dropped to his knees.

"What are you doing?"

"Finishing off my lunch," he said, sliding down my bottoms.

"That's really not necess—" I gasped.

My words just stopped upon the feel of his mouth on my clit. Simon growled, and I could feel it vibrate through me. His warm tongue circled around my lips. I was probably pulling too hard on his hair, but I couldn't help it.

Simon buried his whole face between my legs. It was the most intense oral sex of my life.

"My pussy," he whispered in between lapping his tongue.

He gripped my ass to guide me over his mouth.

"That's it. Ride my face," he groaned.

Simon's tongue was deep inside of me as I came so fast. It was literally the longest lasting orgasm of my life.

When he stood up, he said, "Please tell me I'll get to do that again. That can't be the last time."

"Haven't we broken the rules enough for one day?"

"Technically, not the Clinton rules. We're still in compliance." He rubbed my cheek then pulled me into him again and kissed me hard.

I was surprised how little of my lipstick had actually spread to his lips...or his cock. It was matte, and long-lasting, apparently.

Simon and I safely returned to the emergency room area. No one had a clue that we had been together, let alone what we had been doing on the third floor.

Later that afternoon, Simon and I were attending to the same patient. I caught him staring at me when he thought I wasn't looking. Our eyes locked, and we just smiled at each other for a moment. It was clear we were both still on a sexual cloud nine.

My shift ended before his. I was on my way out but decided to say goodbye to him first.

Simon was looking at someone's chart when I came up behind him.

"I'm off, Simon."

He frowned. "I wish I could get out of here with you."

There was something I had been waiting to ask him.

"I've been meaning to tell you..." I said. "The weekend after next is Brendan's birthday. I'm having a little party for him at the house. I think he would love it if you'd be there."

Simon closed his eyes momentarily then asked, "That's the weekend of the twenty-fifth?"

"Yes."

His expression dampened. "Shit. I would've loved to have gone, but I've booked tickets to the UK. I'm going there for a week."

My heart sank. "Oh. To see your parents?"

"Yes." He seemed hesitant. "And I...also have an interview for a permanent internist position at a private practice in Leeds."

I just stood there with my mouth hanging open. I knew this was coming. He'd always made it crystal clear that he was going back to England once his residency was over, but a part of me really hoped he would change his mind. Apparently, that part of me was just delusional.

"Wow, it's really happening, huh?"

"Well, nothing is set in stone. It's just an interview."

"But if you get it, you'll take it, right?"

"I haven't thought that far ahead."

I didn't know if I was just feeling really emotional because of what we'd done today or if it was the build up from months of worrying about this very thing happening, but my eyes started to water.

Fuck.

Stop it.

I tried to walk away suddenly so he wouldn't notice, but he quickly followed after me.

"Bridget, fuck. Don't go."

"Don't forget where we are, Simon. This is inappropriate. Go back to work."

"Fuck inappropriate. I don't want you driving home upset."

I ran ahead of him and snuck into a closing elevator before he had a chance to stop me.

Chapter 24
Simon

My parents and I were having dinner in the local pub around the corner from their house in the Calverley neighborhood of Leeds, a quiet village-like suburb not too far from the city.

It was great seeing them, but being back home felt a lot different than I'd expected it to.

Had it always been this cloudy here?

I hadn't left the US on good terms with Bridget. She'd started avoiding me more than ever after finding out about my interview. And this time, I let her. I avoided her right back. Because it just wasn't fair to lead her on anymore if I was going to take this job. Her tears were proof that I'd taken things too far.

Making the situation even more difficult was the fact that the interview had gone spectacularly. After an eight-hour day spent touring the facility, the partners of the medical practice unanimously agreed to offer me the position, which would start in two months after my residency in Providence officially ended. They even offered to pay for my moving expenses.

My parents were therefore considering this a celebratory dinner, because they'd assumed I would be taking the job. To anyone looking in from the outside, the decision was a no-brainer. I hadn't told anyone in my family about Bridget. I kept my recent private life under wraps; my parents didn't even know I'd been living with her.

My mother took a bite of her fry. "So, once you move back, it's going to be great for Nan. She's really missed you. I don't know how much time she has left," my mum said.

"I plan to visit her this week before I leave."

"When can we expect you back here for good?" my father asked.

"Well, I didn't formally accept the job yet. They gave me until next week."

My mother seemed surprised. "But surely, it's a done deal?"

I couldn't get myself to give Mum the confirmation she wanted. I hadn't expected them to offer me the job on the spot with an ultimatum. I was still gobsmacked, really. I figured I'd have several weeks to make a decision. But they were looking for an immediate commitment.

My mother further prodded. "Simon...is there something you're not telling us?"

I didn't want to spend the next hour lying to my parents, making up excuses for my hesitation when there was only one reason I wasn't jumping to happily accept my supposed dream job.

Unsure of how to begin, I said, "There's someone back in the States...um..."

"You've *met* someone?" She looked at my father then back at me. "You haven't mentioned anything."

"Well, she's...someone I've gotten to know for quite a while, actually."

Dad grinned. "Is she in the medical field, too?"

"She's a nurse, actually."

"I see."

My mother leaned in. "Is it serious?"

"Well, technically, we're not together, I suppose. But it's...we've gotten close."

"Would she consider a move across the pond?"

Mum could be very judgmental. I hesitated to tell her the whole story, because I knew she would go off on a tangent about Bridget having baggage, not being good enough for her precious son. I really didn't want to hear all that.

I simply answered, "She can't."

"Why not?"

I braced for her reaction. "She has a son."

My mother grimaced. "You're seeing someone with a child? She's divorced?"

"No. Her husband died in a car accident."

My father nodded. "Sorry to hear."

She went on with her questions. "How old is this woman?"

"Thirty-four."

"She's five years older than you?"

"Four, basically. And that's not very much at all."

"You've been spending time with this little boy?"

"Yes."

"Well, it's a good thing you're getting out now. You wouldn't want him getting anymore attached to you."

My mother's assumptions were making me a bit defensive.

"He's a great kid. I'd be lucky if he got attached to me, really."

"Oh, Simon. Listen to yourself. You can have practically any woman in the world that you want. Your life and your family are here in Leeds. You can't stay in the US with some *woman*, not to mention raising another man's child. Don't you want children of your own someday? She could be trying to trap you, you know. This woman is pushing thirty-five, she's hardly—"

"Her name is Bridget. Not 'this woman.' Her fucking name is Bridget." My pulse was going a mile a minute.

Fuck. I can't remember the last time I swore in front of my parents. It was out of character for me. But my mother was really pissing me off.

"I'm sorry, Mum. Forgive my language."

My father was much more easy-going. "Clearly, son, this situation is making things complicated for you. I'm sure you'll make the right decision, and if your dear old Dad's opinion matters at all to you, for what it's worth, I think the right decision is to take the job."

━━━

The following night, I met some of my old friends at a bar in London.

It had been a long time since I'd gone out drinking. The flashing lights, the loud music, and the crowd were making me a bit uneasy.

My voice became hoarse from talking too loud. Even though I was enjoying catching up with friends I hadn't seen in years, I was finding it really difficult to relax.

I couldn't believe I only had a few days to make a decision. It wasn't just a matter of a job. I felt like my entire existence was riding on this, like I was at the biggest crossroads of my life. There were two incredibly different paths I could take, and the decision I would make in the next few days would impact me forever.

It was too much to handle. Abruptly saying goodbye to my friends, I left the bar feeling lost. I didn't want to go back to my parents' home, didn't want to talk to them about this anymore, since my mother, in particular, didn't understand my dilemma.

An hour later, I found myself at Heathrow Airport, boarding a short flight to a place I'd never thought I would have the courage to visit again. Somehow, I knew I needed to be there in order to make this decision.

***

Calliope's parents no longer owned the Scotland lake house that we stayed at when Blake's accident happened. So, I chose a small inn that was the closest in proximity.

Legend had it that this lake had its very own monster, similar to Loch Ness. I tried not to think about that. There were enough bad thoughts associated with it as it was.

Since I had arrived in the wee hours of the morning, I slept a bit at the inn before heading to the lake early to spend some time there. The plan was to fly right back to London early this evening.

I chose a spot off of the loch near the area where I remembered the accident happening.

Sitting at the end of a pier, I looked up at the sky.

"You're probably wondering what the fuck I'm doing here now. I know I should've come a long time ago. I just didn't have the bollocks to face you, really."

Taking a deep breath in, I continued, "Anyway, I suspect you can see everything that's been happening. I often wonder what you would think of me and of my decisions in life, if you'd be proud or if you'd be angry because I'm living life when you can't."

Straining to fight the tears in my eyes, I said, "That's the thing, Blake. Whenever I feel happiness, it's always bittersweet, because a part of me will always feel like I don't deserve it. It should have been me or at the very least, I should have stopped us from going out on that boat. If I could change only one thing, it would be that. We could have done something else that night, lit a fire—anything. I would give my life to take that night back. I hope you know that. I love you so much."

My tears finally fell. The last time I fully sobbed like this was at his funeral.

"I've tried to do what I could to live a life you'd be proud of, to take care of people, save people. I couldn't save you, but I can save someone else in your memory. That's the best I could come up with."

After my tears dried, I sat in silence for a while before I resumed talking to him.

"I'm sure you've seen Bridget. The one with the best arse. Yeah...her. If you were here, I'd definitely ask for your advice on what to do. The truth is, I know a lot of my hesitation when it comes to her—getting close to her son, ironically, has everything to do with you—my fear of hurting them, like I hurt you. I failed to protect you and I'm sorry. I know I have no right to ask you for guidance, but I do like to think of you as my guardian angel. So, if you can find the time to give me your opinion, that would be brilliant. If not, I can go fuck myself. That's okay, too. As long as you're okay, brother—wherever you are. As long as you're okay...that's all that matters."

I stayed at the same spot at the edge of the pier the entire morning. The longer I stayed, the more comfortable I was there. The loch was no longer the scary, murky place I'd remembered. The sun was even trying to peek through the clouds.

At one point, I took out my phone to check if I had any messages. My parents had texted to check in on me. I'd told them where I was going.

I hadn't heard from Bridget, not that I'd expected to. It dawned on me that yesterday was the day of Brendan's party. Bridget didn't post on Facebook much, only when there was an event involving her son.

I checked her page to see if she had posted any photos. Sure enough, there was an entire album of pictures titled *Brendan's 9th Birthday*.

Scrolling through, I couldn't help but smile. There were pictures of Brendan running around with giant water guns with his friends. Bridget had also rented an inflatable slide.

I stopped at a photo of Bridget and Brendan that nearly took my breath away. She was wearing a blue strapless dress that really brought out her eyes. Her caramel-colored hair was straighter than normal. I had never really noticed how deep her dimples were. She and Brendan both looked really happy.

Keeping my focus on the picture, I tried to imagine what it would be like years down the line to have to look at photos like this, what it would feel like to see her inevitably moving on. There was no doubt in my mind that if she put herself out there, that someone would snag her quickly. She hadn't a clue how attractive she really was.

How would it feel, Simon?

How would it feel to truly walk away from her? From them? *Forever.*

I couldn't describe in words how it would feel. But I was experiencing it in my body. That rush of adrenaline and panic. The anger inside of me that always developed when I thought about her with another man.

Then there was Brendan. He deserved someone who wanted to be a father to him—not a big, goofy friend. *A father.* I didn't feel good enough for that role. But did I want it?

Stopping for a moment to look up at the sky, I got chills because there was a faint rainbow forming. It hadn't even rained.

I continued to scroll through the pictures from Brendan's party, laughing at myself for thinking I was going to somehow find the answer to my dilemma in a Pokémon piñata.

Bridget had really gone all out. She'd even had place settings featuring the names of each boy written on a piece of folded paper with a different Pokémon character next to the name. She'd taken a separate, close-up photo of each one.

It wasn't until the last name that I realized maybe I *was* getting my answer in a Pokémon party after all.

BLAKE.

Chapter 25
Simon

I couldn't wait to see her.

Straight from the airport, I drove to Bridget's house. She'd be leaving to pick up Brendan from school in less than a half-hour, but there was no way I could wait. Which reminded me, I needed to have more sympathy for the addicts that came into the ER. Having never experienced being hooked on anything my entire life, I was generally not empathetic when they came in seeking something to hold them over until their next fix. *But I sure as shit could use a Valium myself right now.* I had all the signs of addiction—craving and compulsion, loss of appetite, disrupted sleep patterns, spending an inordinate amount of time planning the next fix in my head, and lying to myself that I didn't need my drug. When I pulled up in front of her house, my hands even began to shake. *Totally fucking addicted.*

There was a black pick-up truck parked in front of her house. I hoped she didn't have company. Even though I still had my key and would have liked to sneak up on her, I knocked and waited.

She answered wearing the most gorgeous smile. "Simon! What are you doing here? I thought you were in London for a few more days?"

I responded by pulling her to me for the biggest hug. Although my heart was beating out of my chest still, a strange calm came over me while I held her. I imagined it was a lot like a junkie who took a hit after a long period of going cold turkey. A physical sigh rolled through my body. And God, she smelled incredible—like lilies and orchids. Oddly, until that moment, I wasn't even sure I knew what those flowers smelled like. I took a long, deep breath in and out and then lifted her off of her feet before swinging her around in a circle. She giggled and it cemented my decision. *This*. This is the sign I needed.

"God, I missed you, Bridget."

"I could tell. I think you might've broken a rib—you're squeezing me so hard."

"Oh. Shit. Sorry." I reluctantly set her back down on her feet.

"It's fine. I'm teasing. But what are you doing back so soon?"

"I have some pressing things I need to do." *You.*

We were still standing in the doorway when something caught my eye over her shoulder—a man had walked into the kitchen. He was coming from the hall that leads to Bridget's bedroom. My blood pressure shot up. I pointed with my chin. "Who's that?"

Bridget turned. "Oh, that's Nolan."

"Did he just come from your bedroom?"

"Yes. I've had him locked up in there for two days. He's doing some work for me."

"Let's go inside." I wrapped my fingers around Bridget's hip and guided her into the kitchen.

Nolan was probably a few years older than me—Bridget's age, I'd guess. He was also pretty damn good looking—*for an asshole.*

"Nolan, this is Simon, my..." she hesitated. "...Simon was my tenant. He used to live here in the converted garage."

Nolan's eyes zoned in on the hand I had possessively holding her hip and then they lifted to meet mine. He extended his hand, which forced me to let go of Bridget. "Was? So you don't rent it anymore?"

I ignored his question and gripped his hand in a shake that was so firm it bordered on assault. "What kind of work are you doing here?"

Bridget answered. "A pipe burst in the bathroom while I was at work a few days ago. It flooded through the wall of my bedroom. Nolan repaired the pipes and now he's fixing up the wall that needs to be replaced. He was just finishing up for the day."

"Why didn't you call me?"

"Umm. Because you were in London, Simon?"

"Well I'm back. So I can take care of whatever's not done."

Bridget stared at me for a long time. She knew exactly what I was not-so-politely trying to say. After our unspoken exchange, she turned back to Nolan with a full smile. "So, tomorrow morning, then?"

The asshat smirked. He looked at me and back at Bridget with a grin that I wanted to punch from his face. "Looking forward to it."

While Bridget walked the predator out, I went to check out her bedroom. Sure enough, the entire wall that abuts her bathroom had been ripped out and new sheet rock was hung. There was dust all over the place, and the top of the Spackle bucket wasn't even closed properly.

"What are you doing, Simon?" Returning to the bedroom, Bridget folded her arms across her chest in the doorway.

"Shutting the Spackle bucket so Asshat's mud doesn't dry up and you aren't sniffing chemicals all night."

"That's not what I meant."

She looked annoyed for some reason. "I didn't mean what are you doing at this moment. Clearly, I can see you're shutting a bucket that was fine the way it was. I meant, what are you doing showing up here and acting like some sort of a jealous boyfriend?"

"Did you see the way that dick was looking at you?"

"That *dick* came highly recommended by your friend, Calliope, and he wasn't looking at me inappropriately. He's also charging me half the price that the other guy wanted."

I scoffed. "That's because he wants in your pants."

"So what if he does, Simon? Why is that your concern, anyway? I'm a big girl and can take care of myself."

This was nothing like I'd imagined our reunion going down. I was acting like a dick, but it was only because the thought of any man taking care of Bridget other than me made me insane. "I'm sorry. I'm protective of you. I was being a jerk."

"Yes, you were." Her face softened. "How was your trip?"

"It was...good. Exactly what I needed, actually."

"So, you got the job then?"

"Yes. I did."

Bridget frowned and turned to walk out of the bedroom. She went directly into the bathroom before I could stop her and say more. I waited outside in the hallway. When she didn't come out after a few minutes, I leaned my head against the door and gently knocked. "Bridget?"

"What, Simon?"

"We need to talk."

A few minutes later, she opened the door, and I could tell she'd been crying. I'd royally fucked this homecoming up. I had visions of showing up and her falling into my arms. We'd make mad, passionate love, and I'd tell her I was in love with her. Instead, her face was red, eyes were puffy, and I'd acted like a big dick.

I stood in front of the doorway when she tried to walk out of the bathroom. "I need to go pick up Brendan, Simon."

"Okay. But we need to talk. Can I wait for you?"

"I'm taking Brendan to exchange his birthday present after I pick him up."

"What did you get him?"

"A bike."

"Black with flames?"

Bridget gave me a sad smile. "Blue with a white racing stripe. How did you know what he wanted?"

"He showed me a picture of it. It's a really cool bike. Think they make it for six-foot-two dicks?"

That earned me a real smile. I put two fingers under Bridget's chin and lifted so she looked into my eyes. "I'm sorry about how I acted. I didn't mean to be a jerk. Let's start this day over. I really did miss you. Can I take you to dinner later?"

"I promised Brendan I'd take him and a friend to Dave & Buster's after the bike shop. My mom sent him a gift card for his birthday."

"Can I tag along? I have a gift for him anyway."

Bridget contemplated it for a minute. "Sure. He'd love that. Why don't you meet us there at seven."

Calliope wasn't home when I arrived at her house, but she was in the kitchen when I walked out of the bathroom after my shower wearing only a towel wrapped around my waist. She shook her head when she saw me.

"What? I didn't even say anything yet?"

"Your abs. I teach twenty yoga classes a week and you, what, bend over to tie your shoes as your workout? Such bullshit."

"I exercise."

"Not like me, you don't. Men have it so easy."

I shrugged. "A woman without a little body fat and curves looks like a boy anyway."

She smiled. "What are you doing home? Did I mix the days up, or were you supposed to come back on Monday?"

"I came home early."

"Everything okay?"

I nodded. "Got a few minutes to talk?"

"Sure. But go put some clothes on first. I don't want your balls slipping out and accidentally touching my kitchen chairs."

"Okay. But now you've just invited me to sit on your chair naked when you're not home. I like to air out my balls after a long day of being cooped up in trousers anyway."

My friend pointed to my room and barked. "*Go!*"

Calliope made tea while I dressed. After, I sat at the table with my balls safely tucked into my pants and sipped as I looked at my friend over the brim. "I got the job in Leeds."

"That's great. Congratulations."

"Thank you. I'm not taking it."

"What? Why?"

I set down my tea and looked directly into her eyes. "I can't leave her."

Calliope smiled from ear to ear. "It's about damn time. I thought I was going to have to stand on a chair and smack you in the head with a two-by-four to knock some sense into that thick skull."

"That's a little harsh."

"You're pretty damn thick headed. You would've barely felt it."

"Thanks."

"Did you tell Bridget yet?"

"No. Not yet."

Her smiling face grew cautious. "Are you sure about this, Simon? It would kill Bridget if you told her you were staying and then changed your mind six months down the road."

"I'm…" I'd never said the words out loud. I took a deep breath and let 'em rip. "I'm in love with her."

Calliope jumped from her chair and practically knocked over mine as she swamped me in a hug. "I'm so damn happy for you two."

After she calmed down, I told her about my trip. "I went to the lake."

"You did? Jesus, Simon. You're full of surprises today."

"It was a long time coming. I needed to do it."

"Yeah. I think you did." Calliope reached over and took my hand on top of the table. "You've dedicated so much of your life to his memory. But it's time. You can't write a new story for your life when you won't let new characters in."

We sat in silence for a minute, and I knew we were both thinking of Blake.

"I better get going. I'm supposed to meet Bridget in a half-hour."

"Are you going to tell her tonight?"

"I plan to. And then I'm going to spackle her bedroom wall."

Calliope scrunched up her nose. "I don't even want to know what that means."

"It means I'm a jealous prick, but what's mine is mine. And no more handyman referrals from you."

Chapter 26
Bridget

"This is wicked awesome." My son's eyes lit up when he pulled Simon's gift from the box. The matte black helmet with flames exactly matched the bicycle we'd just picked up. "They didn't have anything like this at the bike shop."

"I got it from a website. They custom make anything you want. I emailed them the picture of the bike, and they made it to match. It has your name inside."

Brendan turned the helmet over and pointed. *Little B* was inscribed. While my son thought that was the coolest thing ever, it made me sad to think every time I saw it would be a reminder of Simon—especially after he was gone for his new job.

"Can we go play games now?" The boys had gobbled their food and were anxious to attack the overpriced, money-eating machines.

I took out the gift card Mom had sent. "Yes, but no leaving this room. Not even to go to the bathroom, Brendan. I mean it. You, too, Kenny. If you need to go, let me know, and I'll walk with you. You both stay in this big game room only. And don't talk to strangers."

Brendan rolled his eyes. "Fine."

"Go ahead." I'd barely finished the words when the little boys took off running. I looked at Simon. "Am I too overprotective?"

"This feels like a trap question."

"What do you mean?"

"If I say yes, you're overprotective, you're going to argue with me that you're not. If I say no, then I'm lying to you. It's a no-win situation."

"So you think I'm overprotective."

"I didn't say that."

"But only because you're trying to avoid arguing with me?"

Simon smiled. "How about a glass of wine for you?"

"I'd love that. But I can't. I drove here."

"I'll leave my car in the parking lot and drive us all home in your car."

"But then how will you get to Calliope's later?"

"I can stay in my old room, and you can drive me back here tomorrow morning."

While it was tempting since Simon being back had me on edge and a glass of wine would definitely help, it wasn't a good idea. "That's okay. But thank you for the offer."

Simon nodded, looking disappointed.

Since the day we'd met, I'd always felt comfortable around Simon. But now there was awkwardness between us, and I wasn't sure if it was just me, or we both felt it. I hesitated to make conversation because in my mind, all roads led to Simon moving back to England. But that was selfish of me. I needed to suck it up and get it out of the way so we could go back to normal. Well, as normal as the two of us could be until he left.

"So. Tell me about the job in England."

"It's a private practice in Leeds. I'd be an internist with nine to five hours."

"Wow." I did my best to feign excitement, even managed a toothy smile. "You must be looking forward to that after all the crazy shifts you work."

"Set hours would be nice, yes."

It was difficult to look at Simon, because it felt like he could see right through my lies. I traced a figure eight in the condensation on my soda glass. "That's great. I'm happy for you, Simon."

When I didn't look up, he placed two fingers under my chin and gently lifted my head until our gazes met. "I'm not taking the job, Bridget."

"What? Why?"

"Because it's three-thousand miles away."

I was afraid to let hope spark for fear of being burned. "I don't understand."

"I was hoping to have this conversation in private. But you aren't going to let me get anywhere near you and a quiet room. So, I guess this is as good of a place as any."

Of course, Brendan and his friend picked that moment to run back to our table. "Look at all these we won!" The boys were clutching fistfuls of tickets.

"Wow. That's great, sweetheart."

"We're going to leave them with you so we don't lose any."

"Okay."

The boys stuffed the tickets into plastic cups and then ran off again. I turned my attention back to Simon. Just as he was about to speak, the waitress came to check on us. "Can I get you anything else?"

I looked at Simon who was laughing at yet another interruption. "We'll have a glass of Cabernet and the check, please."

"You're drinking wine?"

"No. You are. As soon as she returns with the check, you're going to chug that glass. Then we're going to go beat the boys at a game of two-on-two air hockey, followed by spending a half-hour in the ticket redemption center so the two of them can pick out junk worth a dollar that cost fifty to win. After that, I'm going to drive you home so we can talk in private after Brendan goes to sleep."

"Are you asking me or telling me?"

"Telling. But hopefully you'll be good with that plan."

I squinted at Simon as he put the car into drive. "Did you have something to do with that?"

"What?"

"Brendan's friend just *conveniently* invited him for a sleepover, and now we are going to have the house alone to ourselves? I saw you and Brendan whispering when you kicked my and Kenny's butts in air hockey."

We'd just dropped the boys off at Kenny's and were heading to my house. After the bomb that Simon dropped on me that he wasn't taking the job in England, my one glass of wine had turned into two. It actually worked to loosen me up, and the four of us had a great time playing air hockey. Not to mention, Simon had rolled up his shirtsleeves, and every time he whacked the puck, the muscles in his forearm flexed. So, yeah, wine and air hockey did the trick. But now that it was just the two of us about to be alone in my house, I was nervous. *So nervous.*

"I had nothing to do with that invitation. Everything is falling into place just as Pokémon said it would."

"What?"

"Nothing."

Inside the house, my nervousness escalated. When Simon unlocked the door and put his hand on my hip to usher me inside, I nearly leaped out of my skin.

"You're jumpy."

"You touched a ticklish spot," I lied.

"I'll have to remember that."

Simon set the keys on the kitchen counter, and I went right to the refrigerator for more anti-nerve serum. "Thank you for driving us home. Would you like a glass of wine now?"

"Sure."

I poured us each a glass and invited Simon to sit in the living room. As we entered, I flicked on the light. Simon flicked it off right behind me. "What are you doing?" I asked.

"It's a full moon. The room is lit enough because you have the blinds open."

He was right. The lighting streaming in from outside was beautiful. It gave off a soft glow that was peaceful and relaxing. Together we sat on the couch.

I shut my eyes and tried to let it all sink in—the wine, the moon, the late hour—hoping I'd find my calm. But when I opened my eyes again, Simon was staring at me in the most intense way. "What? You're making me nervous with how serious you look right now."

"Sorry." He brought his wine to his lips and proceeded to down the entire glass in one long chug.

"Thirsty?" I laughed nervously.

Simon set his glass on the table and then took mine from my hand, placing it down next to his.

"What if I wanted to chug mine like you just did yours?"

"You can do that after I'm done. Hell, I'll down another one and join you after I spit out what I need to say."

Simon shifted and turned to face me head-on. He took both of my hands into his, and I realized he looked as nervous as I felt. Once our gazes were locked, he cleared his throat and took a deep breath before starting. "I can't take the job in Leeds or anywhere else because I can't leave you. I think if I even tried, gravity would pull me right back." He paused, and his voice turned soft. "The first time I saw you, I felt it and it scared me. When I moved in and realized it was you again, I thought it had to be a big coincidence, and I was afraid to get to know you. When I kissed you, it scared the living shit out of me, and I wanted to pull away. But when I tried, I realized I couldn't, and that scared me even more. Then I went back to England and thought about what my life would be like without you in it, and I finally realized that I was more afraid of losing you than I was of finding you. I love you, Bridget. So much that it scared me and made me want to run three-thousand miles away. But I can't run anymore because I need you more than I'm afraid of everything else that comes with loving you."

My heart was thundering in my chest so hard that it actually made me a little nervous for my health. A sheen of cold sweat formed on my neck, my forehead, my palms. Simon's nerves must have been shot waiting for me to respond. He squeezed my hands. "Bridget...say something."

I swallowed a lump of tears in my throat and tasted salt. "I don't know what to say."

His smile was nervous. "How about, *Simon – I'm madly in love with you, too. Now get that big rig up and running and drive it into my naughty garage.*"

I scrunched up my nose.

"No? Not working for you, huh? Okay. How about, *Simon – my love for you is brighter than all the stars in the sky. Now let's go put some sour cream on the big burrito.*"

I laughed. "You're really disgusting."

Simon reached around to my ass and pulled me closer to him. His face turned serious and his voice was low. "Oh yeah? But you love me anyway, right?"

Ben was the only man I'd ever said those words to. I'd known for a while that I was falling in love with Simon, but since I never really believed that he'd be saying those words to me, I didn't bother to freak out about how I might feel saying them aloud the first time. Now here it was suddenly, and I felt panicked.

I stared at him like a deer in the headlights.

Simon blew out a shaky breath. "Talk to me, Bridget. What's going on in that head of yours?"

"I'm scared." I finally managed to croak out.

"That makes two of us. I'm fucking terrified."

"What if it doesn't work out, Simon?"

"What if it does?"

"What if you're miserable here in the States and go back home in a few months?"

"What if I stay forever and we're happy?"

I looked down. Simon was being so honest and putting so much on the line, I needed to do the same. A tear streaked down my face. "I've never said those words to anyone except for..."

Simon closed his eyes and nodded. "Except for your husband."

I reached out and took Simon's hand, placing it over my heart. "Do you feel that? You made it beat again. It's yours. I couldn't have changed that even if you'd decided to go back to England."

Simon cupped both my cheeks. "The words aren't important. You'll say them when you're ready." He leaned in and pressed a soft kiss to my lips. "I love you, Bridget Valentine. I'll just tell you twice as much for now."

———

I'd never given any thought to the difference between having sex and making love before. But what Simon and I experienced tonight was definitely the latter. He truly *made love* to me. It was beautiful and moving, and if I had any doubt that the words he'd shared with me earlier in the night weren't genuine, I was certain now. You couldn't fake what just happened between us. Game changing. *Life* changing.

My head rested on his firm chest as he stroked my damp hair. "That was..." he said. "...I don't know what that was, but I've never experienced anything like it."

"I know. It was magical. Makes you almost want to never do it again because there's nowhere to go but down from that."

I suddenly found myself lifted into the air and flipped onto my back. Simon hovered over me. "Not a fucking chance, woman."

I giggled. "You sound a little like a caveman."

Simon caressed my cheek. "How do you want this to work, luv?"

"What do you mean?"

"Should I take that apartment I found?"

God, there was so much to think about. "I don't know, Simon. I guess I need a little time for this all to sink in. It's not just me that I have to worry about. Brendan is already attached to you, and I'm not sure he's ready to see you in my bed."

Simon searched my eyes. "Sweetheart, where are we right now?"

"I'm not sure what you're asking? We're at my house, of course."

"Yes, but where?"

"In the converted garage. In your room."

"Why aren't we in your room? I asked you where you wanted to go. All of your stuff is in your room. This room is practically empty."

I opened my mouth to say it wasn't what he thought, and then closed it.

Simon's smile warmed my heart. He brushed his lips across mine. "It's okay. Brendan isn't the only one who needs some time. Take all that you need. I'm not going anywhere anymore, and you're worth the wait."

Chapter 27

Simon

The doorbell rang while I was finishing up in the shower. Bridget had just left for the grocery store, and I'd planned to fix the flat on her bicycle while she was out. We thought we'd surprise Brendan and take him to the bike trail that ran through town later today when he got home. Hopping out of the shower, I wrapped a towel around my waist and yelled, "One minute!" so I could pull on some pants before opening the front door. But as I passed the window in the kitchen, I saw the truck parked outside and thought better of putting on clothes.

"Nick—buddy. How's it going?" I opened the door and smiled broadly.

Nolan looked me up and down. "It's Nolan. I thought you didn't live here anymore?"

I hung onto the top of the door and made sure to flex. "Ah. That was a little misunderstanding. I'd just returned from a trip back home to England. But I'm back now. So we won't be needing your services anymore. I can take care of the bedroom for Bridget. Sorry to make you come out here this morning. We would have called earlier, but we slept in after being up half the night. You know how it goes when you get back from a trip, mate."

"Uhh...Is Bridget home?" He tried to look around me, but I filled most of the doorway.

"Nope."

"I'll just give her a call then."

Considering she'd forgotten her cell on the kitchen table, I thought that was a great idea. "Good. Yes, you do that."

I shut the door. Change of plans. I needed to spackle a wall before patching a bike tire.

Bridget stormed inside of the bedroom where I was working on the wall.

"What the hell did you do, Simon?"

I was covered in patch paint. "Hello to you, too, luv."

"You fired Nolan and didn't even consult with me. I just got his voicemail. You can't fire someone who doesn't work for you."

"I thought I already made it clear that I had this situation under control. Why pay someone when I can do the work myself?"

"You didn't have a right to make that decision. I had promised him the work."

"I don't want him in your bedroom. You don't know who he is, and I don't like the way he looks at you."

"That doesn't change the fact that you didn't have a right to make that decision for me!"

I could feel my face burning up with anger. "Why don't you tell me what rights I *do* have, then? Who *am* I to you, Bridget? Your boyfriend? Your roommate? Your fuck buddy? What the hell are we doing? I came back from England to tell you that I love you, that I want a life with you, and you haven't even answered me as to whether I should find a new flat or not." I placed my hand on her chin, prompting her to look up at me. "Do you *want* me here?"

Her eyes were moist and her breathing quickened. I hoped I hadn't scared her.

She finally answered, "Yes. I *do* want you here. It just feels...hard to believe, okay?"

My tone softened. "What does?"

"That you're really staying. I can't seem to...truly believe it."

"Was I not clear on my reasons for turning down the job?"

"You were...I just...I guess I don't understand *why* you would choose this life over that one."

Did she seriously believe I would be better off without her?

"If it's hard to understand why I love you, that's because it's not really something I can describe properly with words. It's a feeling of just not being able to live without you."

"It's not just *me* in this scenario..."

"You don't think I know that? You don't think I know what an incredible responsibility this is?"

"Exactly! Why would you *choose* it?"

She seemed to think she was making a point I hadn't already long considered.

"Incredible doesn't mean unwanted, Bridget. I fully understand and accept the magnitude of this."

"He's going to fall in love with you, Simon. Are you going to be able to return it? Can you really love someone else's son?"

I told her the absolute truth. "I already do."

We needed a change of scenery. Things were getting too intense in the house. I convinced Bridget to follow through with our original plans to head to the bike path with Brendan, even though I was far from finished with my spackling job.

Having spent the entire morning working in her bedroom, I didn't have time to finish patching her bike tire before we left. So, we opted to walk together while Brendan rode his new bicycle. He was up ahead of us as we strolled.

I originally figured we would continue our talk from earlier in a less stressful environment, but our conversation on the bike path turned to lighter topics, like the upcoming school carnival. That was just as well since I needed to keep an eye on Brendan and couldn't be distracted too much. The weather was nice, which meant there were lots of people out cycling or rollerblading today. I needed to look out for him.

"Don't go too far ahead, buddy," I shouted.

Brendan promptly slowed down. Even though Bridget and I were chatting, I didn't take my eyes off him for one second. If I saw an adult rider ready to pass him, I'd yell, "Watch out, Brendan! To your left!"

It was interesting. There were certain times when Bridget was the more protective one, but today I was definitely proving to be the bigger worrier. It must have had to do with the body of water nearby. When it came to Brendan's physical safety in this environment, my mind couldn't help wandering to Blake, especially since a lake ran right alongside the path.

"Watch out," I said, pulling Bridget toward me. "You're stepping in goose droppings."

For some odd reason, our town had an influx of geese this time of year. They would all congregate in certain areas like the high school track or especially around the bike path. Bridget checked the underside of her chucks to make sure she hadn't stepped in any residue.

Everything was going great until about a mile into our trip. That was when a flock of geese unexpectedly crossed in front of Brendan's bike, causing him to brake so hard that he went airborne.

For a brief moment, it felt like my world went dark.

Chapter 28
Bridget

Simon ran ahead of me so fast. It took me a couple of seconds to realize why. I must have been glancing out at the lake the very moment it happened.

My heart fell to my stomach as I hurried to catch up to them.

Brendan was lying on the ground, his arm badly scraped and bleeding. But he wasn't crying. My son rarely cried, which I was grateful for, because seeing him in any kind of pain killed me.

Trembling, *I* was the one crying as I helplessly watched Simon lift my boy into the safety of his arms, carefully inspecting every inch of him and asking lots of questions.

"What hurts?"

"My arm and my knee."

"You didn't hit your head, right?"

"No."

Thank God.

Thank you, God.

"Brendan, you need to be more careful," I said.

Simon was quick to correct me. "It wasn't his fault. There was nothing he could have done. Those giant birds jumped right out in front of him. I saw it happen. Completely unavoidable."

"Can you walk okay?" I asked.

Simon carefully put him down. Even though he was still shaken, Brendan moved his legs around and nodded that he was okay to walk. Simon then knelt down and pulled him into a tight embrace. The same massive relief I was feeling was written all over Simon's face as well.

I picked the bike up off the ground and began wheeling it back.

Walking two steps behind them, I watched as Brendan reached for Simon's hand. He hadn't even hesitated to do it, and Simon took it so effortlessly as if it was totally natural. I just kept staring at Brendan's little hand inside Simon's massive one.

When had this happened?

I knew that Simon had grown close to my son, but it had never really sunken in that—whether I was trying to prevent it or not—a serious attachment had already developed.

For the first time, it hit me. Simon's deciding not to take the Leeds job—it wasn't just about *me*. He wanted to be here for Brendan, too. He wanted this. He wanted us.

I'd been so preoccupied with my own fears, I hadn't really opened my eyes to what was actually *happening* around me.

We cut our afternoon outing short and headed straight home after a quick stop for Del's frozen lemonade; it was right on the way back anyway.

When we arrived at the house, Simon treated Brendan's wounds and confirmed he didn't need stitches; he was going to be just fine. It was helpful to have a doctor around in times like these. I would've probably been second-guessing everything and might have taken him to the ER just to get another opinion to confirm that he didn't have some hidden injury.

Once Brendan was cleaned up, the three of us were hanging out in the kitchen.

Simon clapped his hands together. "How about I go to the store and get us stuff to make tacos tonight?" He knew that was Brendan's favorite meal.

My son perked up. "Can you get the Doritos shells?"

"If that's what you want, sure." Simon smiled.

Brendan's next question changed the mood fast.

"Are you going back to your friend's house after dinner?"

Simon looked at me, seeking guidance on a response. It was time to set the record straight. Truthfully, I'd made the decision, just hadn't had the guts to accept it until this afternoon.

I looked over at my son. "No. Simon is staying here with us, Brendan." I looked over at Simon to make sure my intentions were clear. "He's moving back in permanently."

My son looked between us then straight at Simon. "Until you move to England?"

Simon took a moment to gather his thoughts.

"Well, that was the original plan, but actually, I wanted to talk to you about something. I wanted to know how you'd feel if I stuck around instead?"

His question seemed to take a few seconds to register with Brendan, who'd likely never considered the possibility of Simon actually staying.

"You're not leaving us?"

Leaving us.

The way he put it really made me realize how he'd truly felt.

Simon knelt down to be eye level with him. "I went back there to visit. You knew that...to see my parents. I really missed them. But the thing is...I missed you more—you and your mum. And I realized I didn't want to move anymore. I want to stay here with you guys. Because you both make me really happy."

Simon's declaring that to my son meant more than his telling me he loved me. It was more of a commitment than most marriage proposals, even. When you look a child in the eyes—particularly one who'd lost his father—and tell him you're here to stay, that's about as serious as it gets. I knew he wouldn't do anything to hurt Brendan. He would never make a promise to him that he couldn't keep.

Brendan looked stunned, like he'd never expected this, like this entire time had always been about preparing for Simon to be gone, preparing for another loss. His eyes started to glisten. My son, who never cried, was tearing up. Not because he fell and got hurt, but because he loved Simon. It was as simple as that. He'd been holding back from allowing himself to feel that love because he was sure he would lose him.

That sort of sounded like someone else I knew.

Simon looked ready to tear up himself as he smiled. "Please tell me those are happy tears..."

Brendan nodded and said, "Really happy."

"C'mere." Simon pulled him into a hug.

My heart was melting as my son released a breath into Simon's shoulder.

If Brendan was able to finally exhale, maybe I could, too.

That night, after I tucked Brendan in, Simon was waiting for me in the living room. He'd poured two glasses of wine and set them aside. He had his big feet up on the coffee table as he waited for me.

I didn't know why I was so nervous all of a sudden. It was probably because I knew it was time to unload all of the things I'd needed to say but hadn't.

Simon could sense my tension. He opened his arms, encouraging me to join him on the couch. "Come here, you."

I took my place next to him and curled my body into his chest.

He spoke before I had the chance.

"I'd like to stay in my old room indefinitely. It's too much too soon for him, otherwise."

I looked up at him. "I agree."

"I'm not his father. Regardless of what you saw today, it's not my intention to replace anyone. It's a lot for any kid to see someone moving into his mum's bedroom. I don't care how much he looks up to me, that would be weird for him right now."

"Thank you for understanding that." There was so much more I needed to say. I took a deep breath. "I owe you an apology for my behavior when you came back from England. I had gotten into a mode of self-protection, and it was really hard to break free from the pattern. I was truly convinced that you would be gone from my life and that I needed to protect my heart. Today, though, it really sank in that you're not going anywhere."

"I'm not, Bridget. And as much as it pains me to apologize for firing that Noel or whatever his name was, I'm also sorry I overstepped my bounds and angered you."

"You weren't totally off base about him. He *had* tried to ask me out."

Simon looked like the vein in his neck was about to pop. "Fuck. I knew it. I'll break him if he ever comes around again."

Smiling slightly, I said, "I didn't entertain it for even a second. I was so distraught when you were gone. I couldn't think of anything else. And then when you came back, it felt like a dream. You'd told me everything I'd ever wanted to hear. And it just seemed too good to be true. The fear just paralyzed me."

"You want to talk about fear? I know I said the words aren't important, but you don't think my heart skipped a beat when you didn't tell me you loved me back? You don't think I wake up in the middle of the night wondering if you'll ever love me as much as you loved him?"

Ben.

It never occurred to me that Simon had any hang-ups about that.

The vulnerability in his eyes in that moment was something I'd never seen from him before.

My truest feelings were really hard to admit. I'd never uttered them aloud until now. But his openness deserved reciprocation.

"Doesn't God only give you one soulmate? Isn't that the way it's supposed to be? But, Simon, I feel things for you that I've *never* felt for anyone. I will always love my husband. But I love you so much. You wake up in the middle of the night wondering if I can love you as much as I loved him? Well, I've lost sleep feeling guilty that maybe I will grow to love you *more*. And that sometimes makes me so sad for him that I don't now how to handle it."

Chapter 29

Simon

I was a sick fuck that it gave me pleasure to hear her say that— as much as it had also broken my heart that her feelings for me caused her that kind of torment.

She'd felt things for me that she hadn't felt for him.

It's not a contest, Simon.

What mattered most was that she finally said the words I'd longed for—that I'd counted on hearing when I said goodbye to my parents and my nan and told them I'd likely not be returning anytime soon.

As much as she'd given me what I needed tonight, I also realized the way in which she'd admitted her love was bittersweet. The shadow of her late husband would always be present. I should have never made her feel like she needed to compare us. But love breeds insecurity, making people weak and needy.

Still, it was the first night I truly felt like she was mine. And that was making me want to show her exactly how much she belonged to me.

I caressed her hair. "Let's go to my room."

Today was emotionally draining. I needed release and couldn't wait a second longer to bury myself in her.

I knew from the look in her eyes, she needed it, too. Her skin was flush, and her eyes were hazy even though she hadn't had a drop of wine.

Bridget stood up, and I gently pressed my body against her back as I led her to my quarters.

"We'll lock the door," I rasped, my cock painfully hard. "Just in case he wakes up."

The last time we'd made love, we'd done just that—*made love*. Even though that was intense, tonight I wasn't in a gentle mood. Between her telling me that the fucking handyman had tried to get into her pants while I was gone and then her admitting she loved me, my emotions were all over the place. I just wanted to ravage her and stake my claim.

"I need to fuck you hard, but I know we have to be quiet," I said.

Her breathing became more rapid with my words. "The bed will make too much noise. Take me on the floor."

Fuck yes.

"Take everything off but your knickers then get down on all fours," I said as I unbuckled my pants and stripped down.

I knew Bridget loved it when I was demanding. She'd only ever experienced rough sex with me—no one else. And that pleased me to no end.

Her beautiful ass was sticking straight up in the air—so inviting. I took the pleasure of doing something I'd always fantasized about when I ripped her underwear off of her with my bare hands, shredding it one harsh movement.

She flinched, but the smile she flashed when she looked back at me told me she loved it.

"I just fucked up your days of the week, luv." I slid my hands down the slope of her back. "I'm gonna fuck you so good to make up for it."

She felt wetter than I could ever remember as I sank into her. I knew I wasn't going to last very long, because having her this drenched and at this angle was too much.

"You feel so incredible. This beautiful ass is mine," I whispered, plowing into her. "Tell me you're mine."

"I'm yours. Only yours." Her nails were digging into the carpet.

"Say it again."

"I'm yours. Fuck, Simon, you're in me so deep like this. Fuck me harder. I can take it."

She didn't always talk dirty but when she did, it put me over the edge.

Thrust after thrust, I felt my balls tightening until I couldn't hold back any longer. When I knew she was climaxing, I let myself go. Even though I wanted to come inside of her, I pulled out, instead opting to decorate her beautiful ass with my cum. I was marking my territory, and it was a sight I wouldn't soon forget.

━━━━━

My residency would be coming to an end soon; I still didn't have a permanent position in Rhode Island lined up.

If Bridget and I were officially together now, then it really didn't make sense to hide our relationship from our co-workers at Memorial anymore. We agreed that while we wouldn't announce anything, if someone happened to find out, we weren't going to deny it.

The way in which our co-workers actually discovered it, however, wasn't how I would've ever chosen for it to happen.

Bridget didn't realize I was within earshot when a certain conversation was happening at the nurses' station one afternoon. Hiding behind a wall, I listened as several of the women were discussing *me* right in front of Bridget. It was awkward and disturbing, to say the least. This had probably happened before without my knowing; but things were so much different now.

I could hear a few of the nurses theorizing about my sexual prowess among other things.

How fucking hot I was.

How they wouldn't mind trying me out.

How there won't be any eye candy anymore when I'm gone.

Brianna, the nurse I'd had a one-night stand with before Bridget and I became involved, decided to use the opportunity to announce that she *had* in fact once "sampled the goods."

"He was so good in bed. But I know he didn't want anything serious, so I respected that."

"I just have to know…how big is he?" someone asked.

"He's exactly how you'd think he'd be. Maybe even more."

Bridget was standing right fucking there, and I knew she was hurting having to listen to that shit. There was no bloody way I was going to let them disrespect her, even if they didn't realize what they were doing. Not to mention, this was so goddamn unprofessional.

I emerged from behind the wall, startling them.

"Thank you for your compliments. But I think this needs to end right now." I turned to Brianna. "Yes, we had a brief encounter early on this year, but I'm spoken for now. And I highly doubt my *girlfriend* appreciates having to stand here and listen to you talk about it. So please have respect for *Bridget* and not talk about me in front of her."

There were a few gasps. I didn't give a flying fuck.

Brianna looked at Bridget then me. "You guys are together? I had no idea. I thought you said you don't do relationships."

"I didn't—until her," I said.

Bridget chose to remain silent while the women just stood there looking dumbfounded.

Brianna apologized for her little kiss and tell before the other nurses quickly dispersed like a bunch of pigeons.

Bridget was still quiet. I knew the whole exchange had really upset her.

I placed my hand on her shoulder. "Are you okay?

"Honestly? I feel sick."

I couldn't help my smile. I was pretty sure she was ready to smack me, though.

"You think this is funny, Simon?"

"Not at all. I'm not smiling because you're upset. I'm smiling because it means you love me. You feel sick with jealousy because you love me."

"I do love you. And honestly, they have some fucking nerve talking about you like that here."

"I'm sorry you had to hear all that, especially the Brianna thing."

"You already told me about that skank. The last time you took her out, you brought your cock home for me. Remember?"

"Yes, darling. I do."

She tried to shrug it off, even though I knew she was still upset. "Anyway, it's not like I didn't know you had a life before we met. It's okay."

"No." I leaned in, taking in a whiff of her scent. "No, I didn't have much of a life. I just thought I did. My life was nothing until you guys."

Wanting to kiss her so badly, I refrained. We were at work, and she wouldn't have appreciated that. I planned to make up for lost time at home later.

Her nightly visits to my room were what I lived for. In many ways, sneaking around was more exciting than sleeping in the same bed. She always made sure she was back in her own room when Brendan woke up in the morning.

Bridget was blushing. I loved that I could still make that happen.

"I have to go," she said before walking away. I stood there, proudly watching her rear end bounce.

A phone call interrupted my arse gazing. It was someone from hospital administration. Memorial and the previous hospital where I used to work were part of the same conglomerate. They needed me to head to my old stomping grounds after work today to discuss a lawsuit I'd somehow gotten dragged into. A woman was suing the hospital for malpractice, and I was named in the suit along with about ten others. I'd known about the upcoming deposition for months, but it must've slipped my mind with all of the other life-changing shit I was focused on.

Just brilliant.

It was going to be a long night before I'd get to go home to my luv now.

Chapter 30
Simon

I wasn't a fan of lawyers. Especially the disrespectful dipshit I was currently sitting across from.

"The bulging disc in this woman's back is from her double Ds—nothing we did wrong." My attorney pulled a file from a tall stack on his desk, then moved the remainder of them to the top of the cabinet behind him. "But at least we get some good scenery across the table during the deposition."

I prefer my scenery in the form of a certain sexy nurse at work, thank you very much.

"I don't understand why I'm even involved in this lawsuit. I wasn't the treating physician. I saw the woman for maybe two minutes on the way out at the end of my shift."

"Everyone gets sued. It's the American way. Might as well get used to it. Won't be the last time you're sitting in my office if you're going to stay part of the Memorial Healthcare system. Or are you going back home? Is that a brogue you got there?"

"I'm from England."

"Might want to go back. America's the most litigious society in the world."

Great.

"Anyway. Let's get started. I just want to go over your involvement before the deposition tomorrow."

"Tomorrow? I thought it wasn't for a few weeks."

"Got moved up. The radiologist settled out, so you're up next. You're also the last defendant in the lineup, which means the plaintiff's attorney will depose you in the morning and then in the afternoon, we'll begin our deposition of the plaintiff. "

"I'm on shift tomorrow morning at nine."

"My secretary called over earlier and got you coverage from nine to five. You'll be here with me all day."

"Great," I said sarcastically.

He opened the file and looked over some chicken scratch, then grabbed a pen. "So, why don't we run through your interactions with Ms. Delmonico from the top. How did you first come to meet the patient?"

"I'd just finished up a twenty-four hour shift and was on my way out when a double trauma came in. Car accident. I stopped into treatment room six and asked if there was anything they needed help with before I took off."

"Who did you ask that of?"

"The attending, Dr. Larson."

"Okay. And did you view the patient at that time?"

"I did. Not up close—but from the doorway."

"And what did you observe?"

"She had a burn on one side of her face—which I assumed was from the airbag, and Dr. Larson was removing the cervical collar that the EMTs had placed for transport. He asked me to call in radiology orders for a neck and head scan and hang a bag of fluids. It was a busy night, between flu season and the driver who was brought in with the woman, everyone was tied up. Normally a nurse would call in orders and hang fluids, but I'm a resident and Larson is an attending which means he barks, I fetch."

"Anything else?"

"Nothing out of the ordinary. I called X-ray down to the ER, hung the fluids, wrote it in the chart, and took off for the night."

The attorney scribbled something in the file and then looked up again. "About the burn on her face. Do you happen to remember which side of her face was burned?"

I closed my eyes. It had been a few years, but I could still see it on my memory's highlight reel. "The left. Dr. Larson was standing on that side and she was crying. I didn't see it at first, until he moved the collar and her head turned a bit."

"We have a theory on the face burn. A medical team consisting of a group of orthopedics, internists, surgeons, and nurses review all of our medical records involving any lawsuit. They formulate an opinion on whether standard operating procedures were followed and if any malpractice occurred. During the review of Ms. Delmonico's medical records, the team noted an inconsistency with the burn and the injury sustained to her neck."

"What do you mean?"

"She suffered whiplash from the impact of the accident and tore a ligament on the right side of her neck."

"So? That's common."

"Yes. But with the angle of the impact, her head should have snapped back to the right side and caused hyperextending of the ligament on the left side. The burn would be on the left side of her face if she was in the passenger seat like she said."

"So she lied about where she was sitting? Why would she do that?"

"Our guess? She was giving the driver a hummer when the crash happened."

I raked my hand through my hair. Which reminded me, I was going to have to get this mop sheared if I wanted anyone to take me seriously in court. "That sucks. But what does any of that have to do with me and the lawsuit? She's suing for failure to diagnose a lower back bulging disc, right?"

"Shows a pattern of lying. She claims she's got long-term pain and suffering. Bulging discs are difficult to prove one way or the other. Sometimes it's easier for us to get the jury to not trust her than it is to prove we weren't negligent. Not to mention, the driver was her boyfriend—her very married boyfriend. Pick a jury of a few married women, we'll be on easy street."

The law was a dirty business. "Did we do something wrong or not?"

"Doesn't matter. It's not always about right or wrong."

"Really? I thought it was."

The lawyer snickered. "Stay in practice long enough, those shiny ideals you have will dull."

It was late by the time I got home. The attorney had spent hours going over the questions I might be asked, even though I could have summarized everything I knew in under two minutes flat. I found Bridget asleep on the couch, with her e-reader still in her hands. Her beautiful mouth let out a sweet whistle with every exhale. I smiled to myself thinking how wrapped around this woman's finger I was if I thought even her damn snore was cute. Not wanting to wake her, but knowing she wouldn't sleep well on the couch, I gently lifted her and tiptoed toward the bedroom with Bridget cradled in my arms. She woke as I set her down.

"Hey," she whispered. "What time is it?"

"It's a little after nine."

"I must have dozed off in the middle of reading my book."

"Yeah. I'll turn off your reader. I'm going to go take a shower anyway. Close your eyes. Go back to sleep."

She smiled. "Thank you."

I kissed her forehead. "Goodnight, luv. Sweet dreams."

I was at her doorway when she called after me. "Simon?"

"Yeah?"

"Will you lie with me for a little while after your shower?"

I looked at her to confirm exactly what she was asking. "In here?"

She nodded.

"You sure?"

"Yes."

"Alright. I'll be back in a few."

I knew what inviting me into her bed meant to Bridget. So, even though I was exhausted from being up going on thirty hours, I wanked off quick to reduce the chance that my hard-on would be disrespectful the first time she let me in. After my shower, I locked up the house, peeked in on Brendan, and went back to Bridget's bedroom. She was on her side, so I slipped in behind her and kissed her shoulder.

"How was the meeting with the attorney?"

"Fine. I'm being deposed tomorrow, so I won't be at the hospital until dinner time."

"It must be scary being sued."

"I'll let you know."

"Does the lawyer think the hospital did anything wrong?"

"He doesn't seem to give a shit. His focus is on making the woman look like a liar."

"That's horrible."

"Yeah. The guy's a dirtbag. I think he was getting off on the fact that they suspect the woman was giving the driver a jobby while he was driving."

"A jobby?"

"Sucking him off."

"Oh. Wow. That sounds dangerous. Is that what caused the accident?"

"I don't know. But it has nothing to do with her injuries and any possible malpractice. Yet the lawyer plans to make it that way."

She sighed. "I'm sorry you have to go through this."

"I'll deal." I swept her hair to the other side and kissed her neck. "You know what gets me through everything?"

"What?"

"Knowing I get to come home to you."

"You're really a sweet talker when you're not a dirty talker, Dr. Hogue."

I rested my chin on her shoulder and whispered in her ear, "Thank you for letting me lie here with you. It means a lot."

"*You* mean a lot."

I tightened my grip around her waist. "Get some sleep. I set my phone alarm for an hour so I'm not in here when Brendan wakes up."

"Okay."

"Night, luv."

"Good night, Simon. Good luck tomorrow."

"State your full name for the record." It was the afternoon, and the hospital attorney's turn to question the woman. This morning I'd been deposed, and it was rather uneventful. As much as I didn't like Arnold Schwartz, there hadn't been a single question that he hadn't prepped me for last night.

"Gina Marie Delmonico."

"Ms. Delmonico. Is it okay, if I refer to you as Gina sometimes during this afternoon's session?"

"Sure."

"Thank you. I have to go over some formalities before we begin. Can you please tell me your current address, how long you've resided there, and your date of birth?"

"910 East Elm Street, Warwick, Rhode Island. I've lived there for about six years. My date of birth is July 10th, 1985."

"Great, thank you. And are you married, Gina?"

"No."

"Were you married at the time of the visit to the Emergency Room on July 12th, 2015?"

"No, I've never been married."

"Thank you, again. Do you have any children?"

"Yes. I have one daughter, Olivia."

"And her age?"

"She just turned three last week."

"Okay. Thank you. I'm going to begin asking you questions about the night of your visit to the Emergency Room."

"Okay."

"What event led you to visit the Warwick Emergency Room on the evening of July 12th, 2015?"

The small conference room we were in had nothing to look at. The tan-colored walls were barren and the conference room table was empty, except for the files in front of each attorney. I'd been watching Gina Marie Delmonico all morning, and her face hadn't changed—until she had to answer that question. The color of her skin paled, and her eyes glassed up.

"I was in a car accident."

"And were you the passenger or the driver of the vehicle?"

"I was the passenger."

"And who was driving?"

"A co-worker was driving."

"And was the driver taken to Warwick Hospital as a result of the accident, as well?"

"Yes."

"And he didn't make it?"

"No. He died in the accident."

Arnold slid a box of tissues across the table. "I'm sorry for your loss."

"Thank you."

"Did you and the driver have a relationship outside of a professional one?"

Gina turned to her attorney, whose lips drew to a straight line, and he nodded his assurance. Clearly they'd discussed that this issue would likely come up. I felt bad for her—whatever their relationship was, it was obvious that the loss was difficult for her even after a few years. It felt dirty to make her talk about it when it was so irrelevant to the issue of malpractice. She swallowed and answered in a low voice. "We were dating, as well as co-workers."

"And this co-worker, your boyfriend, was he married?"

Her eyes pointed down. "Yes."

"Was he separated from his wife at the time of the accident?"

"No."

"And how long were the two of you a couple?"

"I don't know exactly. Around a year, I guess. Maybe a little less."

"So, you had an ongoing relationship with a married man for an extended period of time prior to the accident."

"Yes."

"And you were aware he was married during this relationship?"

"Yes."

"Alright. And where were you coming from on the evening of the accident?"

"We'd just had dinner at a restaurant, Carmine's."

"And where were you heading?"

"To my house."

"To be clear, you and your married boyfriend were not working at the time of the accident. This was strictly an evening of a personal nature?"

"Yes." A tear fell from Gina's eye. She used the back of her hand to wipe it away, rather than take one of the tissues that Arnold had pushed toward her. I didn't blame her. I wouldn't have taken anything from the jerk, either. This entire thing was wrong, and regardless of whether she was dating a married man, Gina deserved some privacy. The least I could do was not gape at her while she cried. I folded my hands on top of the table and stared at my clasped fingers.

"What was the location of the accident?"

"We had just come off Exit 15 on 95 and onto Jefferson Boulevard."

"And what caused the accident?"

"A car had been stopped in the shoulder and unexpectedly merged into traffic just as we were about to pass. We swerved to avoid the car, going into the lane to the left of us, and sideswiped a car that was already in that lane. Our car lost control and bounced around before being spun into oncoming traffic."

"And that is your own personal recollection of the accident?"

"No. I don't remember any of it. That's what I learned afterward from the police and witnesses."

"What's the first thing you're able to remember from that evening?"

"I remember waking up, and our car was upside down. A truck was smashed into the driver's side, and people were yelling that everything was going to be okay."

The woman paused and then her voice broke when she started again. "There was so much blood. So much blood, and he wouldn't wake up. Everything wasn't okay." I kept my eyes trained on my hands out of respect.

"Thank you," Arnold said. "I'm sorry. I know this must be difficult for you to talk about."

The woman sniffled. "It is."

"Would you like to take a moment?"

"No. It's fine. I'd rather just get this over with."

"Okay then. So, *the cause* of the accident, you're saying, was a car cut you off. But you don't recall seeing that car actually cut you off?"

"Yes."

"So that I'm clear, you don't remember seeing the car, or you weren't able to see the car from where you were seated?"

"I don't remember."

I tried to tune the rest out, knowing where Arnold was going with his questioning and wanting nothing to do with it. "Let's talk about where you were seated during the accident? Were you seated in the front passenger seat?"

"I was."

"Were you wearing a seatbelt?"

"No."

"No seat belt. Why not?"

"I'd just taken it off for a minute."

"Were you upright in the passenger seat, Ms. Delmonico?"

"I don't understand the question," she sounded panicked.

"From the nature of your injury and the angle of the impact, it appears that you weren't facing forward as one might assume is normal when you're seated in the passenger seat of a moving vehicle."

The woman's lawyer jumped in. "This is a new low, even for you, Arnie. My client lost someone she cared about and was injured. None of this is relevant and you know it."

"This is a deposition. Keep your relevance objections for the judge, Frank."

The other lawyer grumbled something I didn't catch.

"I'll go back to my original question," Arnold said. "Were you upright in the passenger seat prior to the accident, Ms. Delmonico?"

There was quiet and then a low answer. "No. I was lying down."

"You were lying down? Where was your head?"

"On the driver's lap."

"So, it wasn't possible to know if a car cut you off or not, even if you remembered that actual accident?"

"No, I guess not."

"Were the driver's pants open while your head was on his lap?"

"I don't remember."

"You don't remember?"

"You asked, she answered," Gina's attorney warned. "Move on."

"Fine."

By that point, I was so pissed off that none of this had to do with the type of treatment she received, that my knuckles were turning white keeping my hands folded. Where were the questions relevant to the woman's medical care, for Christ's sake?

"For the record, what was the name of the driver whose lap your head was on—with or without his pants being open?"

The woman whimpered, causing me to look up. Tears were streaming down her red face, and she was doing her best to keep control. She looked distraught and our eyes caught as she spoke. "Ben. Benjamin Valentine."

Chapter 31

Simon

The door lock clanked closed. Too exhausted to even turn over and see who was there, I assumed it was a fellow resident coming in to get some sleep. Until lips met the back of my neck. Even if I hadn't known Bridget's touch, I was like Pavlov to her smell. Only this dog wasn't ready to face his master quite yet.

Taking the cowardly way out, I pretended to be asleep. She wasn't on the schedule for a shift this morning, so I wondered if they called her in because someone called out sick. For a few minutes, I listened as she tiptoed around the dark room and then she brushed her lips on my cheek.

I waited until the door opened and closed to roll over. There was a small nightstand next to the bed I was pretending to be asleep in. Bridget's handwriting slashed across a folded piece of paper—*Simon*. Next to it was a brown paper bag. I grabbed the note first.

> *Simon,*
>   *I stopped by after dropping Brendan*
> *at school to bring you some treats. Hope*

everything went well yesterday with the lawyers. Looking forward to seeing you tonight at home. I left something to remind you what's waiting for you after shift.
-Your luv,
Bridget
P.S. Yes, I am.

Yes, I am? She'd folded the note in half and sealed it with a lipstick kiss along the crease—she'd been wearing *the* red lipstick. *Fuck.* My head and heart were in pain, but apparently my cock was chipper this morning. I was growing stiff from a fucking note while I was miserable inside. I blew out a frustrated breath and grabbed for the brown paper bag.

The minute I opened it, the smell of fresh-baked, banana nut bread permeated my nose even though it was wrapped in tin foil. I lifted it from the bag to see what was underneath and found it still warm. *She baked me fresh bread.* The bag also had an orange juice, coffee, and what I initially thought was some wadded up napkins. But upon closer inspection, I realized that wasn't what was at the bottom of the sack—it was a pair of Bridget's knickers.

I pulled them out. *Wednesday.* Since that was today, the first thought that ran through my mind was *Is she walking around commando?* It dawned on me that she'd already answered my question. *P.S. Yes, I am.* The woman knew me so well, that she answered my questions before I even asked them. How the hell was I going to lie to a woman who could do that? She'd see right through my bullshit. I hated the thought of lying to her even if I could get away with it. But I hated the thought of hurting her just as much, if not more.

After getting over the initial shock of finding out that the woman who was suing me was my girlfriend's dead husband's mistress, I went into a period of denial. It had to be a coincidence. There could've been two Ben Valentines that died in a car accident a couple of years ago. It was a long shot, but I had nothing else to cling to. When the deposition was over, I asked my lawyer some follow-up questions regarding the driver of the car. Of course, sleazy Arnie Schwartz was happy to tell me whatever dirty shit they'd dug up on the plaintiff.

The hospital had hired an investigator to surveil Gina Delmonico in an effort to catch her doing things that a person with a bulging disc shouldn't be able to do. They'd also done a full background investigation on her, including her relationship with the driver. My heart sank when Arnie mentioned that the driver's wife was also an employee of the hospital—a nurse, and the two of them had a child together. But I felt sick thinking about the last half of the conversation we had.

"Birth records list the father of Gina's child as unknown. Doubt the kid will ever know she probably has a brother," he said.

"A brother?" I was confused, or perhaps it was willful ignorance.

"Wife has a son, girlfriend has a daughter—chances are they share DNA. Hope the two don't unknowingly meet in college and hit it off."

I couldn't face her. I also couldn't break Bridget's heart by telling her that the man she had been married to wasn't the man she thought he was. I'd be opening up old wounds that would never get a chance to heal. But how could I *not* tell her? Brendan could possibly have a sister.

My head was spinning so fast after the deposition that I needed to take some time to think things through. In hindsight, it might not have been the best idea to spend that time thinking in a pub. Nothing was any clearer with my brain marinated in alcohol. I was a bigger mess now than I'd been earlier in the evening. Hence, the reason the alarm was going off at nearly four in the morning, and I was trying to climb in through the living room window. In my drunken haze, I couldn't remember the code to punch in.

Nigel came to the front door carrying a bat and found me wedged half in, half out of the living room window.

"What the hell, Simon? You could have gotten your head bashed in."

I lost my balance and fell face first through the window and yet somehow landed on my very drunken arse. "Good thing you didn't lock the window."

Nigel walked to the keypad and punched a code in. "Yes. We could have kept out an intruder. We wouldn't have wanted that, now, would we?"

I stumbled attempting to get up just as Calliope walked into the living room to join us. She pulled her bathrobe shut and squinted. "What the hell, Simon?"

"That's exactly what your better half said." For some reason, I found that hysterical and started to laugh.

"Are you *drunk*?" Calliope asked

"Are *you*?" I responded, still laughing.

Nigel sighed, "I'll put some coffee on. You two have fun."

I managed to get myself to the couch and plopped down on it.

"What's going on, Simon? What are you doing here in the middle of the night climbing through our window?"

"You changed the alarm combination?"

"We didn't change the combination, Simon."

"Well, then it must be broken."

"Sure, it's broken. But why aren't you at Bridget's? Did you two have a fight or something?"

"Nope. Everything is brilliant."

"If that's the case, then why are you here?"

"Ah." I held up my pointer finger. "Because incest is bad. They could have a two-headed baby. I went to medical school. I know these things."

"What *the hell* are you talking about?"

Suddenly feeling like the room was spinning and a giant weight was crushing my chest, I leaned my head back on the couch and shut my eyes. "I love her, you know."

"Who are we talking about? Bridget or the two-headed baby?"

"I'd love the shit out of a two-headed baby if it was Bridget's."

"Okay, Simon. It's four in the morning and you're talking in drunk circles. Why don't we go into the kitchen and have some coffee. Whatever is going on, we'll figure it out."

The following morning, Bridget was already dressed in her maroon scrubs, getting ready for work when I walked in the door. I'd texted her last night before heading to Calliope's, explaining that I was too wankered to drive. Thankfully, Calliope's house was only a half-mile walk from the pub.

Leading Bridget to believe that it was simply the deposition that had me stressed, I knew she was probably confused as to why I'd chosen to drown my sorrows alone in a bar instead of coming home and relieving my stress inside of her. That was uncharacteristic of me, for damn sure.

I placed my hand around her cheek and kissed her forehead. "Brendan's at school?"

"Yes. I just got back from dropping him off." Bridget seemed oddly sympathetic when I had expected her to be more pissed at me for not coming home. "How are you feeling? Want some coffee?"

"Sick. I nearly honked on their couch. No coffee, thanks."

"Honked?"

"Vomited. I was stupid to drink so much."

"Well, you were stressed. We all deserve an escape once in a while. As long as you don't do it all of the time."

"Believe me, I don't intend to, my luv. I'm fucking miserable away from you at night. Thank you for being so understanding."

Her warm lips covered my stale mouth. "I missed you."

Anticipating what was to come, my heart was breaking as I whispered, "I missed you, too."

I longed to return to the days before this mess came about.

She frowned. "I wish I had more time to spend with you this morning, but I'm already late for work. I just stuck around long enough to say hello. You're off today, right?"

"Yeah. I don't have to go in until tonight. We're going to just miss each other's shifts by like an hour, I think."

"You can catch up on rest today then, stay hydrated."

"I intend to."

God, I hated this façade.

After she left for the hospital, my mind was racing. Calliope had warned me I could probably get in trouble for contacting Gina Delmonico directly because I was a party to her lawsuit. I'd watched enough *Law & Order* reruns to think she was right—but I needed to talk to her privately before telling Bridget anything at all. That way I could go into that inevitable conversation armed with information. As much as it made sense, I dreaded calling the woman. I just wished all of this were a bad dream.

Wandering around the quiet house aimlessly, I stopped into Brendan's room. There was a framed picture of his father atop the chest of drawers. It was in a baseball-themed frame.

I lifted it and spoke to him. "What the fuck were you thinking...messing with that broad when you had Bridget? If you weren't already dead, I'd fucking kill you, you know that?"

This situation was causing me to completely lose my marbles; now I was talking to a dead man and threatening his life.

"Alright, maybe I don't mean that, because you're Brendan's dad. But I'd definitely rough you up a bit, maybe make you watch while I fucked your wife nice and good right in front of you. Although, maybe you've been seeing us from where you are. If so, then you've already bore witness to that. Serves you right."

I looked up at the ceiling before talking to the photo again.

"Thanks a lot for leaving me to clean up your mess, mate. You'd better hope this little girl's not yours. Get to work...talk to some people up there and bloody fix this."

Chapter 32
Simon

Gina agreed to meet me at a coffee shop on the East Side of Providence. Bouncing my knees up and down and surrounded by Brown University students and their MacBooks, I sipped my coffee and anxiously awaited her arrival. The only thing pleasant about this was the smell of cinnamon wafting from the baked goods shelf.

I hadn't told Gina the exact reason for my wanting to speak with her. All I'd said was that I had some information that she might be interested in, making it seem like meeting me would provide some benefit in regards to her case against the hospital. I feared she might not have come if she knew the real reason I needed to confront her.

When she appeared, I waved to her from my seat in the middle of the packed café. She lifted her index finger then pointed to the counter to signal that she was going to order something before joining me.

Five minutes later, Gina placed her coffee down on the table and sat across from me. Her chair skidded.

"What did you want to see me about, Dr. Hogue?"

Needing to cut to the chase, I came right out with it. "My girlfriend is Bridget Valentine—Ben's wife."

Gina froze in the middle of sipping her coffee. Her expression turned to one of fear. She slowly nodded but said nothing as I continued.

"I was dragged into the deposition because I happened to be on shift in the ER the night of your accident. I didn't know Bridget then. We've only gotten together over the past several months. The fact that the driver turned out to be Ben was a very unwelcome surprise."

She blew out a long breath. "I can imagine." Gina was nervous, looking around and fidgeting in her seat.

"Look, I'm not here to judge you. But I can't keep this information from Bridget. I have to let her know what I've discovered. But before I say anything, I need to make sure that I'm not misrepresenting the facts. This is going to gut her no matter how I present it."

She was wearing bright red lipstick, similar to the shade I loved on Bridget. On Gina, it just seemed dirty and unappealing.

"What do you want to know?" she asked.

I figured I'd tread lightly rather than skipping right to the most important piece. I needed her to feel comfortable opening up to me so that she didn't feel the need to hide anything.

In the least abrasive tone I could conjure up, I said, "You indicated you carried on an affair with Ben for about a year…"

"Yes. We never meant to hurt anyone. I had a boyfriend at the time, too. But Ben and I…we just connected. It started as an innocent flirtation at work, just emails and text messages and what not. Then we ended up on the same business trip once and well, you know…"

"Unfortunately, I do know, yes." My blood was boiling. "Did he ever…talk about why he was cheating?"

She shrugged her shoulders. "He loved his wife. There was never any doubt in my mind about that. He never spoke negatively about her. They'd just been together for so long, and I think their relationship lacked excitement in certain areas."

"Did he say that exactly?"

"Well, he'd tell me that he didn't feel comfortable exploring…certain things sexually with her. He didn't feel right because she was the mother of his child."

If that wasn't the sorriest excuse I'd ever heard.

Gritting my teeth to hide my anger, I said, "Right. He'd make love to her and he'd *fuck* you."

"If you want to put it that way…yes."

"Did he ever talk about leaving Bridget?"

"No. I knew he would never consider that because of his son, and I would have never asked him to. But honestly, we didn't talk a lot about his home life when we'd spend time together. That wasn't the point of our affair. We enjoyed the carefree nature of our relationship. The few times he opened up, he did mention that even though he loved his wife, that things between him and Bridget were strained at times. He didn't think Bridget was happy anymore. Ben was with me for an escape, and I was escaping a bad relationship at the time myself. We really didn't set out to hurt anyone. We never wanted anyone to find out about us, certainly never intended it to come out this way."

He wanted to escape his home life.

I looked up at the ceiling and silently continued my conversation with him from earlier.

Bridget wasn't happy? Go fuck yourself, Ben. Maybe if you'd given your wife the same energy you'd given your whore...things would have been different.

I continued, "So, your philosophy is...what people don't know won't hurt them?"

"Basically, yes. I mean, we weren't really thinking about anyone else. It was selfish, but we couldn't help our connection. Once you cross the line the first time, that's it. You can't really go back, nor do you really want to."

I needed to get to the crux of the matter before I lost it on her and flipped this table.

"You have a daughter..."

"Yes."

"I think you probably can guess what I'm going to ask next."

"Olivia is not Ben's," she insisted.

Squinting my eyes skeptically, I asked, "How old is she again?"

"Three."

"Technically, it's possible, then. How can you be sure she's not Ben's?"

"I'm ninety-nine percent sure."

My eyes stretched open. "Ninety-nine. Not a hundred..."

"Like I said, it's nearly impossible."

I leaned in. "How is that the case if you were having regular sex with him?"

"Ben was religious about using condoms. He didn't want to take even the smallest risk of getting me pregnant."

"And this other man you were with...you had unprotected sex with him?"

"Yes. He was my long-term boyfriend. We'd been together almost ten years when I met Ben. Brian and I aren't together anymore."

I checked my phone and realized it was time for me to head to work.

"Look, Gina, I'm not going to push this issue or do anything to influence Bridget one way or the other, but if she ends up wanting a DNA test, would you be willing to have Olivia tested to match for a sibling against Brendan?"

"Yeah. I mean, if it will put this to rest. My ex, Brian, knows about my affair with Ben. I ended up telling him after we broke up. But he's taken responsibility for Olivia. He believes he's her father."

"Alright...well, I appreciate your willingness to cooperate if it comes to that." I stood up. "I have to be going now."

She stopped me. "Before you go...for what it's worth, please tell Bridget I'm really sorry. I don't think she's gonna want to hear that. But it's the truth. It was so hard not being able to go to Ben's wake and funeral. Aside from my own injuries that prevented me from it, I couldn't face her. Ben may not have been in love with me like he loved his wife, but I knew he cared about me. It wasn't *just* sex, you know? We were friends, too. I'll never get over what happened to him. But I certainly wish that this whole thing hadn't come out. Nothing good can come from this now."

"I wish I'd never found out about it, to be honest. Now, I'm faced with having to ruin her memory of him. But I can't *not* tell her."

"I understand. You're in a difficult position."

"Thank you for taking the time to speak with me."

"No problem." She smiled, her eyes landing on my torso before returning upward. "Bridget's a lucky woman."

I walked away, refusing to acknowledge her last comment, which didn't sit right with me at all. It made me feel like she'd do it all over again if given the opportunity. Once a cheater, always a cheater. It was amazing how easy it was for her to justify her actions. *They had a connection, my arse.* Fuck that. He was married to someone who believed in him and who thought their marriage was sacred.

Driving to the hospital, I didn't know how I was going to make it through my long shift. I wouldn't have the opportunity to address any of this with Bridget until our mutual day off this weekend. While the time apart would allow me to gather my thoughts, I wasn't sure there was any way to do this without shattering her world.

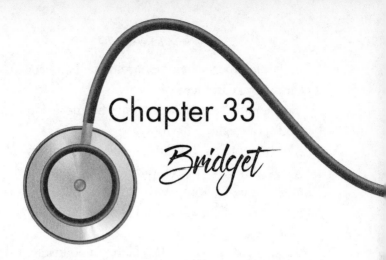

Chapter 33

Bridget

Brendan had tomorrow off because of a professional day at school, so I dropped him off at his grandmother's house for a sleepover. I planned to pick him up on Saturday afternoon.

Driving back from Ben's mother's place, I found myself dreading returning home to an empty house. Even though I had loads of laundry to do and plenty of housework to occupy my time, I was really missing Simon tonight. I hated when we ended up on opposite shifts like this. He'd be working all through the night.

It was a bizarre week to say the least with his unexpectedly getting called into the deposition and then his drunken night away. Simon never lost control like that, and I guess it was a matter of time before stress caught up with him.

Making matters worse, he hadn't nailed down a permanent position here yet, so he was facing unemployment on top of everything. He had some discussions with the management at Memorial about their taking him on permanently, but no one had been able to give him any guarantees yet.

So, I couldn't say I blamed him when he let loose at the bar the other night.

I'd just pulled off the highway when my phone rang. Quickly glancing at the screen, I realized it was Ginnifer, one of the nurses at the hospital. She was the only co-worker I'd really confided in since Simon publicly announced our relationship.

It was odd for her to be calling me outside of work, though. It made me wonder if I'd left something behind.

"Hey, Ginny. What's up?"

"Where are you?"

"I just dropped Brendan off down in North Kingstown. Headed home to crack open a bottle of wine and do laundry. Exciting night." I chuckled. "What's up?"

"Okay, you're driving. Maybe you should call me when you get home."

"Why? What can't you tell me now?"

"Can you pull over for a minute?"

My heart started pounding. She was still at the hospital, and Simon was now on shift. I immediately began to worry. "Did something happen? Is Simon okay?"

"Everyone's fine. It's nothing like that."

"Okay..."

Pulling into the parking lot of a karate studio right off the main road, I touched my hand to my chest and could feel my heart thumping against it. "I'm parked. Tell me what's going on."

"I was doing some shopping on the East Side today before work tonight, and I happened to walk by this café. I saw Simon there with a woman."

My stomach sank.

"What? Are you sure it was him?"

"Positive. I stood in the window for a while to confirm it. He was pretty deep into a conversation and didn't notice me standing there."

"So, they were merely talking?"

"He wasn't doing anything wrong, per se, but I just wanted to make sure you know what I saw. I thought it was odd. It doesn't necessarily mean anything. I just couldn't go about my night without at least telling you."

The nausea was getting worse.

"Have you seen Simon tonight in the ER?" I asked.

"Yeah. I've treated a few patients with him, and honestly, he seems...off. Really downtrodden, not his normal, chipper self."

"What did she look like...this woman?"

"She had long, dark hair—looked Italian. Attractive. Obviously I wouldn't be concerned if he was having lunch with some ugly old lady."

"What else can you tell me?"

Her voice sounded muffled. Or was it my brain?

"She was wearing a navy dress and bright red lipstick."

Bright red lipstick.

My voice was shaky. "Anything else?"

"No. That was it. Like I said, they were talking. They both had coffees. Honestly, it makes me sick to be starting any trouble for you. You seemed so happy that last time we spoke."

"Don't you dare feel bad. I would have done the same thing. I'll talk to him and get to the bottom of it."

After we hung up, I couldn't move. It was like the shock had paralyzed me, preventing me from knowing how to even start the car.

In my heart, I felt that Simon would never do anything to hurt me. But when he'd checked in with me today, he said he spent the afternoon catching up on sleep, nothing more. So, even if this woman was just some friend or acquaintance that he'd never told me about, the fact remained that he had lied to me.

I drove home in a daze, barely remembering how I had gotten there.

Should I text him?

I honestly didn't know what to do. Deciding to pour myself that wine, I started to gulp it down unusually fast. I mindlessly made my way down to the basement and put in a load of laundry, not even paying attention to whether I had mixed whites with colors.

A text came in, interrupting the monotony. It was from Simon.

Simon: I love you so much.

That was so random, that it came in this moment as if he could sense my strife. Tears started to fall. What if Ginny was wrong, and I ended up accusing him of something he didn't do? I valued the trust that he and I'd developed in our relationship. Even questioning him about something like this would damage that, regardless of what actually happened.

My brain was going a mile a minute. If I could only look in his eyes, maybe I would find the answer. He wouldn't be off his shift until six tomorrow morning. I felt like I was going to burst if I didn't talk to him soon.

Bridget: Can you wake me when you get home in the morning? I really need to talk to you about something.

The phone rang almost immediately. Simon sounded concerned. "Is everything okay?"

"I'm fine, physically. But there's something I need to talk to you about. It's important. So please just wake me if I'm not up."

As much as I tried to hide my freaking out, he knew from my tone. "What's going on, Bridget?"

"I'd rather not talk about it on the phone."

I could hear the worry in his voice. "Let me see if I can get someone to cover me. Stay where you are. Don't go anywhere, okay?"

"Alright."

About a half-hour later, Simon sent me another text.

Simon: Managed to get Dr. Lowry to fill in for me through the rest of the night. I'll have to cover for him tomorrow though. Just got in the car. On my way. Be home soon.

Abandoning my laundry, I made my way back upstairs and stayed huddled on the couch while I waited for him.

Fifteen minutes. He couldn't have been more than fifteen minutes away. I felt like I had to cherish these last minutes of hope as scary as they were. Because if it turned out that he lied to me, I might not be able to ever fully trust him again.

When the door opened, I didn't move. Simon looked like he'd literally run home from Providence. Out of breath and with his hair mussed up, he seemed more frazzled than I'd ever seen him.

"You need to tell me what's going on."

I came right out with it.

"Were you with a woman today at a café on the East Side?"

He looked like my words had knocked even more wind out of him.

"How did you know that?"

"So, you were?"

"Answer me. How did you know that?"

"Ginnifer saw you." I was starting to cry. "Who is she?"

"She's the plaintiff in the lawsuit."

My pulse slowed a little. It hadn't occurred to me that the meeting might have had something to do with the deposition. But still, why hadn't he mentioned it to me, then? He'd specifically said he was catching up on rest and never uttered a single word about a meeting with a woman.

Wiping my nose with my sleeve, I said, "You lied to me. You said you were home all afternoon."

Simon's blue eyes darkened in a way I'd never observed before. It felt like my entire world was closing in on me as he knelt down onto his knees in front of the couch and placed both of his hands on my shoulders.

He looked deeply into my eyes when he said, "First off, I need to tell you that there's absolutely nothing going on between me and the woman in the café. Her name is Gina Delmonico, and it was the first time I'd ever spoken directly to her."

My chest grew heavier. "Gina...Gina Delmonico? The woman who Ben worked with? The one who was in the car when he...when he died?"

Simon nodded. "Yes."

"I'm confused. Why were you with her? What's going on, Simon?"

He took a deep breath and closed his eyes for a moment before speaking. "What I'm about to tell you is probably the most difficult thing I've ever had to do in my entire life." When he noticed my hand shaking, he said, "Please don't be scared. We're fine. We're so good, my love. I love you so much. This doesn't have anything to do with us, but it has to do with Ben."

"Ben? What about Ben?"

"In the course of the deposition, I realized that the car accident we were discussing was *Ben's* accident. I was apparently working the ER at Warwick Hospital the exact night he was killed. The woman who is suing the hospital for her injuries is Gina Delmonico, Ben's passenger. We've never spoken about his accident in detail. I hadn't even realized that there was someone in the car with him."

"Yes. Gina was his co-worker. He was driving her home the night of the accident. They were working late, and her car didn't start. I've always felt badly for not sending her a card or calling her. It's just...I was in shock when it happened. I knew she went to the ER, but his office said it was nothing too serious. I never followed up."

Simon frowned, but said nothing.

"So that's why you lied to me? You didn't want to mention that the woman who is suing you is Gina because...because you didn't want to upset me by bringing up the accident?"

The way Simon looked at me, I knew that wasn't it. His face was etched with pain, and he was struggling to say anything at all.

"Simon," I whispered. "What's going on?"

"I'm so sorry, luv." He just kept shaking his head and looking down. When he finally looked me in the eyes, I held my breath to brace myself. "Gina and Ben were having an affair. She admitted to it during the questioning at her deposition."

Even though I was still sitting, the room started to spin as I grabbed onto Simon for balance. I was staring right at him—his mouth was moving, sound was coming out, yet I couldn't hear the words that he said. It felt like I was underwater, everything was so muffled. He paused and tears welled in his eyes. Holding my head with two hands as if I was fragile and he was worried I might break, his voice broke through. "She has a daughter, Bridget. She's three. Gina doesn't think she's Ben's daughter, but she isn't positive. Apparently, she also had a boyfriend at the time."

He looked alarmed after a minute. It might have been because I had grown pale. The room started to spin faster and faster.

"Bridget? Breathe, baby. Breathe. *Shit!*"

I woke up with a cool rag on my head and an extremely nervous looking doctor holding my hand. "You scared the living shit out of me, luv."

"What happened?" I was lightheaded and felt a bit queasy.

Simon went from nervous to full-blown panicked. "Please tell me you remember the conversation we just had. I can't have it again."

It all came back to me.

Ben.

Gina.

An affair.

A child.

For a moment, I'd thought I might need to get up off the couch so that Simon could lie down. "No, no. I remember. I guess I passed out?"

"You did. And you scared the life out of me."

I reached up and touched Simon's cheek. "I'm sorry."

"Don't be. Just tell me you're okay. How do you feel? Physically, I mean." He picked up my wrist and began to take my heart rate. Still not satisfied, he felt my forehead for a fever, lifted my eyelids to get a better look at my eyes, and then began randomly patting me all over."

"What are you doing?"

"Checking to see if you're okay."

"Did I fall?"

"Not really. You were sitting up, and I caught you in my arms and laid you down on the couch."

"So, what are you looking for?"

Simon stopped patting my legs and looked up at me. He seemed to realize for the first time that he was acting a little crazy. He shook his head. "I have no fucking idea."

Even feeling like the world as I knew it had just crumbled before my eyes, this man could make me smile. "I'm fine. You know I have a tendency to pass out."

"You're sure?"

"Yes. I promise." Although I was dizzy still, I sat up to reassure the concerned doctor. I also needed to know more information. "Tell me everything, Simon. I want to know every word that she said—anything you can remember."

Chapter 34
Simon

"**O**h my, God!" Bridget bolted upright from the bed. It was after two in the morning, and we'd just settled in after talking for hours. I'd told her everything I knew. It was terrible to put her through that pain. There'd been a lot of pacing and yelling, but she hadn't passed out again on me. I *thought* she was finally starting to fall asleep.

I sat up. "What? What's the matter?"

"A blowjob. She was giving him a *fucking blowjob!*" Since I'd shared what the attorney had told me the hospital's review panel had discovered—before we had any idea the receiver of said blowjob was Ben—I hadn't bothered to reiterate that part of the story tonight. I was hoping she wouldn't remember.

"I'm sorry. I was hoping you'd forget that."

"My husband died over a blowjob. Maybe if he was paying attention to the road, my son would still have a father."

I didn't know what to say or how to make her feel better. She had bounced back and forth between angry and upset all night. "Come here." I coaxed her back down to bed and rubbed her shoulders, attempting to soothe her. She was quiet for a few minutes, and I thought perhaps she was drifting off.

"Simon?" Her voice was a whisper.

"Yes, luv?"

"Was I not enough?"

I stared up at the ceiling and cursed that bastard. *If you weren't fucking dead already...* Ben and I were going to have a long goddamn talk soon, but right at the moment, Bridget was more important. She needed my reassurance. I gently turned her so she was lying on her back.

"You're not *enough*, Bridget. Enough is the minimum amount that it takes to satisfy something. That doesn't even begin to describe what you are—you're *everything*. You're not the fucking minimum—you're the maximum. What he did is not your fault. Cheating isn't about the person who was cheated on. It's about the cheater—*his own* insecurities. Think about it. Did you ever cheat on a test in school? Everyone has. Why? Because you were afraid you would fail the test—afraid you weren't smart enough or hadn't worked hard enough to earn a good grade. This is about *him*—not about you." I hesitated before continuing, but thought she needed to hear it. "I know you loved him, and he's Brendan's father, but he didn't deserve you. People don't deserve to have things they don't respect. He didn't fucking deserve you, Bridget."

Tears streamed down her face. "How can you sound so sure?"

"Because I am, luv. I've been insecure about having a relationship my whole life—meeting you changed that.

You've made me better, more secure than ever, not the opposite. Love makes you stronger, not weaker."

The next morning, Bridget slept late. I made some calls and had just finished cooking bacon and eggs when she walked into the kitchen. Her face was puffy from a night of crying, but she was still the most beautiful woman I'd ever seen. Usually women became less pretty to me as I got to know them. What attracted me to them initially on the outside, dulled when I got to know the person inside. With Bridget it was just the opposite.

"Morning, beautiful."

"Coffee."

I smiled. "Coming right up. Sit. You didn't eat anything last night. You're going to have some of my eggs even if I have to feed you myself."

Bridget sat at the kitchen table, and I fixed her coffee before plating more food than she could possibly eat and joining her with my own heaping dish.

"I have to be at the hospital in an hour," I said.

"Oh." She frowned. "That's right. I'm sorry. I made you come home last night, and now you're on today instead of being off."

"It's fine. I just hate to leave you alone today."

"I'll be fine. I need to pick up Brendan from his sleepover soon, anyway."

I would've rather have eased into things, but I didn't have the luxury of time today. "I made a few calls this morning."

"Oh?"

"DDC is a chain of labs that does in-home DNA testing. You pick up the kit, swab the cheeks of the people who you want to test, and drop the kit back to the lab. There's one in Providence, Cranston, and Warwick. You can get the results back in three days, right online. I didn't think you'd want to use the lab at work for privacy."

"Oh, yeah. You're right. I hadn't given any thought to the logistics."

"You can swab both children without the parents' DNA. The place I found does more than the average sixteen-marker, standard DNA test. So, it's reliable without a parent to test against."

"Wow. Okay. I'll need to swab Brendan then, too. Of course, that makes sense. I just hadn't thought that far ahead."

"I was thinking maybe you could bring him to the ER when I'm working, and I could take his vitals and swab his mouth. Tell him it's a physical."

"Yes, that would work," she said. "He's comfortable at the ER since I work there. He's also been a patient when he hurt his arm playing soccer, so it won't seem too strange."

"Okay, that's good."

Bridget had only taken two bites of her food. I sipped my coffee and watched as she pushed food around her plate. "You know I don't like a bony arse, so you better eat a little more than that."

She forced a smile. "I don't have an appetite."

"Two more pieces of bacon. Get some protein in your body, at least."

She pouted, but picked up the bacon.

Looking at the time on my phone, I knew I was going to have to jump in the shower soon. I cleared my throat, hating to even mention the name. "I also texted Gina this morning. I'm going to pop over to the DDC office in Providence at lunch today and pick up the kit. She's agreed to meet me this afternoon during my dinner break, and I'll do a quick swab on her daughter."

Bridget nodded but then went quiet for a while. I thought perhaps she'd changed her mind or that I'd overstepped. "Last night you said you wanted to get the testing done as soon as possible. Do you still want to do that? It's not a rush. Maybe you should take some time before moving forward. It's a lot to take in at once."

"No. I need to know as soon as possible."

I nodded but knew something was still bothering her. She looked like she was mulling over saying something on her mind. "Did I upset you by texting her and putting the wheels in motion?"

"No. Not at all. I appreciate you handling everything. I wasn't looking forward to dealing with all of it. But..."

"What's the matter?"

"What time are you meeting her?"

"Five o'clock this afternoon. Why?"

"I'd like to do it myself. I'd like to meet Gina to collect the sample and meet her daughter."

I thought that was a terrible idea. "I'm not sure that's so wise, Bridget."

"Maybe. But I need to do it, Simon. I need to talk to her."

"Bridget—"

"I'm serious, Simon. I need to do this. I'm never going to have closure from Ben because he's not here anymore."

As much as I hated the thought, I could understand her needing some answers directly from the source. "Fine. I'll go with you."

"No. I need to do this alone—woman to woman."

"I'd really like to come along. I want to be there just in case you need me."

Bridget reached across the table and covered my hand with hers. "You *are* here if I need you. You were here last night, you made all of these arrangements this morning, and you're going to be there for me even if you're not physically *with* me. But this is something I need to do by myself, Simon."

I looked back and forth in her eyes and saw sheer determination staring back at me. I fucking hated the thought of her going alone—but I thought about what I'd needed to do with Blake. Some ghosts we just need to exorcise ourselves. Against my better judgment, I finally nodded. "I'll let Gina know you'll be the one coming."

Bridget shook her head. "No. Don't. I don't want her to be prepared for me. No different than I was to find out about her. I want honest answers, not something manufactured. It's better that she be surprised."

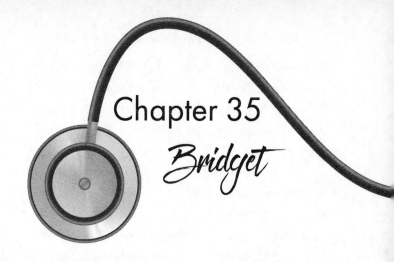

Chapter 35

Bridget

I couldn't stop my hands from shaking.

Simon had arranged to meet Gina at the McDonald's near the hospital, which had a children's PlayPlace. I parked next to the tall windows and looked inside at a half-dozen little girls running around. *One of them could be my husband's daughter. My son's half-sister.* The thought made me feel like I might throw up right there in my car. I had to roll down the window to get some fresh air, then shut my eyes for a full five minutes in order for the overwhelming urge to vomit to pass enough to go inside.

Luckily, my feet were able to move me forward, even though my brain was screaming to run the other way. Opening the door from the restaurant to the kiddie area, I looked around the giant PlayPlace for a woman who fit the description that Simon had given me. To the right, there was a brunette sitting with a redheaded woman chatting— that could be her. Although I figured she would come alone. To the left was another brunette with her back to me, but she was sitting with twin boys who looked to be about three. I was beginning to breathe a little easier, relieved that maybe she hadn't shown up, when I spotted a woman off in the corner near the ball pit sitting with a little girl. My heart started to hammer in my chest as I walked toward her. She was stunning. Simon had failed to mention that.

I considered turning around and leaving, but then a little boy about Brendan's age walked by holding the hand of a little girl about Gina's daughter's age. They were probably siblings. My chest squeezed, and I knew I had to go through with it. I needed to know for my son's sake, even if not for my own sanity.

Without giving myself another opportunity to back out, I walked over to the table where they were sitting. The woman looked up at me and smiled at first.

I stared until that smile morphed into concern. She wrapped her arm around her daughter protectively. "Can I help you?"

My voice was barely a whisper. "Are you Gina Delmonico?"

"Yes?"

When my gaze shifted to her daughter, searching for signs of my husband, signs of my son, she must've figured it out. Closing her eyes briefly, she nodded. "Yes, I'm Gina. You're Bridget, aren't you?"

I stood frozen while the woman spoke to her daughter. "Do you want to go in the ball pit?"

The little girl jumped up and down. "Yes! Yes! Yes!"

"Okay, baby." Gina stood and looked at me. "Excuse me a moment." She disappeared to help her daughter into the ball pit, and then came back. Motioning to the side of the table she'd been sitting at, she said, "I need to be able to keep my eye on her while she's in there. Do you mind if I sit on this side?"

I just kept standing there. After she settled into her seat, she looked up at me. "Do you want to speak to me, or did you just want to swab Olivia?"

"Olivia?"

"My daughter. I assumed that's why you were here instead of Dr. Hogue."

Blinking a few times, I finally snapped out of it and sat down. I don't know what I'd expected—perhaps it was me screaming at her, or her running away from me when she realized who I was, but sitting down to speak in a civil manner was not it.

Gina at least had the decency to look embarrassed. Staring down at the cup of coffee on the table in front of her, she shook her head and let out a shaky breath. "I'm so sorry."

"I didn't come for an apology. I came because I need to know why. Why did he turn to you?"

"He didn't love me. It was...just an affair...just...sex."

Ben and I'd had a normal sex life; at least I thought we did. Sensing her answer wasn't enough for me, Gina continued, "The only thing he ever told me about your marriage was that you were trying to get pregnant again. He'd told me that you guys struggled the first time and... well...he alluded to the fact that you had stopped having spontaneous sex and that it had become something more planned. I guess around your cycles and all. He didn't go into details or anything."

Ben and I *had* struggled to conceive Brendan, which resulted in fertility testing and my eventual diagnosis of polycystic ovary syndrome. A few years ago, we'd tried to get pregnant again. It was probably about a year before he died—which would have coincided with the start of his affair with this woman. During that time, our sex life was sort of scheduled in order to try and increase the chances of my conceiving at certain times. That was enough to make my husband stray?

I shook my head. "You knew he was married from the beginning?"

Gina's face turned red, and she looked nervous to answer. "Yes."

"How could you? How would you feel if it were your husband?"

"I don't have any excuse, other than to say I wasn't a good person before the accident. And it wasn't just what I'd done to you. When my father was sick, I didn't visit him often. When I was up for a promotion at work, I spread rumors about the other candidate having a drinking problem in order to win the position over him. I put myself, and my wants and needs, above everything. Basically, I was selfish and didn't think about the effect I was having on other peoples' lives."

"And now? Are you saying that's changed?"

She looked down. "It has. At least I'm working on it."

I stared out the window for a few moments. Oddly, I didn't want to scream and yell anymore. I just wanted to put this whole thing behind me. "Does she look like him?"

She shook her head. "No, she doesn't. And we always used condoms. Ben was really good about it."

I scoffed. "How big of him."

"Like I told your boyfriend, I really don't think she could possibly be Ben's. But I can't be one-hundred percent positive because...you know."

"Because you were sleeping with my husband at the same time you were cheating on your boyfriend?"

"Yes."

"I'd like to swab her now. Perhaps we can do it in the ladies' room. It will only take me a minute."

"Yes, that's fine."

It was bizarre to go into the ladies' room with my husband's mistress and swab the little girl. Gina simply told her daughter to open her mouth so that the nice nurse could check her cheeks. The innocent little thing was none the wiser. By the time I was done, I was anxious to get the hell out of there. Gina, on the other hand, thought we'd become friends and could talk about boys while I packed up the test kit into my purse.

"So, you're dating Dr. Hogue now?"

I glanced up at her in the mirror as I washed my hands in the sink.

She continued, "He seems like a good catch. Was pretty upset when he realized who I was and the connection we had."

I grabbed a paper towel and attempted to ignore her. She still didn't take the hint.

"Plus, he's a doctor and all."

I wanted to smack that man-eating smirk off her face. But I wouldn't do that in front of her daughter. Finished with what I'd come to do, I knelt down to the little girl. I took her hand into mine and squeezed gently. "It was very nice to meet you, Olivia."

She smiled, and I took once last opportunity to study her face for any sign of Ben. I couldn't find any.

Standing, I pulled my bag onto my shoulder and leaned into Gina so that her sweet daughter couldn't hear. "Keep the fuck away from Dr. Hogue, you home wrecker. You haven't changed at all."

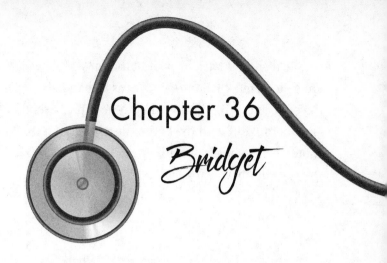

Chapter 36
Bridget

It was the longest three days of my life.

The day after I met with Gina, I brought Brendan to the hospital at the end of Simon's shift for a quick swab. I hated lying to my son, but there was no reason for the memory of his father to be soiled. In just another day and a half, I'd know the truth.

Oddly, for the last day, the object of my obsessive thinking wasn't my cheating, dead husband. It was something his mistress had said that I hadn't been able to shake. She'd reminded me of the struggle I had getting pregnant. I wasn't even sure if Simon wanted kids. But it wouldn't be fair of me to not warn him there was a distinct possibility I wouldn't be able to give him any. It was hard enough almost ten years ago, and now I was getting older.

Simon had taken a quick shower after dinner and went to his room to get changed while I put Brendan to bed. I found him in the kitchen pouring two glasses of wine. "You read my mind," I said.

"I figured you could use it."

He'd slicked back his wet hair after the shower, but a long, blond piece fell into his eyes as he handed me a glass. I eyed it and brought my wine to my lips. "Brendan has an appointment with the barber next week. I'm thinking I should bring you along with him."

"I'll cut my hair if you don't like it."

"You will?"

"Absolutely." He shrugged. "You just have to show me a boob."

I sputtered swallowing my wine. "What?"

"You heard me. I'll trade you a haircut for a peep show."

"You'll cut your hair if I...flash you a boob?"

"Deal?" He arched a brow.

I reached out my hand. "You've got yourself a deal, Dr. Hogue. Maybe Brendan will stop complaining if you get yours cut, too."

Simon took my hand in his, and then used it to yank me flush against him. He whispered against my lips, "I had an appointment set for this Saturday morning, but now I'm gonna get some tit, too."

"You tricked me!" I laughed.

"Sweetheart, I'd shave my damn head just to get this smile for one minute." He traced my bottom lip with his pointer finger. "I've missed it."

I took a deep breath. "I know. I'm sorry. Why don't we go sit in the living room? There's something I wanted to talk to you about."

"If that's code for you're gonna unbutton your shirt and let me lick a nipple, I'm in."

I shoved him playfully before taking his hand and leading him to the couch.

Simon figured out that something was up when I let out a long breath and rubbed my palms.

He placed his hand on my knee. "Are you nervous about the test?"

"I am, but that's not what I wanted to talk to you about."

His expression turned serious. "Alright."

It took almost a full minute for me to gather my thoughts.

"I feel a little embarrassed to be bringing this up to you now, and I'm certainly not looking to freak you out..."

"The only thing freaking me out is not knowing what in the bloody hell is bothering you if it's not the DNA test. Whatever it is, say it."

"I'm going on thirty-five..."

"Total MILF, yes. I'm aware of your age."

"What I mean by that is...I'm really getting to a point where it's going to be more and more difficult to conceive with each year that passes. I'm worried that I won't be able to give you a child of your own, if that's something you want."

"This is what's been on your mind?"

"Yes. Well, it's something I should've given more thought to earlier, but it wasn't until my conversation with Gina that I was really reminded of the struggle Ben and I had trying to have a baby. I have polycystic ovary syndrome. That means that my hormones are out of balance. Add in the factor of my age now compared to then and—"

"Whoa!" He interrupted. "This is all too much for you to be worrying about right now on top of everything else."

"I know. I can't help it. It's a serious concern. It feels so premature even bringing this up to you, but I feel like you need to figure out if you'd ever want a baby of your own. Because I may not have much time left to give you one—that is, if I'm even *able* to give you one at all."

Simon blinked several times in a row and seemed to be absorbing my words. "Wow. Alright. I'm going to be honest here. For many years, I was convinced that I didn't ever want to bear the responsibility of a child. Part of that had to do with my maturity level at the time and an even bigger part had to do with guilt feelings over Blake—fears of inadequacy, things like that."

Interrupting him, I said, "I feel awful bringing this up now. I know it's too soon to even be thinking about this."

"Why are you feeling awful? I always expect you to tell me exactly what's on your mind. We need to always be honest with each other."

"I don't expect you to make any decision now or anything. But I do want you to ponder it. Because if a baby is something you do want, I can't be sure it will happen, and we don't have forever to try."

"Okay...I'll think about it. Give me a few."

"A few months?"

"No, a few seconds." He closed his eyes tightly before his eyes flashed open. "Okay, I've thought about it."

"You have?"

"And my conclusion is that I *don't* need to think about it. Because in my heart, I know that I would love to have a baby with you. But not if it's going to cause you stress and anxiety. Do I want it? Yes. Because I love you, and I would love to experience that with you. And of course, it's crossed my mind before, Bridget—often, actually. So...as long as it's not putting you in any danger, I would be open to whatever you want. But I'm going to make it very clear that I don't *need* a child of my own blood to feel fulfilled. So if it doesn't happen, that's fine, too."

"I think you say that now, because you're still young. But you'll regret it if you don't. You're such a beautiful man. I couldn't imagine you not procreating."

"Let me ask you this. Do *you* want another child? That's just as important as whether I want one. I wouldn't be the person carrying it, you know."

I didn't have to think about the answer to that question. "Yes. I do. I just never thought that would be possible for me again."

Simon pulled me into him, caressing my hair as I rested my head on his chest. He spoke softly. "This entire year has felt like fate to me—the way we met, how I ended up here of all places in the world. Why not leave this up to fate, too? Let's not worry about it so much that it causes stress but rather take the attitude that if it happens, it happens."

"Well, I'm on the pill...so it's not going to happen if—"

"Why don't you throw those out tonight?"

I looked up at him. "Are you serious? You...want to start *now*? Would you be ready if it happened?"

"This baby would be a part of you and me. I don't even have to think about whether I would *want* it. I am prepared for it to happen. We would also have to be prepared to deal with things if it *didn't* happen, either, I suppose."

"Yes. I've been down this road before, and it can be very devastating when you're expecting it to happen and it doesn't."

"Here's what we're going to do," he said. "We're gonna fuck each other a lot and love each other a lot—like we always do. And we'll leave it up to fate, okay?"

I smiled, so relieved that we'd had this conversation. "Okay."

The next day, I'd just gotten home from picking up Brendan from school. Simon was in the kitchen making us an early dinner before his shift later that night.

"You think the results might be in?" he asked.

"I'm gonna head to my room and check."

He put down his pasta tongs. "Want me to come with you?"

"No. I'll be fine. Be right back."

Once in my room, I opened my laptop and logged into the DNA testing company's secure online portal. I punched in my password. To my surprise, the status had changed from *Processing* to *Results* to *Available*. I knew if I clicked, that was going to be it. I would find out if my son had a half-sibling.

Should I wait?

Was I ready?

Without thinking it through too much, I clicked and scrolled down to find the words that would completely change the tone of my night.

Results: Brendan Valentine is excluded as a relative of Olivia Delmonico.

I looked up at the ceiling and screamed, "Yes!"

I could hear Simon running from the kitchen.

He appeared in the doorway in a matter of seconds. "Bad yes or good yes?"

"Good yes. It's negative!"

He lifted me up into the air and spun me around. "I'm so goddamn relieved."

With my hand over my heart, I let out another breath. "Me, too."

Simon kissed me hard then said, "If Brendan's going to have a sibling someday, *we're* gonna be the ones to give it to him."

A week later, it must have been a full moon. Brendan had been in a horrible mood all day. It culminated in him swearing at Simon, who'd merely asked him to do a simple chore. It was unlike my son to be so flippant.

I was doing laundry down in the basement when I heard them talking above me.

Simon was yelling, "Excuse me. What did you say?"

"Nothing," Brendan said.

"You don't talk to me like that. Do you understand? You need to have respect for your mum and for me. Finish putting the bottles away and then I want you to go to your room until I tell you to come out."

Brendan whined, "Simon..."

"Go!" Simon repeated. "I'll call you when dinner's ready."

I rushed upstairs to find Simon leaning against the counter, looking upset.

"I heard everything. You did the right thing," I assured him.

"If I had spoken to *my* dad like that, there would've been hell to pay."

My dad. I wasn't sure if he realized the way he'd said it implied that he considered himself Brendan's dad.

I couldn't help smiling at him.

Simon picked up on my expression. "What?"

"You're cute when you're mad."

"Oh yeah? I'll take it out on you later. How about that?"

"I'd like that. And I think you should move in permanently," I said.

"Um...yeah...I've been living here for quite some time. I'd say it's permanent."

"I meant into my *bedroom*."

He lifted his brow. "Yeah?"

"Yeah."

"Well, alright, then. You're not gonna hear complaints from me on that."

And just like that, on a random night with a full moon, Simon officially became the man of the house.

Chapter 37

Simon

They say when life throws you lemons, make lemonade. I wasn't entirely sure how that applied to infertility, which often seemed like an empty, thankless, process in which there weren't even any lemons to work with.

The ironic thing was that everything else in our life had been going perfectly the last few months. The hospital system finally came around, hiring me for a permanent internist position in their new walk-in clinic just outside of the city. The hours were consistent, 7AM to 5PM, allowing me more time to spend with Bridget and Brendan than ever before.

Even though Bridget and I had vowed not to let the baby thing stress us out, with each month that passed, it seemed to be something we wanted more and more. Bridget's thirty-fifth birthday would be here before we knew it. And it became clear that leaving it up to "fate" wasn't working. If we seriously wanted a baby, we were going to need help.

We opted to see a fertility doctor who checked my sperm count only to determine it was abnormally high. While this was good news in a sense, it only put more pressure on Bridget. And I hated that. We tried medications first, and that led to daily injections. I'm not going to lie—the shots were really tough to watch. But we knew it was likely the only way it was going to happen, and the doctor had said waiting too much longer would only further decrease our chances.

I'd wanted to propose to Bridget for some time, but all of our mental energy had been expended while trying to conceive. Planning for a grand proposal kept falling by the wayside. Even though we'd discussed the fact that neither one of us felt the piece of paper was necessary to define our commitment, it was still something I wanted.

Never had that rung more true than on a certain night when Bridget was standing across from me in the bathroom. She was administering a subcutaneous injection into her abdomen for what felt like the umpteenth time. It just hit me how much she was willing to go through for me. I couldn't say that anyone had ever showed me so much love through actions in my entire life. Suddenly, I realized I couldn't wait anymore. I wanted to marry her— yesterday. Sure, we didn't need the piece of paper to define our relationship, but I *wanted* it.

She was disposing of the syringe in a glass jar when I came up behind her and planted a kiss on her neck.

"What's that for?"

"I love you," I simply said. "I'll go tuck Brendan in. You go relax. Pick out what you want to watch tonight."

Our adult time after Brendan went to bed was always my favorite time of the night after a long day. There was nothing like cozying up to my luv as she fell asleep in my arms. Bridget always nodded off before whatever we were watching was over. That was why lately we opted for sex before turning on the telly. Tonight, though, I could tell she was too exhausted for sex, as much I wanted it.

Brendan was playing on his tablet when I entered his room.

"Hey, buddy. Time to shut down the game and brush your teeth. After you come back from the bathroom, I want to talk to you about something, okay?"

When Brendan left for the loo, I took the opportunity to do something I hadn't done in a while—talk to Ben.

Walking over to the bureau, I lifted the framed photo.

"I don't have a lot of time. So, here it is. You know I'm mad at you for what you did to her and in many ways, I'll never forgive you for it. But the fact remains that in your death, I received so much. I owe you for this life in a strange way. You may have been a shitty husband, but from what I hear, you were a good father. You can rest in peace knowing that I'll take good care of your son, not as a friend but as the dad he deserves. And for what it's worth, I'll continue taking *real* good care of your wife. Take that however you may."

When I could hear Brendan's footsteps approaching, I put the photo back in its rightful spot.

"Come on," I said. "I'll tuck you in and we'll talk."

After he climbed into bed, I sat on the edge of his mattress.

"You know how your mum and I talked to you about she and I sharing a bedroom now and all of that..."

"Yeah. You said her bed was more comfortable than the one in the other room."

"Right. That's part of it. But it's more about being more comfortable with *her* near me at night, sort of like how you like to sleep with your stuffed rabbit, Miffy."

He seemed to understand. "Yeah."

"Anyway...I want to ask you something. And I don't want you to feel like you have to answer me if you're not sure."

"Okay."

"Normally, a guy asks this question to a woman's father, but since your granddad is not around, and since I value your opinion more than anyone's, I'd like to ask you if it would be okay with you if I asked your mum to marry me."

He straightened up against the headboard to better look at me. "That would make us a real family?"

"Well, I feel like we already are. Don't you?"

"Yeah. But sometimes I feel like it's bad to think that."

"Because of your father?"

"I don't want him to be sad that I love you."

His words caused me to close my eyes. Not only had he never said he loved me before, but the other part was hard to hear.

"I love you, too, buddy. I love you exactly how a father loves a son. And I don't think your father in Heaven is sad. I think he's happy that I'm here to look out for you. I know I would feel the same if I were him."

"I want you to marry my mom."

"Yeah? I have your permission?"

The slightly timid-looking grin on his face was adorable. "Yeah."

"Thank you for your blessing. I didn't want to ask her without it."

"When are you gonna ask her? Can we have a party?"

"Of course. But I haven't figured it out yet. I'll let you know before I do. Deal?"

"Deal." He high-fived me and asked, "What would that make you to me if you married my mom?"

"I'd be your stepdad, technically. But to me, that's no different than a father."

"What would I call you?"

"You could call me whatever you want...as long as it's not a curse word." I chuckled. "You could still call me Simon, or you could call me Dad if you want. Or maybe you reserve that term for your father, Ben, and call me something like...Pop. It's what I call my dad from time to time. Because really, Brendan, I hope you look at me like an additional dad not a replacement. I could never replace your father."

He took a few moments to ponder my suggestion then said, "Pop. I like that. Pop for my father here and Dad for my daddy in Heaven."

Rustling his hair, I smiled. "I think that's brilliant, son."

Chapter 38

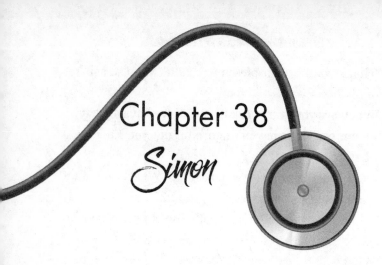

Simon

It took me more than a month, but I finally figured out how I was going to do it.

When we first met, Bridget had mentioned that she'd never been to WaterFire in Providence. My plan was to take her on a gondola and propose to her on the ride. Then, the next day, we'd head to Newport for some family time with Brendan to celebrate the engagement—have the party he wanted.

It was the Friday evening of the proposal. Both Bridget and I had the entire weekend off. She was getting dressed while I paced in the living room, practicing what I was going to say to her later. It surprised me how nervous I was. I wanted it to be perfect.

My cell phone rang, disrupting my thoughts.

"Hello?"

"Simon, it's your mother."

"Mum? It's late there. Is everything alright?"

"Yes, son. Everything is lovely. Your father and I just landed in Boston."

"What?"

"Don't sound so thrilled."

"You're here in the States?"

"Your dad is renting a car. So, we'll be driving up in your direction. Are you still living with that woman? I just punched the address from your Christmas card into the navigation."

Shit. This could not be happening.

"Yes, that's the one."

I let out a long breath. Ever since my last trip home, my relationship with my parents had been strained, particularly with my mother. The few conversations I'd had with her were all about how I was going to regret my decision to be away from my family forever. My dad kept quiet overall, but I knew he agreed with her. I was an only child, and they wanted me to carry on the family legacy in Leeds, take over their properties. My mother was convinced that Bridget wasn't right for me for the sheer fact that she'd been married before and had a child. And as much as I hated to admit it, I knew it was also partly because she was American. The only thing I ever kept from Bridget were my conversations with my parents. I couldn't burden her with their nonsense. It would've broken her heart. The problem with that, though, was that now she wouldn't be the least bit prepared for any kind of confrontation.

"Your father and I thought it was about time we came to check things out."

"Why wouldn't you tell me you were coming first so that I could've prepared?"

"We knew you'd discourage it. Dad had some miles that were going to expire next week, so we decided to call

British Airways on a whim. And here we are. We'll see you in about an hour."

Bloody hell. This was going to be a nightmare.

———

Simon stood at the doorway as I put my earrings on. When I turned to him, I could see from the look on his face, that something was wrong.

"Simon?"

"I'm afraid there's been a change of plans tonight, luv."

"What do you mean?"

"I can't believe I'm saying this...but my parents are on their way over."

"What? They're here? In the US?"

"Yes. They landed in Boston and are driving here as we speak."

My blood was pumping.

"Oh my God."

"I'm so sorry that we have to cancel our date. You have no idea how much."

"Are you kidding? We can always go to WaterFire. It's not every day your parents are here. I've always wanted to meet them. I just expected a little more warning."

"Bridget, there's something you should—"

"I have to run to Shaw's." There was no time to talk. I needed to food shop. "We have nothing to offer them. I can't have your parents here with an empty fridge."

He followed me around in my frenzy. "Why don't we just take them out?"

"I can't do that. These are your parents. I need to welcome them into our home, need to cook for them."

"Bridget, we need—"

"There's no time!" Panicking, I grabbed my purse and ran out of the bedroom. "I'll be back."

———

At the grocery store, I'd run into every problem imaginable. Ingredients I needed weren't in stock, causing me to have to substitute. The lines were long.

Once home, I felt frazzled as I entered the kitchen to find Simon standing there with his parents.

Holy shit. His parents!

Simon's mother was a statuesque blonde, exactly how I might have pictured her to look. He'd shown me a family picture once, but it was taken some years ago. His father's hair was white but looked like it might have been blond as well back in the day. Simon definitely looked like his dad. Both of his parents were really tall.

Out of breath, I rushed toward them. "Mr. and Mrs. Hogue. It's so good to finally meet you."

As soon as the words exited my mouth, the bottom of the brown paper grocery bag I'd been holding gave way, unleashing the entire carton of eggs onto the ground, but worse—onto Simon's mother's feet.

Panicking, I got down on my hands and knees, literally scooping the broken eggshells and yokes up with my hands. "I'm so sorry. Oh my God."

Simon came toward me with a towel. "I'll handle it, sweetheart. It's okay."

Amidst the chaos, I looked up at his mother again from the ground and repeated, "I'm so sorry."

"It's alright," she said, not really looking amused.

When I stood up, I could see Simon's dad staring straight at my chest. In the process of my leaning over to clean the eggs up, my boob had popped out of the black dress I'd been wearing because of our canceled romantic night out.

"Wear something sexy," he said.

Well, that was a big mistake.

Lifting the material over my breast to cover it, I had no choice but to ignore the obvious.

Trying to salvage this disaster of a first meeting, I smiled in an attempt to make light of the situation. "Clearly, I'm a little discombobulated. At least the eggs were only for breakfast and not dinner."

"It's alright. We're the ones who surprised you," his father said.

I turned to his mother. "I'm really sorry again, Mrs. Hogue."

"No need to apologize again. Please, call me Eleanor. My husband is Theo."

Simon looked up from the ground as he continued to clean up the eggs. "Bridget insisted on cooking us a nice meal. I'd suggested we just go out, but honestly she's a wonderful cook."

After several minutes of awkward small talk, Simon finally finished up and washed his hands. "Dad, can I get you a scotch?"

"If you have it."

Simon and his father retreated to the liquor cabinet in the living room.

Shortly after, Brendan came out of nowhere, wrapping his arms around Simon's mother's legs. "Grandma!"

She jumped and nearly toppled over.

Brendan immediately realized his mistake. The poor little guy looked mortified. He'd approached her from the back, thinking she was Ben's mother, Ann, who'd be here any minute to pick him up. Both women had short, blonde hair, so it was easy to see why Brendan got confused.

"Sorry. I thought you were my grandma. She's supposed to come get me and take me to her house."

She straightened her skirt. "That's perfectly alright."

Wrapping my arm around him, I said, "Brendan, this is Simon's mother. His parents came to surprise us."

"Oh." He lifted his hand in a wave. "Hello."

"Hello." She smiled.

Simon reentered the kitchen with his father. "Hi, buddy. I see you've met my mum. This is my dad."

Theo bent down, offering Brendan his hand. "Very nice to meet you, young man."

Theo and Eleanor made small talk with Brendan while I started preparing the rosemary chicken I planned to make. Simon looked tense as he threw back his scotch.

Shortly after, Ben's mother arrived to take Brendan back to her house. After a brief introduction, my son very adorably bid everyone adieu with "cheerios!" instead of "cheerio." He had always though it was *cheerios*, apparently.

Eleanor's eyes had been glued to Simon the entire time he was hugging Brendan goodbye tightly. Simon had also whispered something in his ear, something about a change of plans. I wondered what that was all about.

Relief coursed through me when Simon and his parents headed to the living room, leaving me alone to finish prepping the meal. It felt like the first time I could breathe since arriving back from the market.

Once the food was ready, we all sat down in the dining room that I'd mainly used to do paperwork and bills. Simon had thankfully cleared all of my junk off of the table, which I'd totally forgotten to do.

Dinner was awkwardly quiet. Occasionally his parents would give Simon updates on things back home. But lots of silence ensued in between the clanking of silverware.

At one point, his mother turned to me. "Bridget, everything is delicious."

"Thank you. It's my mother's recipe."

Simon placed his hand on my knee under the table. When I looked at him, he leaned in and gave me a peck on the lips, which certainly didn't go unnoticed by Eleanor.

I got up from the table. "I have to start preparing dessert. It will take a little bit."

"Do you need help?" Simon asked, looking almost eager to join me.

"No. Enjoy your parents. I've got it."

Unlike most dining rooms, mine was located on the opposite side of the house from the kitchen. I never understood the reasoning for that layout, but on this particular day, I was grateful that Simon's mother thought I was out of earshot.

I'd forgotten my phone on the windowsill in the dining room, so when I went back to retrieve it, I heard them speaking argumentatively. I stopped and hid behind the wall to listen.

"That little boy is going to get very attached to you, Simon. It's dangerous."

"It's already happened, Mother. I love him."

"How can you possibly love some other man's child?"

"I consider him mine."

There was a long pause before Eleanor spoke again. "Bridget is lovely. Honestly. I'm actually pleasantly surprised. But you need to realize that she's going to trap you into this situation forever. You'll never get out, Simon. Never."

"Trap me? I'd love to be trapped here. You can't trap someone somewhere if it's the only place in the world they want to be."

His mother continued to argue with him while his father stayed silent.

"You can't be serious, son. You'll never be able to return to England. You'll be stuck here for the rest of your life, away from your family and from the people who love you."

"The people who love me are here.

Simon slapped his cloth napkin down on the table. It sounded like he was going to get up from the table, so I ran on my tiptoes to the kitchen.

Leaning against the counter, I completely lost it. So overcome with sadness about how his parents really felt, I broke out into tears.

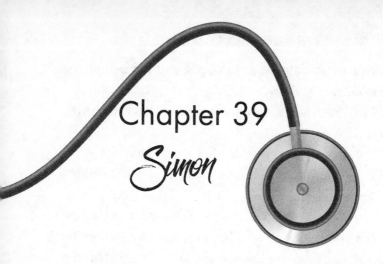

Chapter 39

Simon

I needed another drink, but more than that, I needed to check on Bridget and get the hell away from my parents for a few minutes.

Bridget was layering the ingredients of her fruit and chocolate trifle when I noticed her shoulders were shaking.

Rushing toward her, I asked, "My God, are you crying?"

Tears were streaming down her cheeks. "How come you never told me how your parents feel? I thought they were coming to meet me, not to warn you against me!"

"You heard them from all the way in here?"

"I'd gone back to get my phone to double-check the recipe. I was listening behind the wall. I heard everything."

That gutted me.

I pulled her into my chest. "I'm so sorry you had to hear that rubbish. It doesn't matter how they feel, especially now. I love you so much, Bridget, more than anything in this world. I haven't wanted to burden you with their foolishness, because it doesn't bloody matter."

She stepped back to look me in the eyes. "It matters to me. I want them to like me, to understand how much I love you. They've judged me before I've even had a chance to prove any of that to them."

"Don't you dare go getting upset right now. I'm going to fix this. They can't come into our house and disrespect you like this, even if they think you can't hear them." I knew what I had to do. "You trust me?"

"Why? What are you going to do, Simon?"

"We're gonna face this right now. I'm going to make them understand once and for all. Take my hand. We're going to put an end to any doubts that they have."

She did as I said as we walked back together to the dining room.

My parents both turned in their seats to face us. My heart was pounding as I prepared to lay it all out on the line.

"Mum and Dad, with all due respect, I need you to understand something very clearly. Bridget is here right now because we don't have any secrets in this house. She's aware of your apprehension about us. If you love me, if you've ever loved me, you will stop questioning my life choices. You think you know what's going on, think you know Bridget, but you don't really know anything. I clearly haven't explained things thoroughly enough to you. The fact that you have this fear that she's going to trap me is ironic and terribly painful. Want to know why? I have spent the past several months doing everything in my power to knock her up. You have no idea how badly I want—as you call it—to be trapped. You also have no idea what it's like having to watch the person you love more than anyone in this world go through something as painful as infertility, injecting herself day in and day out with potentially harmful drugs. Why? For me. All for me. Because she knows I want a baby, not with just anyone, but only with her. And that was the only way to get it. She's gone through hell for me."

"My God," my mother muttered.

I went on, my blood pressure rising by the second.

"And that boy isn't someone else's. Brendan is my son. The things you see as complications are blessings to me. You want to know how serious I am? What you interrupted tonight? Bridget and I had a date to go into the city. I was going to ask her to marry me tonight. I'd been waiting for just the right moment to do it."

I hadn't exactly intended to let that cat out of the bag. It just came out in my anger.

Bridget looked at me in shock.

I mouthed, "I love you."

My father finished off the last of his drink as my mother continued to stare at me in silence.

It was time to unleash the big one.

"But see, Mother, even the fact that my big plans were ruined can't dampen my spirits—nothing can. Because earlier this week, I got the most amazing news that I've ever received in my life. Bridget is pregnant...not just with one baby...with two. We're having twins. So, that woman you've been disrespecting in her own house is carrying *your* grandchildren inside of her. And there's nothing you can say or do that is going to change the fact that I am on cloud nine."

Mum let out a long breath, closing her eyes then opening them with a look of empathy. "I had no idea."

"No, I didn't tell you any of this because things have been hard enough without your opinions on top of it all."

Bridget spoke for the first time. "Can I say something?"

"Of course," I said.

She spoke to my mother directly. "I can understand why you've had doubts about me. You don't know me. You only know that I've kept him from you and that I've been married before and that I have a child. I used to think I wasn't good enough for your son, either, to be honest. I tried *not* to fall in love with him, thinking that he would be better off without me. But whether we make sense or not, we love each other. You can't choose love. It chooses you. And I don't want him to have to choose between us and you. No one should have to make that kind of choice. And even if you continue to hate me, I still would never keep him or your grandchildren from you. Because I love him too much to do that."

"We don't hate you." My mother sighed before rubbing her temples.

I put my arm around Bridget and addressed them. "I think we've had enough stress for one night. I love you both very much, Mum and Dad, but I think you need to stay in a hotel tonight."

"No," Bridget insisted.

Surprised, I turned to her. "No?"

"No. They're staying in your old room. They're your parents. They're not going to a hotel. I insist." She let go of me and looked over at them. "If you'll excuse me, I'm feeling very tired and now you know why. I think I'm going to turn in early. The trifle I made is ready, Simon. I want you to serve it to your parents. You never get to see them. Enjoy the dessert and this time together."

Then, she simply walked away.

I went after her, but Bridget assured me that she was okay. She refused to let me join her in the bedroom and continued to insist that I spend the rest of the night with my mum and dad.

They were getting to see firsthand exactly why I was in love with this woman.

Chapter 40

Bridget

I slept like a baby. Even though Eleanor's words last night had hurt me, Simon's had healed me. The way he stood up for us in front of them really made me realize that nothing and no one could ever break us apart. As hard as it was, I was just going to have to accept things with his parents as they were.

I knew that he had stayed up really late with them because I'd heard him come into the bedroom in the middle of the night. Although they weren't crazy about me, it really did make me happy to know that he was getting to spend time with them.

The sun was now shining through our bedroom window. Simon stirred when he heard me get up. He placed his hand on my nightgown, pulling me back into bed with his firm grip.

Resisting, I said, "I need to make breakfast for them."

"You'll do no such thing. You worked hard enough cooking that supper last night. We'll take them out somewhere."

"They need coffee."

"They don't drink coffee. They drink tea. And I set everything out for them last night." He patted the bed next to him. "Lie with me for a bit."

I lay back down and faced him.

Simon placed a piece of my hair behind my ear. "I screwed up when I blurted out my plans to propose. I'd been waiting for the perfect night so that I could orchestrate everything just right, but perfection doesn't always lie in the obvious. Last night, the respect you showed my parents in the face of disrespect made me love you even more. I honestly didn't think that was possible. They see it now. And honestly, for me, there is no more perfect time to ask you to be my wife than this moment."

Simon reached into the nightstand, taking out a small, black box. Rather than get down on one knee, he wrapped his legs around mine and hovered over me on the bed. "Bridget, I know we've done things a little arse backwards. We lived together before we became lovers. I knocked you up out of wedlock. But I wouldn't change a thing. The order may not have been perfect, but you, our son, our babies...are perfect—everything I never knew I wanted."

He opened the box, displaying a ring that had one large, center diamond, surrounded by four small ones.

"This ring represents us. You're the big beautiful stone in the middle. The two stones on the left represent Brendan and me. The two on the right are our unborn babies. Will you do me the great honor of being my wife?"

"Yes!" I jumped up to wrap my arms around his neck. I couldn't help but laugh. "Your parents are gonna shit over this."

"No, they're not. They know."

"They do?"

"I told them before bed that I planned to ask you this morning. I made a promise to our son last night, that when his grandmother dropped him off today, that there would be a ring on his mother's finger. You didn't know it, but our trip to Newport today was meant to be a family celebration of our engagement."

"We're still doing that trip even with your parents here?"

"They're invited to come along. If they don't want to, that's their problem."

When we emerged from our engagement bliss, Eleanor and Theo were sitting in the kitchen, sipping their tea. Simon had his arms wrapped around me.

"Good morning," I said.

"Good morning, Bridget." His father smiled.

My head was pounding, and I couldn't even have coffee because I'd decided to eliminate caffeine.

His mother stood. "Can we have a moment?"

"Sure," I said.

"Dad, let's take a walk," Simon said, before disappearing out the front door with his father.

Eleanor and I were officially alone. I really hoped that she wasn't going to say anything mean to me, because I was in no mood, especially without coffee.

"I need to apologize for my behavior last night. After you went to bed, my son spent the entire evening recounting his experience here. It's evident that he loves you unconditionally and that I was out of place in thinking that I could sway him in some way. But I assure you I no longer wish to do that."

"I understand why you felt the way you did. I can't say I would be any different if it were my son wanting to move to England with someone who had baggage. Until you really know the person or understand the situation, you take it at face value. We all want what's best for our children."

"Well, I can see now that what's best for my son is what makes him happy. And that is you. Thank you for welcoming us into your home."

She smiled, and it actually seemed genuine.

I lifted my hand, displaying the ring. "Did you see?"

"He showed us last night. Congratulations."

"Thank you."

"You know, Simon doesn't know this, but I had trouble conceiving him. It's why he's an only child."

"I didn't know that."

"So, I know how hard that is."

"Well, I'm hoping that these little guys or girls turn out to be just like your son."

She bent her head back in almost evil laughter. "He was a holy terror. If they're anything like little Simon, good luck to you, dear."

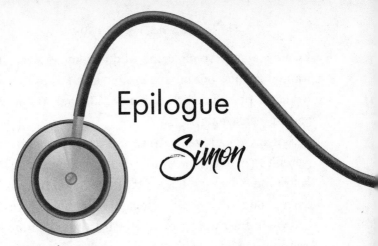

Epilogue
Simon

Seven Months Later

It was like I'd died and woken up in pink-washed heaven. I looked around the room at the pink balloons, pink flowers, and pink clothing items strewn about. The hospital room had vomited pink.

It had been an exhausting day with people in and out of Bridget's suite. First my mother, who'd flown in for the birth, was here. She finally went back to our house to prepare some meals for when we returned.

Then, Bridget's mother came in from Florida along with Ben's mother, Ann. It seemed like they were here forever. Right when they left, Calliope and Nigel showed up with a giant, pink stuffed animal. Now with all of the visitors gone, Bridget was finally able to nap. Brendan was in the corner of the room playing quietly on his tablet.

And Daddy was getting alone time with his girls, one in each arm, sleeping like the babies they were. Eleanor Blake on the left and Elizabeth Simone on the right, both named after their grandmothers.

Eleanor's eyes suddenly opened as she began to cry. I could already see the differences in their personalities.

Eleanor was more like me, didn't like to sleep, never wanted to miss out on any excitement. Loved to suck on Bridget's tits. Elizabeth was more like her mother, calm and a great sleeper.

I'd already proven to be an overprotective father. They weren't even out of the womb, and I'd nearly gotten kicked out of the delivery room for trying to direct the physician during the birth. I couldn't imagine what I was going to be like when they were teenagers. That reminded me that I was going to need backup.

"Hey, Brendan. In about fourteen years, I'm really going to need your help, okay? Be prepared. We'll have some serious teenage boy butt to kick."

"Okay, Pop," he said before turning his attention back to his game.

Bridget's voice was groggy. "What are you saying?"

"Did I wake you, luv?"

"No. Your mini-me, Eleanor, did. She's ready for a snack?"

I handed the twin who had been resting on my left arm to her mother.

Elizabeth remained sleeping on my right. Eleanor latched onto the left breast right away. Bridget had been tandem breastfeeding, which had officially graduated her to my superhero.

"Can I get you anything?" I asked.

"Some water."

I poured her a cup and watched as she drank it down.

"Now that you're awake and the guests are gone, I can finally give you your presents."

"Didn't you already give me enough?" She smiled.

"Well, Calliope told me about something called a push present. So, I'd been planning to give it to you. I have two presents, actually," I said, handing her the first item. "This one's for them."

Bridget ripped open the wrapping paper to reveal two matching sets of onesies.

She giggled. "Days of the week."

"To match your knickers. Now they can dress like their mum."

"Honestly, that is adorable, Simon."

"Okay, next one's for you." I handed her a box and watched as she opened it.

She lifted the white gold necklace and examined the charm, which looked like two letter Js back to back. On the tip of each end was a small diamond.

"Oh my God, it's beautiful. What a unique design. Why does it look so familiar?"

I opened my wallet and took out the fish hook that I'd extracted from her arse the very first day we'd met. "Because it's an exact replica of this."

"That's the same kind of fish hook that was stuck in my butt the day we first met!"

"Not the same kind. The one and only."

"You kept it?"

"Bizarre, right? That day, instead of discarding it, I slipped it into my jacket as a memento. That was probably the most unsanitary thing I'd ever done in my entire medical career, but something told me to keep it, that it was important."

She looked at the hook in my hand and then down at the charm. "This is the strangest yet oddly romantic thing I'd ever received."

I put the hook back in my wallet before adjusting the necklace around her.

"This is what I'm going to wear on our wedding day," she said.

Bridget and I had a date set in England a year from now. We figured the twins would be old enough to travel then. I couldn't wait to show her and Brendan where I grew up.

"Here's the strange thing about the fish hook," I said. "It's a double hook with *twin* ends. Maybe it was a premonition." I leaned in to whisper into her ear so that Brendan couldn't hear. "Even stranger, apparently when Googling *double fish hook*, I found that it's also slang for a sexual act in which two middle fingers are inserted into a woman's arse and then pulled apart. Something we can try when you're ready."

"Aw, and that reminded you of me. The symbolism here is overwhelming." She laughed. "I just can't believe you kept that thing all this time."

"It's proof you hooked me from the very beginning, luv."

Acknowledgements

First and foremost, thank you to all of the bloggers who enthusiastically spread the news about our books. We are eternally grateful for all that you do. Your hard work is what helps to build excitement and introduces us to readers who may otherwise never have heard of us.

To Julie – Thank you for your friendship, daily support, and encouragement. We are so happy that this has been a better year than last for you and can't wait for "moore" of your phenomenal books coming soon!

To Elaine – An amazing proofer, editor, formatter, and friend. Thank you for your attention to detail and for helping to make our projects the best that they can be.

To Luna – What would we do without you? Thank you for being there for us day in and day out as a friend and so much more and for blessing us with your incredible creative talent.

To Dani – Thank you organizing this release and for always being just a click away when we need you.

To Letitia – Perhaps you worked your cover design magic better than ever before with this cover, transforming Simon into the sexy doctor that he is.

To our agent, Kimberly Brower – We are so lucky to call you a friend, as well as an agent. We're so excited for the year ahead and are grateful that you will be there with us every step of the way.

Last but not least, to our readers – We keep writing because of your hunger for our stories. We love surprising you and hope you enjoyed this book as much as we did writing it. Thank you as always for your enthusiasm, love and loyalty. We cherish you!

Much love,
Penelope and Vi

Other Books by
Penelope Ward & Vi Keeland

Mister Moneybags

Playboy Pilot

Stuck-Up Suit

Cocky Bastard

Other Books by Penelope Ward

Drunk Dial

Mack Daddy

RoomHate

Stepbrother Dearest

Neighbor Dearest

Jaded and Tyed (A novelette)

Sins of Sevin

Jake Undone (Jake #1)

Jake Understood (Jake #2)

My Skylar

Gemini

Other Books by Vi Keeland

Standalone novels

Beautiful Mistake

EgoManiac

Bossman

The Baller

Left Behind (A Young Adult Novel)

First Thing I See

Life on Stage series (2 standalone books)

Beat

Throb

MMA Fighter series (3 standalone books)

Worth the Fight

Worth the Chance

Worth Forgiving

The Cole Series (2 book serial)

Belong to You

Made for You